Al

James E Mack was born... childhood abroad, gaining a love of nature, the outdoors and wildlife. He became a Commando in the late 1980s and a member of a Special Operations unit, with a 22-year career serving in many of the world's troubled hotspots. James subsequently specialised as a Counter-Terrorism adviser and assisted in capacity building operations in support of UK and US Government initiatives.

His passion for wildlife led James to assist in the development of counter-poaching programs in Africa. This passion remains and James spends much of his leisure time photographing the very animals that he strives to protect.

When time allowed, James began writing novels based upon his experiences in Special Operations and conflict zones around the globe. *Fear of the Dark* is his second novel.

James lives in Northern Scotland where he enjoys the surfing and the mountains nearby.

Published by Achnacarry Press

ISBN: 978-1719480864

FEAR

OF

THE

DARK

JAMES E MACK

My thanks once again to everyone who supported me throughout the writing process. I remain truly grateful for your help and encouragement and am well aware that this book would not be here but for your efforts. To my partner Teresa goes a special thanks for taking the time to listen to my drivel and read over the (very) rough drafts of the manuscripts. Your insights have absolutely helped in making this a stronger book. To the readers also, must go sincere thanks for your support and enthusiasm for my writing, for without you there would be no books; merely a collection of dusty manuscripts tucked away, forgotten in a cupboard drawer.

James E Mack

Also by James E Mack:

Only the Dead
The Killing Agent

'When I leave the light behind me and enter the night's embrace,
I am become what others dread and cannot bear to face,
I shun the rays of morning and the chorus of the lark,
And turn my soul towards the woods and the
coming of the Dark'

1

It was his regular practice to walk the cliff tops of a morning, taking pleasure in the quiet solitude before the intrusions of work and people impacted his day. No morning was ever the same; the light that painted the landscape an ever-changing palette of pinks, oranges and reds, flourishing in intensity from the east before dissipating into the day that the later risers would awaken to. The sea this morning absorbed the warming reds of the rising sun, camouflaging the frigid cold of the northern waters that lay beneath the crimson cloak. His breath fogged in the freezing air around him and he rubbed his gloved hands together as he paused at the top of the cliff path and enjoyed the stillness.

He wondered if he would still take these early morning walks when he retired, still feel the need to snatch some quiet moments when he was no longer working for a living. He thought of waking up with Susan, both of them sharing the bathroom and breakfasting together. Him kissing her on the cheek as she left for work while he, well, he hadn't quite worked out what he would do with his days at that point.

Mr Colin Duffy. Not Sergeant. Would take some getting used to. Thirty years as a policeman with a title and an identity and in a month's time he would be just another *Mr.* Susan would be happier, had said as much. He smiled at the thought of her, warm and snug in their bed, duvet pulled tight under her chin and smelling of soft lotions and sleep. It would be another hour before she needed to wake. The chill began to settle upon him and he resumed his walk, following the grass path that meandered along the top of the cliffs towards the old fishing station. The sea was on his right and below him, the sound of the crashing breakers rolling up the sandstone walls and reaching his cold ears. A buzzard alighted from a fence post in front of him, large wings slapping the air to gain lift as it regarded him with a glare of reproach, an interloper among the time for animals, not men.

Nearing the bottom of the path he slowed his pace and took care with his footing, the ground loose and uneven after the recent snow. Looking at the old fishing station he felt a small pang of regret at not buying it when they had the opportunity some years ago. Its stunning cliff-top location and traditional charm still retained the capacity to impress. He'd only been a constable back then though and the mortgage would have crippled them. The gravel crunched under his feet as he walked between the buildings, the right of way cutting through the station's accommodations. Some English man and his wife had bought the place a few years ago and were running it as a bed and breakfast but Colin hadn't really had anything to do with them.

The path narrowed and the grass was higher as he negotiated his way along the more precarious section. Below him, waves hurled themselves against jagged rocks, the echoes of their assault cracking like gunshots in the natural amphitheatre of the bay. The light was losing its red hue as the sun rose and ushered in the day. His thoughts turned to his workload for the coming day and any impending problems. He gave a small chuckle at this. *Problems?* This was St Cyrus, not Glasgow. Problems to Colin and his team were generally related to secondary issues such as traffic or flooding. Police Scotland's return to community policing had been good in terms of providing family stability and a sense of belonging but the trade-off was that by choosing such a rural location, there was precious little police work to be done. For Colin, this was no bad thing. He'd done his time mixing it with drunken oilmen in Aberdeen and drug dealers in Dundee, felt the pressures of budget cuts and poor morale in the large urban stations. His team however, had not. Tess and Mitch, like most young constables, yearned for the excitement and drama of big city policing, felt they were missing out on *real* police work. He understood their frustrations. Was only natural that they'd prefer to be hammering down a drug dealer's door in Torry to chatting with primary school kids about safe bicycle riding on public roads. They'd only been with Colin this last year and he knew he was lucky that they

3

didn't have the option of moving on, their first assignment being a mandatory two year posting.

They would, of course, head off at the first opportunity, but he would be well out of the game by then. Tess in particular, he could see already, was destined for better things. A smart policewoman with a good instinct for detective work, Colin saw a great future ahead of her. She had a mature head on her shoulders that belied her physical years, probably as a result of having spent some time in the Army. Mitch was a typical young copper. Straight from training at Tulliallan, he'd arrived in St Cyrus convinced that he was God's gift to rural policing. He was taking longer to settle in and Colin used as much of his time mentoring as managing the young constable.

A strong gust of wind caught him unawares and he staggered backward slightly, adjusting his footing to compensate. The stinging cold on his exposed face brought with it the promise of more snow that the previous day's forecast had predicted. Looking out to sea he could make out the forms of the dark, roiling clouds racing towards the land, their bellies pregnant with precipitation. The forecast had warned of heavy snow to follow that of the weeks before and of subsequent road closures for some areas. Colin had no doubt that his team would be busy once the storm struck in earnest. Standard Scottish winter conditions, he mused, although to hear the weather report and the media sensationalising of the briefest of snow flurries, one would think the apocalypse was setting in.

Taking the farm track back towards the village, Colin removed his woollen hat and scratched at the centre of his head, fingers rasping through the short-cropped, greying hair. He felt the cold immediately and jammed the hat back over his head, pulling the materiel down to cover the tips of his ears. He would be at the station for over an hour before Tess or Mitch showed up and he would use that time to shower and don his uniform. More importantly, he would put the coffee pot on and take fifteen minutes or so reading the morning's headlines in *The Times*, the daily ritual he had carried out for many years now. Then he would ease into the day, prioritising their requirements and allocating troops to tasks, although *tasks* was stretching the term somewhat.

He opened his stride as he passed Jasper Cottage and his eye was drawn to the light in the window and some movement within. A face looked out, smiled in recognition and waved. Billy Ritchie, a local man who worked, as some did despite the drop-off in the industry, offshore on the oil platforms. Colin returned the wave and carried on up the small rise towards the Kirk. He wondered if Billy was heading back offshore today, wasn't sure when he had returned to the village. Turning right, the wind abated somewhat as the cliffs to his rear took the brunt of the gusts and deflected them from the older section of the village. As he passed the Old Schoolhouse a deep, booming bark greeted him and he smiled as he glimpsed the two huge Newfoundland dogs shuffling towards the gate of the property. A woman's face at the front window investigated

5

the dog's barking and waved as she saw Colin walk past. Gina and Andy Wellstone had done the old building up some years before and made a really good job of it. Colin and Susan were regulars at the Wellstone's Christmas party that they held in the house each year and Colin was always impressed at the sensitive and tasteful conversion the Wellstone's had managed.

Crossing over the bridge that spanned the rise where the old railway had once been, Colin glanced at the new houses that had just recently been completed. Although well-constructed and clearly aimed at wealthier patrons, he was a little saddened by their presence. This was the third development in the village since he had moved here and the fabric of the small hamlet was changing as a result of the increase in residents and the general demographic. Thankfully the increase in people had not brought a correlating increase in crime, most of the newcomers being families seeking a quiet rural idyll in which to raise their children.

As he passed the inn on the way to the station house, he reminded himself to pop in after work and have a quick pint with John, the owner. Colin had heard some loose talk about a couple of the local offshore lads leaving the pub after a few beers and driving their cars. He would have a chat with John tonight, ask him to make his staff aware of it and get them to pass on the informal warning to those who needed it. Smiling as he opened the wrought iron gate of the Station House, he reflected that he was actually quite proud of the fact that much of his work could be conducted through such informal chats with people without the need for bureaucracy or form-filling. Closing the gate behind him, he removed his glove and fished a set of keys from his pocket, separating two from the bunch. He opened the locks on the blue-painted wooden door and entered the key-code to the internal entrance, heeling the door closed behind him then reaching up and switching off the alarm at the panel above his head.

Colin opened the inner door and felt the warmth on his face, removing his other glove and hat as he made his way to his office. Opening his door, he entered and placed his gloves and hat over the back of a chair, removing his coat, which he laid over the other items. He was reaching for the coffee pot when his phone vibrated in his pocket. Frowning at the unusual intrusion upon his morning routine, he took the phone out and looked at the screen. It gave him the caller's identity and the first line of the message. This was enough for him to let out a deep sigh, knowing already from the sparse information at hand that the morning was going to be troublesome. He sat heavily on his chair and opened the text fully, stroking his moustache and shaking his head as read the contents. The message was from Susan and was brief and straight to the point: *Steven's been attacked! You need to speak to him ASAP. Call me x*

2

Munching on her last piece of toast, Tess Cameron scrolled through the overnight Facebook posts, lingering on some and skipping most. In truth, she couldn't really say why she was still using the platform as she rarely posted anything, preferring face-to-face meetings and phone calls to keep up with her small social circle. Still, there was the occasional funny post that made her laugh. The radio presenter in the background introduced the news and she glanced at her watch, noting with surprise that she should be leaving for work. She took her plate and cup to the sink and washed them before placing them on the wooden draining board to dry. As she left the kitchen, she turned off the radio and the lights before making her way into the bathroom. Brushing her teeth vigorously she inspected her face, content that the make-up she had applied earlier when she was less awake, was adequate. Satisfied, she rinsed her mouth, holding her long black hair away from the sink as she spat the foamy residue out. She stood and dabbed her lips on the towel then reapplied some lip balm in anticipation of the cold outside. Leaving the bathroom, she turned the light off and closed the door, walking along the hallway and into the porch. She took her heavy police jacket from the coat hook and put it on over her uniform, pulled on her cap, slung her bag over her shoulder and opened the front door.

The cold was instant, a gust of frigid air hitting her face and threatening to dislodge her cap. Looking up she raised her eyebrows in surprise at just how dark the sky remained under the mantle of black clouds. With one hand she jammed her headgear in place while with the other she slammed the old wooden door closed. She didn't bother locking it, like most of the villagers she hadn't ever seen the need. Turning on her heel she rammed her hands into her pockets and pulled her chin down into the collar of the jacket. The snow began just as she reached the bottom of Ecclesgreig Road and she thought briefly of her cosy bed back at the cottage. Fat, heavy flakes were driven against her as the storm pushed in from the sea, the village before her now seen through a filter of television screen static. She hurried along the road, keen to get out of the weather to the point where she merely glanced at the warm glow of the shop on the way past rather than popping in to buy her customary morning newspaper and biscuits for coffee.

As she opened the gate, she saw the lights inside and Sergeant Duffy moving past one of the windows. The snow was already clinging to the front door and accumulating in the corners. Tess opened the door and slammed it closed, stamping her feet to dislodge the flakes that were attached to her clothing and boots. She shouted a hello down the corridor and heard Colin's muted reply from his office.

Removing her hat, coat and gloves she made her way to the main office, acknowledging the warmth in contrast to the cold outside. Opening her drawer, she placed her gloves and bag inside then hung her coat and cap on the wall-mounted hooks. She returned to her desk and, still standing, logged into her computer, knowing that it would take a little time for the system to boot up completely. Smiling at this blatant disregard for information security procedures as she remembered how logging on then leaving your workstation unattended was one of the more heinous crimes they had been warned against during their training at Tulliallan. But St Cyrus was hardly Glasgow; with only three officers here it was pretty obvious no one was going to mess around on your computer.

Leaving the machine to its own devices Tess crossed the small hallway to Sergeant Duffy's office, frowning as she identified what was missing from the morning's usual routine.

'No coffee this morning Sergeant Duffy? That's not like you!'

Colin turned and smiled at his subordinate. 'Not this morning PC Cameron. Just got in when Susan messaged me about her brother.'

Tess shook her head as she watched Colin putting his coat and cap back on. 'What has he done this time, if you don't mind me asking?'

Colin unlocked a small wall safe and removed a set of car keys before closing the safe but leaving it unlocked. 'Apparently *this* time, someone has beaten *him* up.'

Tess raised her eyebrows in surprise. Steven Wylie was well known to her and the rest of the village as the area's chief troublemaker. Fighting, drunkenness, falling out with his neighbours or some anti-social behaviour were his usual clashes with the law. A truly unpleasant man, Tess always thought it a terrible irony that he was related by blood to Colin and Susan, two of the nicest people you could hope to meet. Even in her short tenure as a constable here, Tess had already encountered Steven in an official capacity more than any other individual in the village. He was barred from entering the Village Inn, a result of one too many drunken fights earlier this year and had a caution for violent behaviour hanging over his head. Colin had always treated Steven in exactly the same manner as anyone else, unwilling and unable to open himself up to any allegations of nepotism or favoured treatment.

'You heading out to see him?'

Colin nodded as he zipped up the heavy jacket. 'Yes. No doubt it will be something he's brought upon himself again. I just want to make sure that nobody else has been hurt.'

'Do you want me to come along?'

'No, no. Let's get the story first and see what's what. No point going in heavy handed if it's a load of rubbish, which if Steven's past is anything to go by, it probably is.'

11

Tess smiled and shook her head. Steven didn't know how lucky he was having Colin as a brother-in-law. She felt fortunate to have been mentored by Colin, to have seen his sensitive and pragmatic approaches to rural policing that struck the balance between upholding the law and maintaining good community relations. Not an easy task in a small Aberdeenshire village.

Colin patted her shoulder as he brushed past. 'You hold the fort here until PC Logan gets in. There's nothing crucial happening but the road closures will start coming in soon so just be prepared for requests for traffic assistance.'

She followed him as he made his way to the door. 'Sure, no problem. It's really coming down out there isn't it?'

'Yes, it is. Forecast said it would be heavy. I'll call in as soon as I'm done with Steven and you can let me know if there's anything you need while I'm mobile. Obviously if there's any problems get me on the radio.'

Tess nodded and winced as a blast of wind and snow came through the opened door. Colin slammed it shut behind him and she was left in the quiet of the station house with only the sound of the wind whistling around the corners of the building. She gave a brief shiver before turning and walking back to the coffee maker, keen to get the morning back on track.

3

'You'll be late.'

The hand didn't stop, continued its slow caress up the outside of her thigh, contoured under her pyjama top and cupped a breast. Cathy sighed and pushed it away. 'Seriously Mitch, you're going to be late for work.'

The hand was jerked away and she felt the cold as the duvet was thrown from him in childish reproach. The bedroom door banged shut and she sighed as she listened to his footsteps stomping towards the bathroom. She hugged the duvet tighter around her and was glad Mitch had to go straight to work. He would sulk for hours over this and she really couldn't be bothered with him this morning. He'd been bad enough last night when she'd laughed at the handcuffs he'd pulled out from under the pillow with what he obviously regarded as an erotic flourish. *Handcuffs, for crying out loud! Could he be any more of an idiot?*

Listening to the shower running, Cathy wondered how to best break the news to Mitch that she was done with them. It had only been a month but it was long enough. He was a child in a man's body; moody, defensive, vain. And the sex was rubbish. Once he had finished, he would simply

13

roll off her or push her off him and make some noise indicating satisfied exertion. Never once asking if she had come or even enjoyed it.

Breaking up was going to be awkward as they both lived in the same village and Inverbervie only had one pub so it was inevitable they would meet again quite often. Still, she knew he was, if not actually seeing other women, definitely pursuing them. She'd glimpsed the odd Facebook and Instagram post from various women before he'd turned his phone away, seen from the flirty nature of the conversation that they were more than friends.

She screwed her eyes up at the thought of being single again. At twenty-eight she assumed she would be married with a family by now, living in one of the big houses in Glebe Crescent while hubby worked offshore earning the cash they needed to fund the big house and the cars. Instead here she was, shagging a policeman whose idea of foreplay was to rub his dick against her buttocks until she turned around.

Today. Do it today. She had two days off work and would use them to go and stay with Jean, her sister, in Aberdeen. Call Mitch at work and tell him then. Truth be told, she didn't think he'd be that upset. Probably turn up in the pub tonight with some other bint he'd picked up, acting the big man. She was fine with that though; she was a local and Mitch was not so he would tread with care in terms of how far he went out of his way to punish or humiliate her. Her brother's friends still kept an eye out for her and policeman or not, Mitch would not be exempt from a smack in the mouth if they deemed he was out of order. Yes. She would call him later and end this, move on with her life, maybe even look at moving up to Aberdeen like Jean was always asking her to do.

Tightening his stomach, he ran his hand along the ridges of muscle, pleased mostly with what he saw and felt. Not *quite* a six pack but not far off. Straightening his arm, he bent his wrist and turned to his side, observing himself in the steam-clouded mirror. He nodded, satisfied with his triceps. Remembering the time, Mitch grabbed his toothbrush and scrubbed at his teeth, watching the reflection of his body. He flicked his hair back, sleek and jet-black after the shower. *Looking good Mitchell my man, looking good.* His eyes were drawn below his waist where his penis lay against his thigh, still thick and swollen from earlier. He rinsed his mouth and listened for a moment before picking up his phone. Standing back from the sink he took a selfie, checked the results, deleted it, adjusted his position and took another. Satisfied with this effort he typed a quick message and sent image and text, grinning widely. *That will give her something to smile about when she finishes her shift!* Bronwyn would be coming off nights at the hospital around now and he congratulated himself on his perfect timing. He hadn't shagged her yet but it was only a matter of time. She'd sent him a picture of her tits yesterday so it was definitely on.

He glanced at the bathroom door as he thought of Cathy's earlier rebuff. The fleeting sense of guilt he felt was immediately surpassed by anger. *This* was why he was chasing other women. He needed more sex than Cathy would give him. It wasn't his fault that he had a higher sex drive. It was genetic; his old man had been the same, had split with Mitch's mother after a string of affairs. Confided in Mitch years later that he just needed more than his wife could ever provide.

His phone buzzed on the counter and he glanced at it hoping that Bronwyn was replying but it was just a work e-mail. Noticing the time, he cursed and hurried his ablutions, already late for work and with a ten-minute drive in front of him. A flurry of applications of deodorant, after shave, moisturiser and hair gel saw him ready to dress and he picked up his phone, left the bathroom and strode into the spare room where his uniform was hanging, ready for wear. He dressed quickly, checked himself in the long mirror then made his way to the front door glancing at the bedroom as he passed. Cathy would let herself out when she woke and he couldn't be bothered going back in to say goodbye. He would text her later.

Shit! The back end of the Freelander corrected itself as Mitch strained his eyes to see the road in front. The snow was already lying and making the road surface slippery, even in a four-wheel drive. Easing off the accelerator, he concentrated on the road ahead. He was late but could easily blame the weather conditions. Although he could already hear Duffy's answer to that as he had heard it on countless other occasions; *Well Mitch, you've been up here long enough now to know the conditions and prepare for them accordingly.* The Sergeant wasn't a bad bugger, just old-fashioned and a bit stuck in his ways. As well as that, community policing rural villages was boring beyond belief and Mitch couldn't wait for his two years to be up and intended requesting a transfer to Glasgow. *Real* police work in a big city; that was why he'd joined in the first place. Catching criminals instead of putting up 'road closed' signs every winter and attending minor traffic collisions.

The snow was really heavy and his heart sank as he could foresee a day of attending to stranded motorists and reassuring terrified pensioners that the power would come back on. Sighing, he slowed down as he entered the winding bends into St Cyrus, the windscreen wipers struggling to keep the screen clear of snow. Approaching the Station House, he noted that one of the vehicles was already gone and wondered what emergency had caused this. He parked with care and jogged to the door, skidding a little as he stopped, keyed in the entry code and pulled it open. Stamping his boots, he removed his jacket and walked down the corridor, the smell of freshly brewed coffee filling the small building and reminding him that he had not yet had breakfast. 'Morning!' His shout echoed a moment before Tess popped her head out from the small kitchen further along the corridor.

'Good morning to you too. Your timing's good, I'm just about to pour a brew. Want one?'

'Is the Pope a catholic? Too right I want one! Where's the Duffer?'

Tess frowned at Mitch's derogatory spin on the Sergeant's name. 'He's had to shoot off. Problem with his brother in-law.'

Mitch laughed. '*Again?* Wasn't it just last week that he was accused of bullying some neighbour of his?'

'Yeah but this time apparently, it's Steven that's the victim.'

Mitch smiled. 'Well, you know what they say; live by the sword...'

'I couldn't agree more. Just a shame that the Sergeant and Susan are always dragged into it.'

Mitch brushed past her and opened the small cupboard above the cooker, removing two mugs which he placed on the worktop. 'Ah, the Duffer will be fine. He always finds a way to deal with it.'

'I wish you wouldn't call him that! He's a good copper and from what I hear was a bit of a legend in his time.' She felt her cheeks flush as Mitch chuckled and held his hands up in mock surrender.

'Okay, okay PC Cameron. I was only kidding. Geez, somebody got out the wrong side of the bed this morning! I take it that it *was* your bed you got out of?'

She spun to face him. 'Oh, piss off Mitch. Firstly, I was in a perfectly good mood until you showed up and second,

18

my sleeping arrangements are nothing to do with you at all.' Grabbing her mug, she stormed from the room to an accompanying low whistle from her colleague.

'Wow Tess, maybe you should email us when you know it's *that* time of the month and we'll tip-toe round you till it's over!'

She resisted the urge to retort to his puerile remarks and settled for a muttered insult under her breath. *Arsehole! Who did he think he was?* She sat at her desk and began trawling through her emails trying to shake the black mood she now found herself in. She knew that it wouldn't last long; she'd been here many times before with Mitch. He infuriated her. Some days he could be charming and funny, was even a decent policeman when he put his mind to it. Then, as reliable as clockwork, he would revert to being the dick that he inevitably could not help being and say or do something to cause an argument.

Her thoughts were diverted by the contents of a recent missive and she read it once again before turning to face Mitch who was now seated at his own desk. 'Hey *Dick,* this will interest you as well.'

Mitch looked over and grinned at her. Tess shook her head. You had to hand it to him, he had skin as thick as a rhino. Seeing that she had his attention she continued.

'There's two Firearms officers from Glasgow coming through here on their way to Aberdeen today. They've got time to drop in and give us a capability brief in the next couple of hours if we're spare.'

19

Mitch was already nodding enthusiastically. 'Too right! Firearms is where I'm looking to specialise once I'm out of this dump. Tell them yes, we'll be here.'

Tess picked up her mobile and began typing a message to Colin, making him aware of the officers' impending visit. She then returned to the email and sent off the confirmation message. She looked over at Mitch who gave her a nod of approval.

'This'll be really interesting Tess. Some of the jobs the Firearms boys do are really hard-core. Surprised you're not that keen on it considering your Army background.'

She shrugged and turned her attention back to the computer. 'Guns are guns Mitch, whether they're Army or Police it's just the same. I left the Army to look for a different career, not to do the same thing in a different uniform. No, it's Detective for me I think.' She heard his chair wheel across the carpet and the excitement in his voice.

'Yeah but think about it; stacking up quietly at the back door of some scumbag who has no idea that you're there, weapon in the shoulder and ready to go, a team of like-minded guys behind you ready to back you up. Don't tell me that's not awesome!'

Smiling, she nodded her assent. 'Yes, it's awesome, but not *my* awesome. *My* awesome is slapping the cuffs on some scumbag that I've nailed through solid police work and good detective skills. Horses for courses Mitch.'

'Mmmm, if you say so. Still think I'll be the one having all the fun mind.'

The office was silent save for the muted clicking of the computer mouse and keyboards as they filtered through the dozens of emails that each officer accrued overnight. Almost lulled back to sleep by the contents of an Aberdeenshire Division HR memo, Tess looked at her phone lying on the desk beside her and wondered how Sergeant Duffy was doing.

4

Colin knocked on the door a second time and waited, rubbing his gloved hand across his face to clear the snow from it. Hearing no reply, he turned the handle and opened the door, stepping into a small entrance hallway littered with muddy boots, wellingtons, and coats smelling of damp. 'Hello Steven, it's Colin. I've been hammering at your door but there was no answer.' Colin moved into the hallway with care, knowing that Steven had occasion to answer his door carrying a shotgun from time to time. He heard a grunt from the direction of the living room further down the hall. 'Steven, that you down there?' Another unintelligible grunt followed but Colin could tell it was Steven's voice. He removed his cap and entered the small room, turning on the light to illuminate the gloom within.

'Fuck's sake man, turn that thing off!'

Colin turned towards the strangled voice and his mouth opened in surprise. His brother in-law was propped up on the sofa holding a bloodied pad against his head. The rest of his face was almost unrecognisable, a deformed mass of swelling, bruising and deep gashes.

'Hell's teeth Steven, what happened to you?' As he rushed to the side of the sofa Colin saw that the injuries were serious. Steven's bones were broken and shattered molars protruded from swollen lips in a grotesque parody of a smile. Even as he was studying the injuries to the face, Steven coughed and clasped at his ribs emitting a low-pitched whine of pain. Colin removed his gloves and began lifting Steven's bloodied sweatshirt from where it covered his chest and abdomen. Steven moaned in protest but Colin shushed him, peeling the garment up slowly until he saw what he was looking for. The rib area was a madman's palette of purples and yellows, deep bruising and more than likely some broken bones. Of more concern to Colin however was the tight, hot swelling in Steven's abdomen; a sure sign of internal bleeding.

Colin stood and reached for his radio. As he brought it to his mouth Steven spat a wad of bloodied material from his own and raised his hand.

'No…no police or ambulance. No… can't…'

'Steven, you're hurt badly and need to get to a hospital now. Don't worry, we'll sort this out.'

'NO!'

Colin started in surprise at the plea in Steven's voice.

'No…can't…don't want help…'

Colin knelt and put his face close to the injured man's. 'Listen, you stubborn idiot, you have to go to hospital or you'll die. You have broken ribs and internal bleeding and there's only a surgeon can deal with that. It doesn't matter what you've done Steven, we can deal with that later, but if you don't get medical help soon, you're going to die in agony.'

He watched as his brother in-law cracked open a blood-crusted eyelid and regarded him through a watery eye, his breathing rasping loud in the quiet room.

'Okay…call ambulance…this really…fucking…hurts…'

Colin stood and spoke confidently into the handset, registering Tess' voice as the reply. He paused only when a question was asked before replying.

'Farming accident.'

'Okay, roger, fifteen minutes, out.' He regarded Steven's contorted face as the man struggled with the agonies he was suffering.

'Steven, we've got fifteen minutes before the ambulance arrives and I need you to tell me who did this to you, okay?'

In spite of his injuries, Colin expected Steven to be his usual uncooperative self and was therefore unprepared for the silence and the tears running down his brother in-law's cheeks. Colin didn't speak, waited for Steven to break the quiet.

'Aw Colin, it's not just me. I think he might have killed Bobby.'

Remaining calm, Colin took Steven's hot hand in his own and was surprised to feel pressure as Steven gripped him hard. Bobby would be Bobby Bruce, a bit of a local rogue who Steven hung around with occasionally. If there had been any doubt before, Colin was sure now that Steven had been up to no good.

'Steven, who? Who do you think killed Bobby and why do you think he's dead?'

His brother in-law's chest heaved as a spasm ran through his system and he hawked up another clot of blood. Colin's brow furrowed with worry and he checked his watch, wishing the time to move faster and get the ambulance here.

'Steven please. You need to tell me what happened so that I can go and see if Bobby's okay.'

The tears continued to trickle down Steven's face, funnelled through his wrinkles and into the stubbly growth on his chin. Colin was really concerned: He had never seen or heard of his brother in-law showing any emotion that was not related to aggression.

'Steven…'

A heavy, broken sigh was followed by a sob of pain and then Colin saw the briefest of nods and his brother in-law began to speak in slow, fractured sentences punctuated by deep rasping coughs the sound of which filled the room.

Colin withdrew his hand, pulled out a small black notebook and pen and began to write.

'He's on his way back Mitch and wants us both here.'

Mitch nodded and stared back at her with undisguised excitement. 'You don't really believe it was a farming accident, do you? Steven Wylie's never farmed a day in his life!'

She was silent a moment before replying. 'No, of course I don't, I'm not stupid but I'm sure the Sarge has his reasons.'

'Must be pretty bad though for him to call it a medical emergency. You think Steven's maybe been shot?'

Tess sighed. 'No, you idiot, I don't think he's been *shot*. A little hard explaining a farming accident callout to the ambulance crew that arrives only to find they're treating a GSW.'

Mitch laughed. 'Yeah, fair one. Still, can't wait to hear what the hell happened though can you? This is the most interesting thing that's happened since I've been here.'

'Yeah okay, but let's calm down a bit. Remember, Steven is Susan's brother and the Sarge's brother in-law so don't be insensitive, right?'

Mitch's reply was interrupted by the sweeping headlights that shone through the frosted glass of the window, indicating that Sergeant Duffy had returned. Both officers returned to their computers, maintaining the façade of being busy with other duties as the front door opened and closed and the sound of footsteps rang down the corridor. Tess looked up and watched as their Sergeant walked straight over to the large-scale map of their part of southern Aberdeenshire. She caught Mitch's eye as the silence in the room extended beyond comfort and Mitch raised his eyebrows and gave a small tilt of his head, indicating that she should speak. As she was thinking about what to say, Sergeant Duffy turned and looked at them over his shoulder.

'Either of you two know much about the guy who owns this property here?'

Tess rose from her chair and walked over to join her superior at the map. She looked to where Colin was indicating and heard Mitch join them from behind. Tess frowned and studied the spot. A wooded property extending to some size with a small cove, jetty and a couple of buildings marked on the map. It had a private access track that meandered through the woods and had markings to indicate that the remains of some old ice-houses were present, a legacy from the days when this area had been known as the silver coast for the proliferation of fish that were caught and exported.

'Not really Sarge, I've never had call to go out there. Mitch?'

They turned to face their colleague whose brow was furrowed in concentration.

'I don't know much about him but I've seen him a couple of times, fuelling up in Montrose. I only know it's him as I saw him coming on to the main road from that direction one day and his place is the only one out there.'

Colin nodded. 'Do you know his name?'

'No. I did ask around the bar one night just out of curiosity. If I remember correctly Barbara from the shop said that he was English and had come up here a few years ago.'

Colin stroked his moustache as he assimilated the information. 'How come I've never seen him in all these years?'

Tess spoke up. 'Maybe he works offshore, or abroad and isn't back here that often.'

'Still, you'd think that we'd have seen him in the shop or the pub, or at the Village Fete or something.'

Mitch cleared his throat. 'Maybe he just keeps himself to himself, you know? And if he's never been on our radar before, we wouldn't have any reason to be aware of him at all. Mind if we ask why you're interested in him Sarge?'

Colin sighed and turned away from the map. He removed his cap and jacket as he walked to a spare chair in the room and sat heavily. 'Well, whoever he is Steven *says*, and I emphasise *says*, that this guy attacked him and Bobby

Bruce last night. Steven is seriously injured and will need surgery and he thinks Bobby might be dead. I quizzed him on that and he thinks this because he managed to escape but, in the confusion, he and Bobby became separated and he hasn't been able to contact Bobby since.'

The room was quiet for several moments before Tess spoke. 'What's your thoughts Sarge?'

Colin leaned forward, elbows on knees and regarded his charges. 'Whatever Steven was doing on this man's property was obviously illegal. The mess that this man has made of Steven however is way beyond self-defence or spur-of-the-moment retaliation. That said, Steven being Steven, maybe this guy is in bad shape also. I won't know for sure until I interview him. So, we need to go out and speak to him. I intend bringing him in for an interview, see what he's got to say.'

Mitch stepped forward. 'I'll go with you Sarge. This guy could be dangerous if he's already done a number on Steven.'

'I appreciate that PC Logan but I'm going to take PC Cameron in the event that there's a wife and kids to deal with. You stay back here and hold the fort.'

Mitch struggled to keep the disappointment from his face and turned back to the wall map to hide it. Tess was jubilant but did not want to upset Mitch unnecessarily by showing it.

Colin stood and gathered up his things. 'PC Cameron, get your stuff together and be ready in ten. I'm going to call

Susan, fill her in on Steven's progress then make a few enquiries, see if we can find out a bit more about our mystery resident.'

Tess had just zipped up her heavy jacket when Colin came out of his office and walked back to the map. 'Okay, I've made a few calls to various people and here's what we've got.' Looking around to see that he had their attention, Colin continued. 'He's an English guy, possibly ex-Army,' he nodded towards Tess, 'came up here years ago and bought this place before the market went mental.' He paused and stabbed his finger at the location on the map. 'And *that* is it, believe it or not. None of the local gossips can give me any more than that. Which is a first.'

Tess spoke up. 'There must be more than that, surely. I mean, he must pop into the shop from time to time at least, eat a meal in the pub, have kids that go to school. He can't just have been here for years with nobody noticing.'

'Well, apparently he can, PC Cameron. Now, we don't have any idea what we will be dealing with down there so I'm authorising the carriage of Tasers as a precaution. Follow my lead on this PC Cameron and we will be fine. PC Logan we'll stay in regular comms with you and if you don't hear from us every fifteen minutes then get on to Stonehaven and get some back-up sent down okay?'

Mitch coloured and spat his words. 'Bloody hell Sarge, I'm more than capable of driving down there and giving you all the back-up you'll need.'

Colin maintained his calm, reasoning tone. 'I know that PC Logan but I'd need you here, coordinating the operation as the officer in charge. You're the one with the local knowledge to direct and guide the assisting officers. This is where I'll need you.' Without waiting for an answer Colin nodded to Tess and left the room. Tess gave a sympathetic look to Mitch before following her Sergeant out of the office and into the tiny armoury where the Tasers were kept. Colin had already unlocked the metal grille hatch and was filling in the signing-out sheets. He then unlocked the main cage and stepped into the small room, punched a numbered code into a keypad and opened the metal locker. Colin withdrew two hard plastic peli-cases, placed them on the floor and opened each one in turn. He checked both of the weapons before handing one to Tess and watched as she secured it to her belt order. 'You happy with how these work PC Cameron?'

She nodded. 'Yes Sarge. We got the lessons at Tulliallan and I did the mandatory refresher a couple of months back.'

Good. Like I say, it's only a precaution, as we know nothing about this guy. Sign the booking out sheet and let's get on our way.' As Tess completed the paperwork, he reversed the opening-up procedures, ensuring everything was secured once again. He pocketed the keys and gave a confidence check on his radio, which squelched through Tess's and the main base station in the main office. They strode off and Colin called Mitch as they passed the office. 'That's us away PC Logan. Will call every fifteen minutes to keep you updated.' The non-committal grunt from within satisfied him that Mitch had understood. He knew the lad wasn't happy but he wanted a level head out there with him and Tess was well ahead of PC Logan in that regard. As they left the building, he felt the drag on his feet and looked down through the howling blizzard, surprised at how deep the snow was already. They hurried to the car and Colin took the driving seat, starting the car and turning the heating dials up. Tess closed her door, cutting off the shriek of the wind.

'Wow Sarge, this is coming in really heavy.'

Colin nodded. 'Yeah, this is a lot worse than the forecast. Let's hope it eases up soon.' He put the vehicle into the four-wheel mode and moved forward, wipers battling to clear the snow that covered the windscreen.

They took their time heading north out of the village and Colin noted that there were no fresh vehicle tracks on the road. He was pleased by this thought as he had anticipated being called out to assist stranded Aberdeen commuters. The car was beginning to warm up as they approached the Tangleha sign and he slowed and took the turning to the right, rolling slowly over the hump-backed bridge and into the sharp bend. The world beyond the windscreen was little more than a blur of snow driven by a furious gale, now hitting the vehicle head on. The noise from the windscreen wipers dominated the sound in the vehicle until Colin spoke.

'Last time I was down here was for one of Ellie Stuart's wee pottery exhibitions. Not really my thing but just flying the flag of local support.'

'Oh yeah, I came to one of these things down here, a photographer's exhibition. Lynne someone or other.'

Colin nodded. 'Lynne Mackie. Does a lot of large format shots of the sea.'

'Yes, that's her. Lives in one of those sea-front cottages.'

'That's right. She's neighbours with Ellie. There's four or five artists all live in that wee row of cottages down there.'

Tess turned to face him. 'We should have called a couple of them. Asked about our mystery resident, they'd probably know more than anyone as they live the closest.'

Colin grinned and changed up a gear. 'Not to steal your thunder PC Cameron but that's where what little I found out about our mystery man came from, but good thinking anyway.' He slowed the vehicle down as he peered through the windscreen, looking for the next junction. 'Right, I think that's us there…' He turned right onto a narrow road where the snow had accumulated in deeper drifts. 'I think we go to the end of this road and where it stops at Woodston cottage we turn right and his drive should be on our left near there.'

Tess pulled out her iPhone and attempted to pull up Google Maps but the network was down. She stretched her legs in the foot-well and thought about their task. *How the hell could someone have lived here for years without anyone even knowing his name?* St Cyrus was one of those rare close-knit communities where close-knit meant looking out for each other rather than looking into each other's business. She loved that about the place and really enjoyed living here in the Police-funded cottage she called her home. There was a real community feel to the place, despite the increase in houses being built and she could just not conceive of anyone willingly avoiding the village and its activities.

Colin brought the vehicle to a halt and picked up the radio handset from the mount on the dashboard. 'Bravo Alpha this is Bravo Sierra, check over.' There was a squelch of static before Mitch's voice responded, informing them that the radio check was clear. Colin replaced the handset and turned right. 'Keep your eyes peeled for that turning PC Cameron, will be quite hard to see if he doesn't have a gate up.'

They crept forward, staring through the snow until Colin gave a grunt of satisfaction. 'Got it.' He turned the wheel into the gap he had spotted and stopped as a five-bar gate halted their access. Straining to see through the snow, Colin shook his head. 'It's chained and locked by the looks of it.'

'We'll need a warrant to enter then.'

Colin pulled on his gloves and donned his woollen hat. 'Absolutely...unless of course we have reason to believe that someone is in imminent danger. For example, Bobby Bruce. According to Steven, nobody has heard from Bobby since last night. I'd better fetch the bolt cutters.'

Tess smiled as Colin slammed his door shut and made his way to the back of the vehicle. He was a wily old fox, no doubt about it. The wind gusted in as the back door was opened briefly then closed again. She watched as Colin passed her window and made his way to the snow-covered gatepost. He studied the chain for a moment then lifted the cutters and pressed the ends together. The chain fell slack and he pulled it from the bars of the gate, throwing it off to one side. He pushed the gate open and walked it back, leaving the opening to the property clear.

Colin jumped back in the vehicle and placed the bolt cutters on the rear seat behind him. Tess felt the cold radiate from him and the warmth of the vehicle's interior was replaced for a moment by the gust of wind that exploited the open door. Colin closed the door and put the vehicle into gear. As they rolled forward, he looked at Tess. 'Right, let's get to the bottom of this nonsense.'

6

The urge to hurl the phone at the wall was all-consuming and only by turning away from the small screen could he regain a small element of control. Taking a deep breath, Mitch again read the contents of Cathy's message.

He had been binned. Chucked, punted, broken-up with. *Fuck!* He jabbed his finger at the iPhone's control button to remove the offending message from the screen. Slamming the phone down on his desk he stood and glared down upon the device as though the inanimate object had somehow colluded in his misfortune. Thrusting his hands into his pockets he forced himself to take another deep breath. *Calm down ya muppet. She was only another chick, loads more fish in the sea and all that.* He picked up his mug from the desk and walked to the kitchen, the act of making coffee as good a distraction as any.

Stirring the steaming brew, he felt his anger subside and its insidious replacement, self-doubt, creep in. Sipping the hot liquid, he stared off into space as he dissected the elements of their relationship, attempting to identify any signs or indicators that could have alerted him that this was going to happen. Cathy *had* been acting a little strange recently, not wanting sex as much, laughing at his attempts to introduce a bit of excitement into their love-life. *Is it another guy? Is that it? Am I being replaced?* No. Mitch was sure that this wasn't the case. Inverbervie was too small a place for anything like that not to have been common knowledge. Her message had been short and to the point; they weren't working anymore and there was nothing to be gained by continuing with something that neither of them believed in.

Shaking his head as he digested this, Mitch struggled to find any signs that she had felt this way. Sure, they'd had their share of fallings-out and arguments but didn't everyone? Mitch didn't know one couple that didn't seem to fall apart on a regular basis. A flush of red coloured his face as he recalled her mocking dismissal of his handcuffs the previous evening. Was this a sign that she thought of him as a figure of fun? Were there other moments, similar to this that he had somehow not picked up on? The creeping thought that perhaps it was a problem in himself entered his mind and took hold with a relentless tenacity. A brief montage of break-ups with previous girlfriends ran through his memory as he sought to identify a common thread that might highlight the reason for Cathy's behaviour. To some women, he had been unfaithful and caught out through the discovery of indiscreet messages and Facebook posts, while with others it seemed to Mitch that they just lost interest. *Why?* He was a fun person to be around, liked a good laugh and a joke, nights out, football, going to the gym.

Walking back to his desk he reflected that he really hadn't had a long-term relationship with a woman for as long as he could remember and at his age, that wasn't necessarily a good thing. While he enjoyed the freedom of not being tied down, he was well aware that as a thirty-year old man he should by now have at least experienced a serious relationship. Sighing heavily, he sat at his desk and placed the mug of coffee on the placemat to one side, staring into the contents of the cup for some time before rousing himself from his reverie of self-pity. *Come on man, you didn't even love the woman.* Which was true; he didn't love Cathy but liked being with her. *Fuck it. Time to move on big man, time to move on.* He jumped slightly at the loud cackle of static from the radio speaker that preceded Sergeant Duffy's message.

'Bravo Alpha this is Bravo Sierra, we are on the property now, over.'

Mitch rose and acknowledged the message, wishing he was out assisting his Sergeant rather than being alone in the stillness of the station with no distractions to help divert his maudlin frame of mind. Pulling his phone from his pocket he thumbed the Facebook icon and checked his feed, scowling when he saw that there was still no response from Bronwyn to his earlier picture that he had sent. Stabbing at the keys of his handset, his mood darkened further by Bronwyn's indifference, he stopped short of sending the message. Reading its contents, he ran a hand over his chin as he pondered the tone. *Too much; you sound like a spoilt child.* Starting over, he typed the new missive with more care and a lighter weight to the contents. *Much better. At least you've actually asked her how she's getting on for a change.* Message sent, he returned to his desk, determined to find some work to take his mind off his personal problems. He wiggled his computer mouse to refresh his blank screen and logged back in to his terminal. Checking his e-mails, he groaned aloud as he read the contents of a HR message informing him that he was loaded on an Equality and Diversity Course next month. *Could this day get any worse?*

7

The track they followed through the woods had less snow cover than the roads but still required some care as they drove further into the property. Colin leaned forward in the driver's seat peering through the windscreen as the heavy snow continued to fall between the pines. Tess remained silent, watching the dark, arboreal avenue ahead, wondering what they would find. A grunt from Colin drew her attention and she turned her gaze in the direction that he was looking. He slowed the Freelander to a crawl as they approached the point of interest. A junction in the track left them with an option of taking a left fork or a right turn that was barred by a gate, chained and padlocked like the first. As he turned the steering wheel to the left, Colin looked down in surprise as Tess laid her hand on his arm.

'Sorry Sarge, but I'm not sure that left is the way to go. Look at the way the bushes and trees at the side of the road are all hanging over. They haven't been cut back in a long time and it doesn't look like anyone has driven down there for ages either.'

Colin thought for a moment before accelerating slightly and continuing with his turning of the steering wheel.

'Yeah, I see what you mean but let's take a wee drive down there. I'm sure it must take us around to the back of the property, which might be handy if we can arrive without being announced so to speak.'

Nodding, Tess continued to observe the gloomy thoroughfare before them, the thick foliage dimming what little light was entering the forest. She turned to Colin and was about to make a quip about getting lost in the dark woods when the front of the vehicle suddenly dropped, throwing them forward as it crashed, airbags exploding, causing Tess to yell an involuntary curse as the car crunched hard against an unseen obstacle. Colin reacted first, turning off the engine and turning to Tess, puzzled and blinking rapidly, pushing the deflating bag from his face and chest. 'Are you okay PC Cameron?'

Tess nodded, rubbing her chest where the seat belt had restrained her on impact. 'Yeah, I'm all good Sarge. What the hell happened?'

Colin spoke over his shoulder as he opened the door. 'I don't know. Think we might have driven into a wee ditch but I'll have a look.'

Unbuckling her own belt, she decided to join him. Pushing the flaccid airbag down, she opened her door and stepped out, footsteps crunching on the dry snow. She saw that Colin had been right in his assessment. The front of the Freelander had tipped into a small, deep ditch, the bumper crushed and resting against the dark earth of the opposite bank. Colin was looking beyond the vehicle and shook his head.

'This isn't good PC Cameron.'

'An accident's an accident Sarge, there was nothing you could have done.' She watched as her superior pointed to the ground either side of their vehicle and to the track that meandered further to their front.

'No, I don't mean that. Take a good look at what we've fallen into and then have a look around it and tell me what you think.'

Tess did as she was asked, noting with surprise that Colin seemed agitated, scanning the woods around them as though searching for something. She continued to study the area and was almost ready to ask Colin what he had been talking about when the answer became clear to her: The ditch had been deliberately placed under the track. There were no other troughs either side of the track and as she bent forward for a better view, she saw an array of shattered branches beneath the wheels of the Freelander. Standing and looking at her Sergeant she cleared her throat.

'This was deliberate Sarge. Someone built that ditch then covered it with enough small branches to conceal it. With the snow on top it was even harder to see. If you'll pardon my French I have to ask, what the fuck is going on here?'

Colin regarded Tess for a moment, his grey eyes narrowed as he assessed their situation. 'This was a trap PC Cameron. Plain and simple. Whoever did this, did it with the sole intention of stopping any vehicle coming down here. Question is, why?'

A heightened sense of awareness washed over her as she acknowledged the significance of Colin's words. The same sensation she'd felt in Iraq and Afghanistan when out on patrol, waiting for that inevitable contact with the enemy. 'What are we going to do?'

Colin was already busying himself around the front of the vehicle. 'We can get it out using the winch and the engine isn't damaged to any degree that will stop it being driven, so let's concentrate on that for the moment then deal with anything else once we're mobile again.'

Tess nodded and stepped down into the ditch to assist her Sergeant. They worked in silence as they accessed the winch and began feeding out the cable. Colin took the shackled end and walked out towards a stand of sturdy sycamores. Tess continued to feed the cable out but monitored the woods around them with renewed vigilance. *Who the hell built traps like this on their own land? And why? What the hell did they have to hide or protect? Drugs? Smuggling?* Her thoughts were interrupted as Colin let her know he had attached the winch cable. She pressed the release button again, this time halting the mechanism. Colin walked back to her, brisk strides crunching the snow under his feet. He continued past her without a glance and she heard the back door of the vehicle open and him rummaging around inside. The door was closed again and Colin came back to the front of the car with two shovels, one of which he passed to her.

43

'Okay, we're going to dig away the lip of this ditch so that when we winch it up, the front of the car will clear it and the wheels will get some purchase. As the winch pulls it forward the back wheels will do the same, then once we're clear we'll spin it round in that wee clearing over there and head back out of here. Sound good?'

Tess nodded and studied the ground before her before taking off her cap then hefting the shovel in her hands. A moment after she heard Colin's shovel bite into the hard earth on his side of the car, she dug her own into the side of the bank, feeling the blade struggle to penetrate the frozen soil. The physical activity warmed her and she soon fell into the rhythm of dig, lever and scoop, watching with satisfaction as the harsh edge of the ditch was eventually transformed into a manageable slope. Colin looked over and nodded at her progress.

'That'll do fine PC Cameron. Chuck your shovel in the back with mine and I'll get in the driver's seat and give you the nod to start the winch.'

Tess followed her superior's directive while still maintaining a wary eye around the woods. As she approached the front of the vehicle once again, she heard the cough of the engine starting and smelled the pungent diesel fumes being emitted from the exhaust. She knelt by the winch at the front and directed her gaze up at Colin who nodded immediately. Tess pressed the winch button and stood back clear of the vehicle as the small whirring motor took up the slack of the cable. Sergeant Duffy's plan worked exactly as he'd explained and after a bumpy climb the back of the car cleared the obstacle and Tess ran forward, stopping the winch. She made her way to the tree and removed the cable, the cold metal stinging her bare hands. Back at the winch she flicked the retrieval switch and watched as the cable was withdrawn back on to its coiled spool. She secured the shackle and turned the device fully off before climbing back in to the vehicle. Colin nodded to her and spun the car around a small clearing between the trees, taking care to avoid the ground they had recently just been trapped in.

'Right. Take two. This time let's just make our way from that gate on foot, shall we? I'd rather have no more surprises like that one.'

'Okay Sarge, I'm with you on that. What's the plan?'

Colin slowed the vehicle as they approached the gate they had passed previously. 'Let's get this gate open and block it with the car just in case anybody tries to get past us.'

Tess nodded, impressed once again with her superior's ability to anticipate problems and implement measures to deal with them. Mitch would never have thought of something like that and she thanked her lucky stars once again that she was out here with Colin rather than her excitable colleague. Without prompting she jumped from the vehicle as it came to a halt and walked briskly to the rear, opening the door and removing the bolt cutters. She made her way to the gate and studied the chain and padlock for a moment. *Sturdy and expensive gear. They haven't skimped on this.* Pulling a loop of the chain to one side she opened the jaws of the tool and settled them each side of a link. Bracing herself, she pushed down hard on the handles, feeling the resistance of the metal before the levered tool did its work and cut through the chain. She pulled the chain and the padlock fell from the broken link, making a soft thud as it disappeared into the snow at her feet. She hurled the now useless chain into the trees and pushed the gate wide open, noting that it moved with ease, obviously well maintained. Colin spun the vehicle around in a tight circle then reversed it until it sat in the centre of the gate's opening, ensuring no-one could get in or out until it was moved.

The engine was switched off and Tess watched as Colin alighted, adjusted his vest order then locked the car with the fob, a confirmatory couple of beeps and a brief flash of the indicators showing all secure. He joined Tess beneath a large conifer and handed her cap to her. 'Better at least look the part PC Cameron. Right, from what I remember of the map I would say we've got about a quarter of a mile or so of track before we get to the house.'

Nodding her agreement, she listened as the Sergeant continued.

'Okay then, let's make our way down there and see what's what when we get to the house, alright?'

Colin turned the power on his portable radio and gave a brief call to Mitch. When there was no reply he tried again.

Still nothing. After a third try yielded no results he turned the volume down and looked at Tess.

'Probably in a dead spot here. We'll try again further along, see if we can't get comms again once we get nearer the water.'

Tess was just about to agree when her heart leapt as a man staggered towards her from the dense gloom of the forest.

8

Colin reacted to the man's appearance first, walking towards him and holding out his hand indicating the man should stop.

'Bobby, it's Sergeant Duffy and Constable Cameron, you need to stop and have a wee chat with us, it's you we've been out here looking for.'

Tess stared, transfixed at the state of the man as he stumbled through the snow towards them. She had not even known that it was Bobby Bruce who had staggered out of the trees even though she had met the man on over a dozen occasions. The swollen, battered face before her gave no clue as to its owner and she was amazed that Colin had managed to identify who it was so quickly. Bobby's thin jacket looked to almost have a camouflage pattern as a result of the dark bloodstains that covered the garment. His jeans looked soaked through and had large swathes of mud adorning the lower legs. Even his thinning fair hair was a sticky mess of coagulated blood. Colin began approaching the injured man, who for his part continued his jilted progress towards them through the snow.

'Bobby, I can see you're hurt there and you need to let us help you. I've already seen Steven and he's had to go to hospital so let's make sure we get you the treatment that you need eh?'

An unintelligible moaning sound came from the swollen gash that served as Bobby's mouth but neither Tess nor Colin could identify the words. Colin made to put his arm around the other man's shoulders. 'Bobby, we can't understand you but I'm going to take you into the car, get you warm and have a look at those injuries okay?' Bobby shoved the arm away then let out a howl of anguish, clutching at his ribs and doubling over, a cloud of breath escaping into the cold air. He recovered quickly and pushed Colin's hand away again. He yelled something through his smashed mouth that both police officers understood: *Leave me alone.*

Colin sighed and walked alongside Bobby. 'Look man, you're in a bad way and only going to get worse. You're beaten half to death and frozen the other. Let us help you, you stubborn old fool!'

Once again, the offer was rebuffed and the other man continued on his rambling way, arms wrapped tight against his body as he tried to retain what little warmth he could. Tess looked at Colin for guidance.

'Nothing much we can do PC Cameron. I suspect his car isn't far from here and it's a four-wheel drive so he won't be stuck.' Looking her in the eyes she noted that his demeanour had changed, a more determined countenance

49

now apparent. 'That's two people this individual has seriously assaulted so we need to be on top of our game down there. This guy could be a nasty piece of work.'

Tess nodded her understanding and felt a small wave of excitement course through her. They hadn't experienced anything like this since her time in St Cyrus and she was feeling that strange combination of anticipation and fear in equal measures. She watched as Colin shook his head at the departing figure of Bobby Bruce, his form soon lost to the swirling snow. Colin tried the radio again but to no avail.

'Right PC Cameron, let's go.'

They walked in silence; the worst of the wind kept at bay by the barricades of thick woods either side of the snow-covered track they were following. Walking side by side, their footsteps muted by the soft snow underfoot, Tess continued to peer into the trees, still wary from their encounter with the ditch. She knew from his head movements that Colin was doing exactly the same thing and was glad that she wasn't out here on her own. Colin's voice shattered the stillness causing her to start a little.

'There's been no vehicle through here in the last twenty-four hours at least. Nothing since the snow started at any rate.'

'Who the hell is this guy Sarge, and what's with the ditch trap and heavily secured gates? I mean, I get that everybody wants their privacy but this seems excessive.'

Colin sighed. 'I'm as clueless as you on this one PC Cameron. Could be he's involved in something where he needs the privacy to protect him from discovery. Drugs? A smuggling operation? Until we get to speak to him it's all just speculation, I'm afraid.'

'That was pretty much the line I was thinking Sergeant. That with all this security, his lack of engagement with the community and his heavy beatings of Steven and Bobby, it seems he must have a good reason for it all.'

Colin tried the radio again but received nothing other than a burst of mocking static. He mouthed a silent curse and pulled out his mobile, scrolling through the numbers before selecting one and putting it to his ear. 'Constable Logan, the radio's down so I'll give you a wee bell on this from time to time until we get comms established again okay? What? No, we're all good, had a couple of interesting developments but I'll fill you in on those on our return. Two things I need you to do for me though, okay? One, give Stonehaven Duty Officer a call and just let them know where we are and what we're doing. Second, give it half an hour then ring Bobby Bruce at home and make sure him or his wife let you know that he's there. I'll be back after that and take care of everything else. Happy? Good, we'll speak again soon, bye.' Colin replaced the handset back into his vest pouch and indicated to his front with his head. 'That's the building coming into view PC Cameron. Let's just make sure the Tasers, batons and handcuffs are at hand eh? Not saying we'll need them but better to be ready I think.'

Tess checked all her equipment, the adrenalin building as she concluded her task. *An arrest!* It really looked like this was going to happen, and not just of a simple drunk either. She looked her superior in the eye and nodded to show that she was ready. Colin gave a slow blink and the pair made their way towards the building that appeared at intermittent intervals through the snow.

9

Mitch Logan was picking up the handset to call Stonehaven when the intercom interrupted him. Frowning, he replaced the telephone onto its cradle and walked over to the small screen on the wall. Although he did not recognise the face, the cap and uniform were those of a fellow officer and he remembered with a jolt that he had forgotten all about the Specialist Firearms Officers', or SFOs as they were referred to. He mumbled a curse as he pressed the speak button. 'Hi there, you the Firearms' boys we're expecting?'

There was a brief pause and he watched as the figure on the screen leaned into the camera.

'Aye, that's us mate. Sergeant Fletcher and Constable Armstrong. Any chance of opening the door, it's Baltic out here!'

Mitch pressed the release button and heard the harsh buzzing noise and a moment later the sound of stamping feet and hands being rubbed together. He walked out into the hallway to greet the visitors. The two men were busy brushing the snow from their clothes with their hands.

'How's it going? I'm Constable Mitch Logan, welcome to St Cyrus.'

Both men looked up with the older of the pair walking forward and offering his hand. 'How you doing? I'm Sergeant Fletcher and that's Constable Mark Armstrong.'

Shaking the proffered hand Mitch indicated behind him with his head. 'Come on through and I'll sort you out with a hot brew.' The appreciative grunts from the men told them that his suggestion had been a welcome one. He entered the small kitchen area and pulled two mugs from the rack above the sink. 'What'll you have?'

The Sergeant replied for both men. 'Tea, white, one for me and coffee, black, one for PC Armstrong.'

Mitch nodded and set about making the beverages as the two men looked around the main office from the doorway. The Constable leaned back over the threshold.

'Nice wee nick, eh? How many of you here?'

Mitch stirred the drinks as he answered. 'Three of us; me, the Sarge and another PC.'

'Cool. You busy?'

Mitch laughed. 'Er…no. One drunk a month and a lost cat if we're lucky!' Picking up the mugs, he joined the men in the main office, handing each one their brew and nodding at the murmured thanks. He took a moment to discreetly observe the pair, not wanting to appear in awe of them. The Sergeant was older but obviously kept in shape, lean and wiry but with an inherent strength about him. The constable looked to be about ages with Mitch but had a big mop of ginger hair and a semi-permanent frown. Mitch indicated that they should take a seat beside Tess' desk as they enjoyed their hot drinks.

'What is that snow like out there Mitch? We've nearly been off the road three times since leaving Glasgow, eh Sarge?'

Mitch nodded at the constable. 'Yeah, it's been bad all morning with no sign of letting up. Thankfully we haven't been called out to any stranded motorists, touch wood.'

The Firearms' Sergeant nodded at Colin's door. 'Where's your Sergeant? Out and about or has he got some time off?'

'No, he's out with PC Cameron bringing someone in for an interview.'

'Oh aye, anything serious?'

'Nah, not really. Suspected assault on a couple of toe rags who probably deserved it.'

The Sergeant grunted his acknowledgement of a common situation. 'Any idea when they'll be back in? We weren't in any rush but with this snow settling so heavy I think we'd rather get the last leg done sooner rather than later.'

Mitch pointed to the telephone. 'He's literally just off the blower saying they were at the suspect's location so I shouldn't think they'll be much longer.'

'No dramas, it's only a capability brief as I said. Bring you guys up to speed with who we are, what we do and how you can make best use of us.'

Mitch leaned forward, elbows on knees, eyes shining with enthusiasm. 'We're all looking forward to it Sarge, me especially as I'm going to put in for Firearms after my two years are up here.'

The Sergeant grinned and held up his mug. 'Tell you what mate. Give us a refill and square us away with some biscuits and we'll give you a warts and all insight to the job until your *compadres* return. Deal?'

Mitch's grin and the speed with which he left the chair told the Sergeant that it was definitely a deal. As Mitch busied himself in the kitchen the Sergeant turned to his constable and raised an eyebrow. He was answered with a nod and a soft grin. Both men were accustomed to the high regard in which they were held by junior members of the force and were not above exploiting it, depending on what was on offer and who it was from.

Mitch handed the men their respective drinks and left an opened pack of Jaffa cakes between them. The Sergeant winked his thanks, stuffed a whole biscuit in his mouth and rinsed it down with a large swig of his tea before speaking. 'Actually Mitch, we've just finished a wee job down in Cambuslang that is probably a good example of a standard tasking for us. Why don't I give you a quick brief on that and you can ask any questions you have? Sound good?'

Mitch nodded his assent and sat forward again, giving the pair his undivided attention. The Sergeant took another drink before beginning.

'So, Cambuslang has a huge drug problem, as you may or may not be aware…'

10

The house sat among an enclave of mixed conifers, a dwelling of dark sandstone, the accumulating snow on the gables contrasting with the umber hue of the walls. Other than the wind caressing the branches, there were no other sounds around the property. Colin stood still as he took in all the relevant details of the house, looking for anything that might supply him with further information about the owner. It was a typical cottage constructed in the local vernacular, with two bay windows on the ground floor and two dormers on the first floor. A white door matched the frames of the windows and neutral-coloured curtains seemed to be the fabric of choice in all the rooms that he could see. There was no vehicle apparent but he remembered from the map that there was an abundance of outbuildings to the rear and further back towards the jetty and slipway.

Tess remained silent, taking the lead from Colin and observing the area for anything of interest. There was still no let-up in the snow and she strained her eyes to look beyond the building and into the area behind. She looked down as she felt a gentle pressure on her arm and saw

Colin's gloved hand attracting her attention. He leaned in and spoke quietly, never taking his eye off the house.

'I'm going to go to the front door and give it a knock, see if anybody answers. I want you to go to the back just in case they decide to take off. Give me two clicks on the radio to let me know you're in place and I'll do the same.' He paused and turned to face her, his grey eyes locked on her own. 'Do NOT take any chances Tess. If this guy comes barrelling out of there either Taser him or get out of his way and give me a yell. I'd rather we both got out of here unscathed even if it means our guy gets a pass for a few more days, agreed?'

She nodded her understanding and set off to take up her post, making her way around the building using the dense woods to cover her from anyone who may have been watching from the house. As she was about to pass the gable end, she looked back to her superior who gave a slow nod of encouragement and began making his way to the front door. Tess lost sight of Colin and quickened her pace past the side of the house and into a large courtyard with several stone outbuildings. More interestingly, a black Toyota Hilux sat parked by the double doors of a former stable, its windscreen, roof and bonnet thick with snow. *Well that hasn't moved for a while.* She kept her back close to the wall as she made her way towards the back door of the cottage. Encountering a large window, she got down on her hands and knees and crawled below the sill, keen to keep her presence unseen. Her heart was racing and she was almost light-headed with excitement. *Calm down woman, there's probably nothing going to happen.* Standing up again she crept slowly towards the back door and took a position beside it, noting with interest that the accumulation of snow on the step remained undisturbed. She paused a moment before giving two firm presses on the radio handset, the pre-agreed signal that she was in place. After a moment a muted two bursts of static came from her own radio: Sergeant Duffy was also in place.

Colin took his hand from the radio and grasped the wrought iron knocker then gave the door three hard raps, the sound fracturing the stillness around the clearing. He stepped back from the door slightly and waited. After several moments had passed, he stepped up again and carried out the same action. Again, there was no response to his knocks. He tried the door and was not surprised to find that it opened with ease once the handle was turned. Very few people in these parts locked their doors and he was glad that his suspect was one of them. He removed his extendable baton from its pouch and gave a flick of his wrist, the weapon now opened to its full length. The house was dim inside and utterly silent. His footsteps seemed very loud on the hardwood flooring and he took more care when placing his feet, attempting to remain as silent as he could. He found himself in a hallway with a door at the far end, open and leading into what looked like a kitchen area. He pushed the door to his left and saw a living room with a sofa and a couple of chairs but no sign of life. The door to his right was only open a fraction and he pushed against it gently, wincing at the creaking groan it emitted as it swung open. A dining room this time with a dark wood table and matching set of chairs, but again, no one present. He made his way carefully along the hallway, past an open door that led into a simple bathroom and a small utility room where some cardboard boxes were stacked.

Looking through the open door of the kitchen, he could see that there was nobody in there either and decided to check out the upstairs. The old floorboards conspired against him, emitting groans of protest under his weight that seemed to echo around the silent house. *No point trying to be quiet after that.* Colin climbed the wooden staircase faster and entered each room with confidence, finding nothing other than tidy rooms, each with a double bed made up with pillows and duvets, matching the neutral colours that seemed to dominate the house. Sighing, he made his way back down the stairs and into the kitchen. This room was similar to the others; clean tidy and with no clutter or anything homely. A single glass and a small white plate stood up in a wire drying rack, accentuating the atmosphere of emptiness. He shook his head and pulled the back door open.

Tess leapt back, baton in hand, eyes wide with shock. She lowered the baton and scowled at Colin's quiet chuckle.

'Not funny Sarge and you wouldn't be laughing so hard if I'd Tasered you.'

Colin beckoned her inside and she entered and closed the door behind her. 'PC Cameron, go take a look around this house and tell me what you think.'

Tess wandered the house as Colin had before her, pausing in each room and taking the time to observe her surroundings. She walked back down the stairs and could hear Colin attempting to raise Mitch on the radio. Colin had just pulled out his mobile when Tess entered the kitchen and addressed him.

'Nobody lives here Sarge, or if they do, they haven't for a while.'

'Why do you say that?'

She swept her arm taking in the area behind them. 'Look at it. No signs of life. No television, computer, phone chargers, books, magazines, mail; nothing.'

Colin nodded and pointed to the draining board. 'Well, someone has been here at some point. But I agree with you, this place is definitely not lived in.'

'What do you think?'

Colin sighed, removed his cap and placed it on the counter. He rubbed his short-cropped hair and thought for a moment before speaking. 'Let's have a look at those outbuildings. Could be this is only used as guest accommodation or even a holiday let, with the main residence being out there.' He replaced his cap and put the mobile back in its pouch. He would call PC Logan once they'd finished in the outbuildings.

Tess followed her Sergeant out of the kitchen and closed the door behind her. The snow was falling thick and heavy as they disturbed the pristine blanket covering the courtyard. Colin pointed to the first building and she nodded. All the buildings were constructed in the same red sandstone as the main house but had no windows, only large, oversized wooden doors, their black paint peeling with age and neglect. She stood at Colin's side as he reached for the dark metal latch and noted with surprise the ease with which the mechanism operated. She had expected the latch to be stiff and rusted in keeping with the general condition of the door but it was clearly better maintained than the wood.

The space inside was dim and they waited a moment, each pulling their torches from their respective vest orders. Colin entered and waited for Tess to join him before pulling the door closed behind them. Tess jumped as the room was suddenly bathed in light and turned to see that Colin had flicked a switch on the wall and a row of lights hanging from the ceiling illuminated the room. In silence, the officers conducted a survey of the building from their positions by the door. Practically empty other than some disused lobster creels, nets and buoy markers in one corner and a cluster of engine parts in another. The remainder of the space was a simple flagstone floor, clean and with nothing else of interest. Colin caught Tess's eye and indicated with his head back towards the door. Tess nodded and followed him outside, switching off the lights and closing the door behind her. Kicking their way through the snowdrifts that had accumulated against the wall of the building they approached the second door, an exact copy of the first.

Colin entered first once again and repeated the procedure of closing the door and turning on the lights. In contrast to the first outbuilding they had entered, this one was much bigger and clearly well used. To Tess's eye it reminded her of some of the larger gyms that she'd seen in FOBs in Iraq and Afghanistan. The floor here was covered with exercise equipment, and lots of it. Barbells, dumbbells, kettle bells, weight plates, gym mats, heavy ropes. In one corner a heavy punch-bag dominated what seemed to be a boxing area with several other types of bags that she couldn't identify and a padded, life-size man's torso mounted on a large sprung device. Colin turned to her.

'What do you think PC Cameron?'

'I think that someone definitely uses this place a lot Sarge. This is all serious kit and well used at that. It's also, really…*macho*…is that the word I'm looking for?' She caught his raised eyebrow and continued. 'This reminds me of the gyms I saw on the bases in Iraq and Afghanistan, set up with basic equipment for testosterone-fuelled blokes to beast themselves on their time off. This is not a place where women or even your average office worker would come to train.'

'That's interesting PC Cameron. Remember what Mitch said about this guy possibly being ex-Army? That might explain this set-up and the very tidy house.'

'Good point Sarge, but this is a massive set-up. Whoever uses this place trains *hard*. And I think it might be used by several people. Look at the boxing corner; there's several pairs of gloves and head protectors stacked there.'

Colin nodded in agreement. 'Yes, I noticed that myself. I see also that there's no heating in here, so whoever trains here obviously works hard enough to be warm in the winter cold.'

Tess took a few steps towards a set of tyres that were stacked against a wall. They ranged in size from a car tyre to what she could only assume to be a tyre from a truck with a large, heavy ribbed tread. A pile of knotted ropes lay beside them and stood erect alongside these was a sledgehammer. Her mind connected the disparate elements and she realised she had seen people using these before. Again, returning to the memory bank of her former life as a soldier she recalled seeing guys dragging tyres behind them from crude rope harnesses and repeatedly smashing prone tyres with sledgehammers. Crude but effective training, perfect for tightly wound soldiers in FOBs to vent their frustrations upon.

Colin interrupted her thoughts. 'Let's check out that last building then take it from there eh?'

'Yeah sure Sarge, lead the way.' As she turned the lights out and closed the door behind her she realised that her previous sense of excitement had been replaced by a creeping sensation of dread.

They repeated their drill and entered into the final building. The lights shone on a floor space similar to the first room they had found. As Colin looked around, he saw a stack of simple chairs against one wall and a pile of old trestle tables folded against each other. A projector screen in its retracted state was also placed neatly against the wall.

'Sarge, did you notice the heaters?'

Colin hadn't but followed the direction of Tess's pointing hand and saw the four portable radiators stood at the far end of the room.

'Unless I'm mistaken, this room is also for training but probably for lectures or something? Do you know what I mean PC Cameron?'

'Yes Sarge, again, it reminds me of a basic military classroom that you'd see put up during an exercise or deployment. And what's that smell? It's faint but really familiar.'

Colin shook his head. 'Yeah, I got it as soon as we came in but I can't quite put my finger on it. Look; there's electrical sockets and a couple of extension leads as well. Definitely used for training. I'm going to take a wee peek around the back of these buildings. You have a look through this room and see if you can find anything else then join me once you're done okay?'

'Okay Sarge, see you soon.'

Colin made his way out of the building and Tess began looking for anything of interest. She pulled the tables apart but there was nothing between them. The chairs were a similar disappointment, yielding nothing. She walked the perimeter of the room and was about to leave when she noticed a small waste-paper bin in the far corner. Walking over to it she thought that it was empty however on standing above it she saw a small white object stuck to the bottom of the bin. She reached in and pulled the small item away from its metal receptacle. It was a small rectangle of white cloth with a faint red line running through it and it took only a moment for her eyes to widen in recognition. It was a piece of flannelette, the cloth cleaning materiel issued to British soldiers for weapon cleaning. Her nostrils flared as a second recognition was sparked by the cloth. She now knew what the smell was they had been puzzled by on entering the room. Gun oil. The sickly-sweet petrochemical tang that smelled like nothing else. Another realisation hit her: She had to tell the Sarge.

11

Colin stood back in order to see the rear of the buildings in their entirety. Nothing. No back doors or entrances that they had missed. That left the old icehouses further back in the woods. He started to walk back to the corner of the outbuildings where he intended meeting back up with Tess. He had just turned the corner when he saw a man step out from the trees between the house and the outbuildings. Colin started a little but recovered and stepped towards the individual. 'Sir, I'm Sergeant Colin Duffy and I need to ask you a few questions okay?'

Colin watched the man come to an abrupt halt and turn his attention to the policeman. He estimated that there was perhaps fifteen feet between them and he took the opportunity to take in all the stranger's details that he could between the falling snow. Despite the weather, the man was wearing a t-shirt, jeans and work boots yet showed no sign of discomfort. Colin could see the individual was muscular, the rounded shoulders, bulky biceps and corded arms prominent through the thin garment. He stood with legs slightly apart, arms loose by his side and stared at Colin with no hint of emotion. Colin's policeman's eye looked for an adjective to describe his initial impression of the stranger and he found himself settling on one that Tess had used earlier; *Hard*. If Colin had to describe the man in one word, he would say he looked hard. The man's dark hair was very short, almost shaved and his eyes black against the tan of his face. *An outdoor man then.*

He repeated his statement and again, the man showed no response. Colin's mouth felt dry and he realised that he was anticipating a confrontation. In a slow but casual move he lowered his hand to his belt order and flipped the retaining loop from the Taser's holster.

'Sir, I really need you to come over here and identify yourself so that we can talk, okay?'

This time the man moved his head slightly, looking to Colin's sides and rear. He then took a step forwards but Colin could see it was not a gesture of compliance. Feeling his heart race Colin held out his hand. 'Right sir, I want you to stop there. Do NOT come any closer. Do you understand?' The man continued closing the distance, his body relaxed, almost sauntering casually across the snow. This state of indifference gave Colin more cause for concern. In all his years of experience he'd only encountered a couple of people who seemed truly without emotion and they had been very dangerous individuals. The man had closed the gap to under ten feet when Colin aimed the Taser.

'Sir I am ordering you to stop RIGHT NOW! If you do not, I will shoot you with the Taser and arrest you. Stop right now.' Colin could see the shaking of his hands as the end of the Taser jerked up and down in small increments. As the man took another step, regarding Colin with his cold, dispassionate eyes, the policeman fired. A short whine emitted a split second before the two barbed projectiles shot out from the black and yellow plastic body. Colin's eyes followed the path of the projectiles and widened in disbelief. The man had hurled himself to the ground and rolled towards Colin, avoiding the Taser completely, the projectiles flying aimlessly through the snow. Colin's mouth opened in astonishment and he let out an involuntary yell as he watched the man propel himself towards his legs. Colin dropped the neutered weapon, stepped back and drew his baton. As he was retreating to create some distance his foot caught against something hard under the snow and he tumbled backwards over it. The wind was knocked from him but he knew that he had to get back on his feet immediately. Gasping for breath he rolled on to his side and got to his knees only to see the man stood before him. Acting on instinct Colin raised the baton but the man's hand shot out and with what seemed to Colin to be an effortless grace, twisted the weapon from his hand and held it in his own. The man looked at the baton he was now holding with the same empty stare then turned his attention back to Colin. The policeman was sucking down huge gulps of cold air in an attempt to get his breathing back but keeping his eyes on the man before him.

The man turned his head briefly and studied the area around them. Seeming to come to a decision, he turned his attention back to Colin fixing him with the glare from his cold black eyes. He spun the baton in a smooth flourish and raised it swiftly above his shoulder. Colin threw his arms above his head in reflex, squeezed his eyes closed, gritted his teeth and braced himself for the impact. A strange grunt and groan caused him to look up again and his eyes widened in surprise. The man was now on his knees, the baton dropped by his side and his face contorted in agony. Two wire filaments trailed from his body and back past Colin. Turning his head to look behind him, Colin saw Tess stood in the classic shooting position, Taser raised in front of her. He felt his breathing coming back and stood on shaking legs and waited for a moment before leaning forward and retrieving his baton from the snow. As he approached the man, the individual raised his head and yelled as Tess applied a further charge to subdue him. Waiting a further moment, Colin stepped forward, handcuffs at the ready then halted in surprise as the man slowly raised a hand and spoke.

'Stop, stop, stop.' The words came with difficulty and were shouted, the sounds echoing around the buildings and woods. Colin noted the English accent and watched as the man held his strange pose of surrender, his right hand raised in a clenched fist, head lowered in supplication. The man spoke again, yelling his words at them.

'Where are you taking me?'

Colin took a breath and yelled back, considering the possibility that the man had a hearing problem. 'We're taking you to St Cyrus Police Station now but we'll be transferring you to Stonehaven as soon as we can, although with this snow it might not be today.'

The man nodded and dropped his hand, collapsing on the snow. Colin glanced at Tess who nodded and continued her control of the man through the Taser while Colin approached with the handcuffs. Tensed for any trickery, Colin applied the handcuffs and hauled the man to his feet, reading him his rights. He saw Tess removing a small pack from her webbing vest and was grateful he'd chosen a switched-on constable to accompany him. As she opened up her small surgical kit for the removal of the Taser barbs, Colin pushed the man until his back was against the wall and informed him that they were removing the projectiles and that he wasn't to move.

Tess stepped closer to the man and Colin saw she had her examination gloves on and the dressing ready. Stepping slightly to one side, Colin readied the baton in anticipation of the man trying something. He watched as PC Cameron worked quickly, cutting the cloth around the entry holes, swabbing the area and then removing the barbs with a small push to extend the wound slightly then a deft removal. The whole time she was working, Colin noticed that the stranger stared off into the middle distance and reacted to nothing, not even the pain of the removal. Tess secured the dressing on the stranger's chest and nodded to him to confirm she had finished. Colin took the man's arm and pulled him firmly away from the wall. As Colin walked the man before him, he could feel the strength in the individual's arms and for the first time since the incident had begun, felt a flood of gratitude for Tess's actions. He would tell her later rather than now in the presence of the man they had arrested. Colin continued walking the man along the track towards their vehicle and spoke to him.

'What's your name sir?'

The man said nothing, merely continued with his compliant shuffle ahead of the policeman. Colin sighed.

'Look, you might as well tell us your name, it gives me something to call you and we'll find it out down the station soon enough.' Again, there was no response from their arrestee.

'Alright Mr no-name, is there anyone you want us to contact to let them know you've been arrested?'

Colin raised his eyebrows in surprise as the man shook his head and spoke softly.

'No. There's only me.'

Colin nodded and they conducted the remainder of the walk in silence, the police officer's watching the suspect closely for any indication that he intended further resistance. Colin waited for Tess to open the back door of the Freelander before helping the man into the rear seat. Closing the door, he walked around to Tess and put his hands on her shoulders.

'Thank you for that today Tess. I think that man might have hurt me very badly if you hadn't stopped him. Thank you.'

Tess felt a flush of embarrassment at the praise and lowered her head, busying herself with her Taser holster.

'Was just doing my job Sarge. You'd have done the same.'

'Well, you done good all the same and I'll shout you a few drinks tonight. Meanwhile, let's get our mystery man back to the station and see what he has to say.'

They climbed into the vehicle and Tess turned to look at their detainee who was looking out the window into the forest beyond. *Probably wondering when he'll see it next.*

As the Freelander turned around and left the area a white-clad figure stirred from the side of a rhododendron bush. The figure motioned with his arm and a further two individuals emerged from separate positions in the forest, again, covered head to toe in white camouflage gear, rendering them almost invisible in the snowy environment. The three came together and stood looking up the track before the first individual spoke, his face covered with an intimidating white mask with only his eyes and mouth visible.

'We need to get him before they move him to Stonehaven or they'll have him. You know what to do so let's get the equipment together and ready for orders in fifteen.' The other two nodded and all three jogged into the forest and out of sight, the fat flakes of snow already covering their tracks and evidence of their presence.

12

The Jaffa cakes were finished and Mitch had just walked over to the kitchen to make another round of drinks when he heard the squawk of the radio. He dropped the mugs in the sink and rushed to the base station, picking up the handset. Before he could say anything, the Sarge's voice came through the speaker, distorted and muffled but understandable.

'Bravo Alpha this is Bravo Sierra, over.'

Mitch spoke into the handset. 'Yes, Bravo Sierra, send, over.'

'Bravo Alpha, we are returning with suspect. Can you ensure custody suite is ready for use, over?'

Mitch raised his eyebrows in surprise. 'Bravo Sierra, will do. What's your ETA, over?'

'Bravo Alpha, weather slowing us down but ETA in fifteen, over.'

'Bravo Alpha, Roger and out.'

Mitch put down the handset and looked over at the two visiting officers who were regarding him with expectation.

'Guess they must have found the guy and are bringing him in.'

The Firearms' Sergeant looked at his watch. 'Well, if they're only fifteen minutes out we're as well waiting and giving you all a briefing at the same time.'

His partner nodded and stood stretching his arms above his head and yawning. 'I'll go and grab all the gear inside Sarge.'

'Cool. Mitch, you mind if I clear a space on that table there? Just need to move those leaflets and folders over so we can display our kit there.'

Mitch stood and started making his way to the key press in the Sergeant's office. 'Yeah, no problem, I'll leave you to it while I get this sorted.'

He retrieved the keys and walked along the corridor to the rarely used holding cell they generously referred to as the custody suite. St Cyrus Station had actually been a Police Station up until the 1980s when it had been sold as a private house and converted into a residence, aptly named 'The Old Nick'. In a strange quirk of fate, when Police Scotland initiated their Community Policing placements in towns and villages, the house was up for sale at the time. It was purchased and converted back into its original role, albeit modernised for current Police use. As such, the custody suite was located where the original cells had been in the old building and still retained an old-fashioned jail feel despite the modern door and sterile interior.

Mitch flicked on the lights and looked inside the main cell. It was, as always, clean and ready for use. He then walked behind a small counter and bent down, retrieving several items that he then laid on the counter top. He ran through a mental checklist of everything the Sarge would require on his return and pointed to each item as he silently mouthed his list. *Booking-in ledger and pen, belongings bag, permanent marker, gloves for the search, lap top.* He nodded his head, satisfied that everything was ready then turned on the lap top, hearing the whir and beeping of the machine as it came to life. All the details could be entered on here by one of them so that there was a digital and paper copy of the in-processing in compliance with Police Scotland's procedures. When the desktop picture appeared on the screen, he made his way back to the main office and smiled as he saw the display that the Firearms' team had laid out on the table.

'Wow! That's some serious hardware, eh?'

Sergeant Fletcher regarded the younger man and gave an indulgent smile. 'Well, it might look like it here but believe you me, there have been a couple of times when I've wondered if it was enough!'

Mitch's eyes widened. 'You're kidding?'

The Sergeant spoke as he continued laying out the weapons and ammunition on the table. 'Nope. We got into a bit of trouble about a year ago when we went head to head with some Bulgarian drug-runners in Glasgow. The intelligence wasn't as good as it should have been so we rocked up expecting pistols and shotguns and faced automatic rifles and grenades. A bit of a cheeky wee day eh Constable Armstrong?'

The other officer grinned and nodded. 'Yeah, was like the wild west there for a while!'

Mitch gave a low whistle. 'Man, that must have been insane! I can't wait to put my request in for you guys.'

The Sergeant regarded him quietly for a moment. 'That's great Mitch and I'm sure you'd love it but in the spirit of full disclosure we do spend a lot of our time sitting on our arses or doing training scenarios.'

Mitch smiled and waved his hand to encompass the room behind him. 'That's no problem to me Sarge; I've had plenty of practice sitting on my arse around here!'

The Sergeant laughed, remembering how keen he had been to join the Firearms unit when he had been a young constable like Mitch. 'Fair enough, just don't let me see you moaning about it two years from now!'

'No chance: I've been wanting to join Firearms since the day I graduated from Tulliallan.'

The radio squawked again and Mitch bounded over to it as Colin's voice came through the speaker.

'*Bravo Alpha this is Bravo Sierra. Our ETA now five minutes, over.*'

Mitch looked at his watch and acknowledged his superior's transmission. He wondered who this guy was that they were bringing in and what Steven had done to deserve the hiding he no doubt had earned. His train of thought was interrupted by the Firearms Sergeant.

'Hey Mitch, come and have a wee familiarisation on these before your colleagues arrive.'

He looked up to see the Sergeant holding an assault rifle and Glock pistol in his hands while smiling at him. Mitch grinned with the enthusiasm of a schoolboy and approached the Sergeant who turned the rifle over in his hands and demonstrated the safety checks to be carried out before passing the weapon to another individual. He took the proffered weapon, surprised at the weight and examined it closely as the Sergeant pointed out the component parts and what they did. Cocking handle, safety catch, fire selector lever, flash eliminator, magazine release catch, ACOG sight system. Raising the rifle up to his shoulder Mitch lowered his head and looked through the sight, the room before him blurred but the reticules, cross hairs, and numbers all in sharp relief. The Sergeant explained how the sight worked and its partnership abilities with night vision devices and laser target marking. Mitch was listening but in his head was picturing entering a derelict squat in Glasgow, weapon in his shoulder just like he had now, ready to take down some Bulgarian gunman. He couldn't wait to be doing this for real.

Sergeant Fletcher took the rifle from Mitch and laid it down on the table beside the other weapons and equipment. He picked up one of the Glocks and cleared the weapon before handing it to Mitch. Again, the Sergeant talked Mitch through the elements of the gun as the younger man went through the motions of drawing and aiming the weapon. A flash of light beamed through the upper portion of the window and Mitch handed the weapon back.

'That's the Sarge and Tess back. I'm going to open the back door so they can take the suspect straight to the custody suite then I'll get the Sarge to come and speak to you guys.' He hurried to the rear door where a small passage linked it to the bottom corridor that led to the custody suite. This was particularly useful as the suspect didn't have to go through any other part of the station to be taken to the cell. Turning on the light he undid the two deadbolts at the top and bottom of the door then turned the large key, the mechanism moving with reluctance but engaging nonetheless. He pulled the door open and grimaced as the snow assailed his face and the peak of a small drift fell into the passageway, covering his boots. Through the heavy snow he could see the Sarge and Tess getting out of the vehicle before they both moved to the rear door.

He watched as Tess opened it and a man was helped out, restrained in handcuffs and head lowered. The door was closed and the trio approached Mitch, one officer each side of the individual. As they got closer Mitch saw that the man was wearing a t-shirt on his top half and must have been freezing. He also noted that this guy was in very good physical condition. As a regular gym user himself he was accustomed to comparing his own body to others and was impressed by this individual's physical shape. And it wasn't soft muscle either; he had that well-toned look that was common to some of the boxers and mixed martial arts fighters Mitch had known over the years.

He stepped aside as Tess led the man inside with the Sergeant behind him. They didn't say a word as they passed but Colin nodded to Mitch as he drew level with him. Mitch shivered in the cold and pushed the heavy door closed, slamming the bolts home and locking it once again. He made his way to the kitchen, knowing that Tess and the Sarge would want to process the individual themselves. Taking down a couple of mugs he set about making the pair a hot drink, having felt the cold radiating from his colleagues when they had passed him in the small passageway.

Tess could hear the frustration in the Sergeant's voice.

'Look, there's nothing to be gained by not telling us your name. We'll get it soon enough and it just saves a bit of time and we can speak to you like a human being and not a prisoner.' When there was no reaction from the man Colin sighed and indicated that he should raise his arms. 'Okay no-name, I'm now going to carry out a personal search. Do you have anything in your possession that could potentially hurt or injure me? For example, any needles or open blade knives?' The man shook his head slowly and Colin began the search, alert for any signs that might indicate the man was thinking of resisting.

Tess removed her Taser and placed it in the shelf behind the desk alongside Colin's. She didn't want to leave Colin and the stranger alone while she returned the weapons to the security locker but she would do it later when their detainee was safely locked away.

As he ran his gloved hands around the waistband of the man's jeans, Colin again was surprised by the individual's compliance. Since his Tasering back at the house the man had shown nothing other than silent cooperation. Continuing the search down the man's body, Colin removed a wallet and set of keys from the jeans' pockets, passing the items to Tess who opened the wallet and noted the contents, the sound of the keyboard under her fingers a sharp staccato that reverberated around the room.

Tess noted with satisfaction that there was a driving licence in a clear plastic compartment of the wallet and removed the item, adding this new information to the on-screen document. Looking up, she saw that the Sarge had finished his search and was handing her the man's brown leather belt and bootlaces. She placed all the items in a serialised, plastic property-bag which she then wrote some details on before sealing. Turning around, she keyed a code into a number pad and opened the secure locker, depositing the bag inside it before closing it again. Reaching behind her, she pulled a log book from the shelf and recorded the details of the deposit, glancing at her watch to identify the time. The processing now complete she joined Colin on the other side of the desk as he led the man into the cell.

The man gave no resistance or acknowledgement of his predicament but meekly allowed himself to be directed into the room. He walked over to the far end of the room, his unlaced boots scuffing on the hard floor, and sat heavily on the end of the single mattress. Colin closed the door and turned the key until the loud clang of the locking mechanism was engaged. He looked through the open portal in the door at the man. 'As you've made no answer to me regarding the retention of a solicitor, I'm going to see if we can get the duty one down from Stonehaven or, if not, we'll take you up there. Though, as you saw from the drive up here, I'm not altogether sure the roads are passable.' He was surprised to see the man react to this and watched as the prisoner raised his head and turned to look at Colin, his dark eyes betraying no emotion but with a faint smile upon his lips.

'Don't worry about it Sergeant. I'm not going to be here that long.'

13

Tess took the mug from Mitch and wrapped her hands around it, grateful for the warmth. She heard Colin approach from behind and Mitch handed him a large, steaming mug as he drew level with her. Mitch nodded with his head towards the direction of the main office. 'Hey Sarge, we've still got the SFOs here for that capability brief.'

Colin sipped from the mug and gave a small sigh. 'Oh right, completely slipped my mind.' He looked down at his watch. 'Okay, let's go next door and I'll tell them to cut it down to about twenty minutes. That'll give our mystery man some time to cool his heels and then we can get on with contacting Stonehaven and filling out the Arrest and Taser Deployment reports.'

They filed into the main office and Mitch made the introductions, the visitors shaking hands with Colin and the Tess. Colin apologised for the men having to wait but the Firearms' Sergeant held up his hand.

'No need Colin. Mitch explained that you guys were out lifting a lad. As I said to him, we were quite happy to wait and bring you all up to speed with who we are and what we do. So, about fifteen minutes of chat and showing you the equipment then we'll be out of your hair.'

Colin nodded his agreement and the three rural officers wheeled their chairs into a small semi-circle facing the SFOs. The Sergeant took the lead and for around ten minutes spoke about the role of the SFOs and the authority and circumstances in which they could be deployed. At the end of this delivery Constable Armstrong took over, picking up each weapon and piece of equipment from the table and explaining its purpose. Once he had finished, he asked if they would like to approach the table and handle any of the weapons. Colin waved a hand towards his subordinates and Mitch stood immediately, making his way to the collection on the table. Sergeant Fletcher looked at the female constable with surprise, wondering why she showed no enthusiasm in joining her colleague.

'You can have a look you know Constable Cameron. The guns are all in a safe state. They can't hurt you.'

Tess sighed at the patronising assumption and turned to address the issue but Colin's dry chuckle stopped her.

'Tess spent quite a few years in the Army and in some very intense places where she used her gun a lot more often than any of us ever will.' He looked down at his constable, the mirth still evident in his grey eyes. 'It's not that she's *afraid* of guns, more like she's had enough of them.'

A crimson flush suffused the Sergeant's face and he stuttered on his words. 'Well...yes, of course...erm...I didn't mean you were afraid Constable Cameron...just some

85

people can be a bit intimidated by the weapons you understand.'

Tess stood and smiled at him. 'You mean some *women* can be intimidated by guns?'

'No, no. Not just women, quite a few men we brief to are very uncomfortable around guns. My comment was in no way meant to suggest that females are any different to men in how they view weapons.'

Colin laid a hand on Tess's shoulder, grinning at her deliberate exploitation of the Service's discrimination directive. 'Constable Cameron, if you're finished here could you start doing some background research on our guest along the corridor please? Thank you.'

Tess gave the flustered Firearms' Sergeant a saccharine smile then turned and pulled her chair over to her computer.

Colin beckoned for Sergeant Fletcher to follow him into his office. Taking a seat, he indicated for the other man to follow suit. 'Don't worry about Constable Cameron Fletch, she was only having a wee dig back at your implication that she was scared of guns. She's a good officer, saved my bacon today and holds her own.'

Fletch smiled and shook his head. 'To be fair to her, I had that coming so I'll take it on the chin. Was just concerned she would bang in a discrimination complaint about me.'

'No. As I said she's a good officer who prefers to deal with things head on rather than bury issues in a mountain of paperwork and investigations. If she wasn't happy with the situation, she would let you know about it, make no mistake.'

'Fair enough Colin, fair enough. It's just that it's so easy to get pulled up for silly mistakes that end up snowballing into disciplinary actions.'

Colin nodded sympathetically. 'Aye, I know. It's a very different Police Force now, Fletch.'

Fletch wagged his finger in mock rebuke. 'Oh no, no, no. Police *Service* Colin, not Force. *Force* implies physicality, pressure, exertion and a whole host of negative connotations!'

Colin laughed at the sarcastic retort and stood. 'Aye, point taken funny man. Come on, let's get you and your lad squared and on your way before you get stuck here.'

Tess was oblivious to her surroundings, her full focus on the computer screen before her and the notebook she scribbled into at regular intervals. Accessing the secure database, she had entered the details she had gleaned from the man's driving licence. *Westley Adams*. Well, the name was a start at least. Although there was nothing outstanding in terms of warrants against him, there was an interesting historical entry. Seven years ago, Adams had been the subject of a restraining order, banning him from any proximity to the family home in Hereford, England. Face frowning in concentration she continued digging for further information. She was rewarded with the barest of details but this at least gave her some start points for further research. The restraining order had been the final element in what appeared to have been a bitter divorce settlement.

The wife had claimed that Adams was violent, unstable, and an unsuitable father to their kids. She had also claimed the family home and access to his military pension. This was nothing that Tess had not seen before, in fact she knew very few divorces that could be said to be anything other than bitter. The pension element was interesting; confirming that Adams was ex-military and, from experience, Tess knew how precious these pensions were to the individual who had spent twenty-two years or more earning it. Even as she thought this through, old conversations with male soldiers going through divorces were recalled, veiled threats muttered towards absent ex-wives if they dared try to take any of their pension. There was another entry for a speeding offence four years before but it was a mere SP30 and had earned him three points and a small fine.

Tess rubbed her eyes and looked down at the meagre notes before her, representing more questions and queries to follow up rather than supplying any substantial information. She chewed on her lip as she ran down her written checklist. *Which regiment? Why did he leave; honourable discharge or other? Call Donna and see what she can dig up?* Donna was now a Major at the Army Personnel Centre in Glasgow, responsible for all the records and documentation of Army soldiers. They had last seen each other a couple of months ago when Tess had travelled to Glasgow for a night on the tiles with her former colleague. She had also done Donna a favour in her capacity as a serving Police Officer. A small favour but a favour, nonetheless. Yes, she was sure Donna could provide some more background on Mr Adams. *Wife and Kids; where now? Custody/Visitation rights? New relationship?* He'd said he was alone so it could be the case that there wasn't anyone else but she would like to be certain of that fact. *Call Hereford Police for background info.*

Looking up she saw Colin leading the two SFOs to the door and caught the eye of the departing Sergeant. She gave him a smile and a wave to show there was no hard feelings and saw his acknowledgement in a sheepish grin and wave back. Turning back to her computer she searched for the telephone numbers she would need in order to begin her research in earnest.

Colin opened the front door and the snow blasted through the aperture, causing the three men to grimace. Out in the driveway the visibility was so bad that Colin could not see the parked vehicles until they were almost upon them. Each car had a thick mantle of snow covering it, the Freelander only slightly clearer than the others. As the Firearms' team began loading their vehicle Colin looked at it with concern. 'This a four-wheel drive Fletch?'

Sergeant Fletcher looked up from where he was bent loading the middle compartment. 'Erm...no, it's got all traction control and stability stuff though so I think we'll be fine.'

Colin was unconvinced. 'Mmmm…just take it easy out there. I haven't seen a plough or a gritter all morning so I can't guarantee that the road will be clear. We had a bit of difficulty getting back here earlier.'

Fletch rubbed the snow from his hair. 'We'll take it slow Colin and give you a wee bell once we're back at base, let you know we arrived.'

Colin shook the men's hands and watched as they drove out of the station, turning left and north towards Aberdeen. He shivered, the snow clinging to him and the cold easily permeating his thin sweater. Turning back towards the station, he jogged to the front door and rubbed the snow from his body, already feeling the warmth from inside.

Making her way to the store room, Tess scrolled through the contacts list on her mobile and found Donna's details. She stepped into the small room and turned on the light, heeling the door closed behind her. It wasn't that she wanted to make the call in secret but rather keep her enquiry as discreet as she could, bearing in mind the data protection issues involved. After several rings her friend's voice and throaty chuckle came down the line.

'Hey TC, what you calling for? Wanting to be drunk under the table again, lightweight?'

Tess laughed. '*Me* drunk under the table? As I recall it you were the one who had to be poured into a taxi at the end of the night!'

'Yes, but that's because I was just bored of your crap banter!'

'Hey, my banter's world class I'll have you know. Probably just too intelligent for your tiny brain to understand!'

'Ha ha, nice one Cameron. Right, unlike you I actually work for a living so what can I do for you?'

Tess outlined the nature of her request and could almost hear the frown in her friend's voice.

'Well...you know of course this isn't strictly above board. That said, I owe you one so if you want, I'll give it to you verbally. Best I can do Tess without leaving a trail of breadcrumbs to show I've been digging. I'll have a look into it now before my meeting and call you back, okay?'

'Brilliant Donna, really appreciate this.' Tess ended the call and left the room, taking a seat behind the computer and sighing as she began the laborious form-filling documenting her justification and use of the Taser earlier that day. She scrolled through the online form, acquainting herself with the unfamiliar document. Seeing nothing that she didn't understand she began populating the various elements of the form.

Mitch glanced over and saw Tess was occupied with something on her computer. He pulled out his personal telephone and read Cathy's text again. His mouth drooped in a frown as he assimilated the contents and considered a response. He was surprised to realise that he wasn't as angry as he had been earlier, his ire replaced by a melancholy sadness that was less preferable. After a moment his thumbs were moving furiously, typing out his response. *WTF???? THIS is how you tell me we have problems? Why didn't you say something before if you were so unhappy? FFS Cathy, I deserve better than this.*

Running his hand over his face he sighed and stared into space, contemplating his situation. Lost in thought, he started when the phone vibrated in his hand. Looking at the screen he was surprised to see that Cathy had replied to him so quickly. In fact, he'd thought that she probably wouldn't reply to him at all. He opened the message fully but there was little more than what he had read on the main screen. *We're done Mitch. There's no point going over it anymore, let's just move on.*

Mitch felt the anger return and fired out his terse reply. *Fine. Have a nice life, you stupid cow.* He didn't wait for a response but stood up, ramming the telephone into his trouser pocket and walked into the hallway. Grabbing his jacket, he made his way to Colin's office as he struggled into the heavy garment. 'Sarge, popping to the shop for a couple of pies. You want anything bringing back?'

Colin looked up from his screen. 'No thanks Constable Logan, I'll probably pop home for a bowl of soup once I get this done.'

'No worries.' Turning back to the main office he addressed his colleague. 'Tess, you want anything from the shop?'

Without taking her attention from the screen in front of her, she waved her hand in his direction. 'No thanks Mitch. All good.'

When he opened the door, Mitch was immediately buffeted by the wind. Hauling it closed behind him he dragged his feet through the drifts of snow, startled to see how deep it now was. He hunched his head down into his shoulders to cover the exposed flesh against the icy fingers of the wind and block that fat flakes of snow attempting to penetrate his collar. *Shit, this is serious snow.* Looking around him he noted that there were no vehicle tracks on the road, the good citizens of the village keeping to their homes where they were warm. He wondered how long the blizzard would last, remembered something from the weather report about disruptions to travel for several days. His thoughts returned to Cathy and what she would be doing today. He still couldn't believe that she had dumped him by text. It was the kind of thing you read about or heard in a pub before shaking your head at the coldness of it. He was shaking his own head in disbelief when the sound of a large bang carried on the wind. Mitch stopped and listened, squinting his eyes in protest at the relentless snow falling on his face. When there was no repeat of the noise, he shrugged his shoulder and turned towards the warm glow of the village shop, his stomach rumbling in Pavlovian anticipation of the promise of a hot, greasy pie.

14

Bravo had given the orders, which lasted almost thirty minutes as he'd detailed the plan and their individual responsibilities. He'd cut the briefing down to the bare minimum, well aware that time was their enemy. If Alpha was taken to Stonehaven, there would be very little that the team could do to secure his release. But they had planned for events like this. Planned *and* practiced for them, with each individual team member confident in their role and responsibilities.

The team had dressed in the white winter camouflage suits and applied white netting and tape to similarly mask the shape of their weapons. Guns were loaded, spare magazines checked and stowed in the pockets of the combat vests. There had been very little conversation, each individual running through their own mental checklist and preparations for the mission ahead. Bravo had watched with approval as Charlie and Delta had then checked and loaded their specialist equipment with quiet efficiency.

As the explosives and demolitions specialist, Bravo would be lead on this mission. Charlie and Delta knew the plan and their role in it, which would be secondary to Bravo until phase two. Timings were crucial to the success of phase one; if they failed at the first hurdle then Alpha would be gone and there would be nothing that they could do about it. Charlie had checked the communications and distributed the radios and earpieces before conducting a check with each of them. Delta passed around the field dressings and personal medical kits then showed them where the team med-bag was located in his backpack so that they knew where to find it if things went south in a hurry.

They'd been ready on time and Bravo had conducted a final inspection, ensuring all necessary equipment was with them and the team was mission ready. The team had made their way silently to the edge of the woods before donning their snow shoes and pulling the white hoods over their heads. They'd jumped up and down on the spot to identify any loose equipment or noise that might betray them but other than minor strap adjustments on the backpacks, they were ready. Nodding to each individual in turn, Bravo had taken the lead and jogged out of the woods and into the white world beyond, the other two following with a small gap between them, crossing the terrain in smooth, rhythmic strides.

Bravo scanned the land before him as he led his team over the snow-covered fields. He was warm from exertion but his breathing was even and he'd found his rhythm, a cadence driven by the placement of his snowshoes on the soft covering underneath. Visibility was limited to around ten to fifteen feet which he was pleased with. Coupled with their winter camouflage, they would be practically invisible to anyone at a distance. He gave periodic glances over his shoulder to monitor the progress of Charlie and Delta but this was more through habit than necessity, each individual maintaining both the pace and the tactical spacing between.

Bravo arrived at a fence which was blocking their path and without any hesitation, pushed the body of his AR-15 down on the top strand of barbed wire and waited until Charlie jogged up to his side. Without a word between them, Charlie stepped straight over the fence and took up a kneeling position a few yards into the field, his own rifle at the ready, pointing ahead into the blizzard. Delta approached and carried out the same action but faced the opposite direction once knelt in the field, ensuring the team had front and rear cover. Lastly, Bravo stepped over the fence and jogged forward, patting each team member on the shoulder as he passed, letting them know he was over the obstacle and that they were moving once again. Charlie and Delta fell into line and the team continued with their advance across the undulating white landscape.

Bravo slowed to a walk as he identified the corner of the woods that he had been looking for. His rifle in the alert position, he advanced into the cover of the trees for several feet before kneeling and monitoring the area to his front, seeking any indication that there was activity in the area. He felt Charlie and Delta kneel alongside him and knew without looking that they would each be covering a different direction, three points of the triangle, ensuring they had three hundred and sixty-degree coverage around them. They waited several minutes in silence then Bravo stood, followed by the others. He nodded in the direction of the northern edge of the woods and watched as each confirmed with a responding nod of their own that they understood.

They walked, slower than before and closer together, their gait the same high-leg lift to accommodate the snowshoes clearing the ground beneath. The raised level of the main road loomed out of the blizzard in front of them and Bravo altered their direction, squinting hard through his goggles until he found what he was looking for. He knelt and beckoned for his team to close up alongside him. When Charlie and Delta took a knee beside him, he pointed to the drainage culvert that ran beneath the road surface. It was barely visible under the snow drift and he had almost missed it but they had now reached their first objective. Again, no words were necessary as Bravo took off his pack and began removing the equipment he needed. Charlie crawled up the edge of the bank and scanned the road area for activity. Delta remained where he was, rifle at the ready covering the immediate area for any threats while Bravo continued his preparations.

Bravo scooped handfuls of the snow away from the mouth of the culvert, exposing the hollow concrete pipe that ran below the road. Taking the first of his shaped explosive charges, he scuttled to the far end of the pipe, glad that the cold had frozen much of the water that would have been streaming under his body. He placed the charge, activated the receiver and reversed out on his hands and knees. Taking the second charge he repeated the procedure before putting his pack on and taking the transmitter from his combat vest. He patted Delta on the shoulder then made his way to Charlie's position. Reaching up the bank, he patted Charlie's leg and saw Charlie begin to slither back down the icy slope to join them.

Back at the corner of the woods, they resumed their three-point coverage of the area. Bravo placed his rifle on the ground before him and readied the transmitter. The green light showed the device was good to go and he spoke one word quietly into his radio mic.

'Standby.'

He flicked the lever on the transmitter and the explosion was instantaneous. Even over the wind, the sound of the blast was enormous. Looking around he caught the others' eyes through the clear plastic of their goggles and returned their mischievous grins. *Everybody loves a good bang!* He raised his eyebrows at Delta and received a nod in return, watching as he stood and led them towards their second objective. Following behind Charlie, Bravo gave a quick glance towards the road but could see nothing beyond the raging blizzard. Not that he needed to check his handiwork; he'd used the well-practised formula of 'P for Plenty' and knew that the amount of explosives would have blown the whole junction to pieces thereby cutting off the northern approach to the village. *Objective one of Phase one complete.*

15

Mark Armstrong burped and the waft of garlic soon filled the car.

'You dirty bastard…' Fletch toggled his window control and a blast of icy air drove a flurry of snow through the small crack.

Mark tried to stifle a chuckle at his superior's discomfort. 'I'm sorry Sarge, just couldn't hold it in any longer.' He risked a glance across and burst into a fit of laughter at his Sergeant's expression of disgust.

Fletch glared back at his Constable. 'Oh yeah, 'cos you sound like you're really fucking sorry!'

'I am Sarge, honestly. Good idea to stop though, that food was lovely.'

Fletch nodded. 'Yeah, not too shabby was it? Might bring the Mrs down here for a meal sometime.' Shivering, he gave an exploratory sniff of the air and concluded that the worst of the smell had dissipated and closed the window. He had enjoyed the meal at the Village Inn, a last-minute decision on the way out of St Cyrus. He'd had the steak pie and chips, and despite being full his mouth watered at the memory of the chunky meat and golden pastry swimming in a sea of beef gravy; perfect. His mind was brought back to the present as he felt the rear end of the car sliding in the snow. 'Easy PC Armstrong, we can hardly see anything beyond the front of the car so let's keep the speed to a minimum eh?'

'Sorry Sarge. I'll take it steady. This snow's really something eh? Don't think I've seen it this deep.'

Fletch stretched out in the seat and yawned. 'Yes, we don't tend to get the snow too bad on this coast but...SHIT...' The car lurched into an unseen chasm, the front end plummeting before crashing hard in a cacophony of shrieking metal and the explosion of airbags deploying. Fletch pushed his deflating airbag down and out of his face with one hand and rubbed his strained neck with the other. He looked over at his subordinate but couldn't see much of him other than the airbag shrouding his features. 'You okay PC Armstrong?'

Mark rubbed at his chest where the seatbelt had ratcheted hard against him. 'Aye Sarge, I'm alright.'

Fletch could smell mechanical fluids and hear the ticking of relaxing metal. 'Right, you stay put just now, I want to take a look at what we've driven into.' Struggling with his own seatbelt he eventually released the mechanism and opened his door. The door opened easily, the weight of it offset by the downhill incline they now found themselves upon. Stepping out the first thing that he noted was that there was brown earth all around them, not snow. *What the hell happened here?* He concluded that it must have happened

100

recently as the snow was already beginning to settle and the whole area would be white again before long. *Gas explosion?* He knew that it didn't really matter what it was, he and PC Armstrong were going to be the butt of every car crash joke and jape for a long time to come. He bent to examine the underside of the vehicle and sighed when he saw the viscous covering of black oil on the earth. They'd obviously ripped the sump off. In addition to the heavily crumpled front end there was only one conclusion to be drawn: They weren't driving anywhere.

Returning to his open door, he reached over the seat and opened the middle console while addressing his subordinate. 'Come on Mark, get all the gear unloaded, we're not driving out of this one.' While he was sure the car wouldn't be tampered with in this weather, there was no way he would leave their weapons and equipment. Bad enough to be the buffoons who crashed the car, let alone the buffoons who also lost weapons. Grabbing the black canvas bags from the boot, both men set about removing the weapons, ammunition and equipment from the car.

With the weapons and gear loaded in the duffel bags, they donned their respective burdens and began walking slowly back to the station. Fletch had tried to radio through to Aberdeen but nothing was coming back. They had no phone signal and it was obvious nobody was going to be passing anytime soon so Fletch had made the decision to return to St Cyrus nick and deal with the recovery from there. He could already imagine the reception they would

receive when the information that two of the Firearms'
prima donnas had totalled their car. *Shit.*

16

Tess closed the door of the store room and sat back at her desk lost in thought. Donna's return call had given her a lot of information about their current guest in the custodial suite although her former Army colleague had to do a lot of digging to get it.

According to Donna, Adams had been a Parachute Regiment soldier who had left the Army under a cloud some time ago. When looking at his files, she'd noticed how little information there was until she went into his service history and found the explanation. As a young corporal in the Paras, Westley Adams had passed selection for the SAS and consequently was administered by Special Forces and not the Army Personnel Centre. Calling in a favour of her own, she'd contacted a trusted colleague in the manning and personnel department at Directorate of Special Forces and was given all the background available.

Westley Adams had joined D Squadron, 22 SAS as a trooper and been allocated to Boat Troop. He'd served in Northern Ireland, Bosnia, Kosovo, Iraq, Colombia and Afghanistan before being seconded to MI6 for a two-year posting. During his secondment he was awarded a Military

Cross for his role in saving two Case Officers from a Taliban ambush. He returned to the SAS and was almost immediately redeployed to Afghanistan, this time as a Team Leader in a Sabre Squadron tasked with mentoring a local Afghan Task Force.

According to Donna's source, Adams had confronted senior officers over the fact that the local Task Force commander was a paedophile and rapist of young boys. He was told that what the commander did in his private life was of no concern to the coalition mission; the commander wielded great influence over the area and it was important that he was kept onside. When Adams stepped outside of the chain of command to push his complaints, he was threatened with the ultimate punishment for an SAS soldier, RTU: Returned to Unit, sent back as a Corporal to the Parachute Regiment he had left all those years before. He had backed down. At some point later in the tour however, something had gone horribly wrong: Adams had killed the commander. The Afghans had reacted instantly, turning their guns on the Special Forces soldiers. Three SAS soldiers, including Adams, were wounded and seventeen Afghans were killed. Adams was immediately removed from theatre and investigated for his conduct.

Donna's source explained that the enquiry identified that Adams's team had been visiting the commander's compound when they had heard a young boy screaming from one of the rooms inside. They had asked the commander for an explanation but been told it was Task

Force business. Adams had persisted and when no further explanation was given, he had pushed the commander aside and entered the dwelling. Inside, he and his team had found a young boy shackled to the commander's bed, naked and bleeding from his nether regions. Adams had cut the young boy free and was leading him out when the commander pointed a gun at him and screamed at the SAS team to leave and never return. Adams knocked the gun to one side and shot the commander where he stood, initiating the bloodbath that followed.

The Special Forces mission was withdrawn from the area soon after when it became apparent that the commander's Task Force, in an act of revenge, had aligned themselves with the Taliban, using the special training they had received from the SAS to great advantage. Adams was lucky not to have been handed a manslaughter charge, his solicitor arguing and winning the case that his client had acted *in extremis*. A settlement was hammered out in that Adams would see no jail time but he would be dishonourably discharged from the Army. A judgement that would deny him the prospect for any of the prime jobs on the circuit that former SAS men regularly stepped into. Adams had apparently been extremely bitter about his treatment, voicing his ire to anyone who would listen. He had been given several warnings about anti-government rants he had posted on social media, reminded that he had signed the Official Secrets Act and Non-Disclosure Agreements that remained extant. His wife had alerted social services to his anti-establishment indoctrination of their children and he soon found himself on the losing end of a divorce and custody battle in addition to fighting the system.

Reading her notes, Tess felt an element of sympathy with Adams. The matter of a local government official, funded and protected by coalition forces, being a paedophile or criminal was not unusual. Many soldiers she met during her own tours mentioned their unease at being forced to work with such odious individuals. Looking down the page further she read what she had scribbled about Adams's family circumstances. *Wife has full custody, family emigrated to New Zealand some years ago, Adams no contact, moved around a lot, Army no idea of current whereabouts.*

Tapping her teeth with her pen, she thought about this for a moment. Adams's property was a large one with coastal access and that didn't come cheap. There was nothing in the information before her to suggest that he could have afforded something like this unless he'd got the mortgage while he was still serving. But surely the Army would have had the address on file? It also seemed way too large for just one man. Was there another wife or girlfriend? There had been something really off with the place that she just couldn't put her finger on. The deliberate ditch, the minimalist accommodation and the disproportionately well-equipped gym. *Very strange.*

Standing and stretching, she closed her computer down and walked to Colin's office, a smile forming at the corners of her mouth as she watched his face, frowning in concentration at the glowing screen in front of him.

'Getting through it Sarge?'

Colin looked up, tipped his glasses back on his head and rubbed his eyes. 'Bad enough when paperwork was actually *paper* work. These online forms though…'

'Nobody likes them Sarge, well, except the geeks that design them that is.'

'Ain't that the truth. What can I do for you PC Cameron?'

Tapping her small notebook with her pen she met his eyes. 'I've dug up a little bit of background on our guest from some…external sources.' She watched as Colin raised an eyebrow at the euphemism. 'There's some interesting stuff but I want to go back and take a look around his place again. There's something there we're missing and I'd like to know what it is before we interview him.'

Colin leaned back and gazed at the ceiling, considering his response. 'Okay. We don't have a warrant to conduct a search and he's said there is no other *person* living there. But as he's not talking, we can't be sure there are no *pets* going to be suffering in the cold while he's not home.' He looked her in the eye and she smiled again at the avuncular mischief evident in his expression. 'So why don't you take a good look around to make sure there's no *Tiddles* or *Rovers* that are going to be missing their owner?'

Tess laughed then addressed her superior with mock gravitas. 'Yes, Sergeant Duffy, you can count on me.

Whether cat, dog or budgie, I will make sure any pet on the property is found and accounted for.'

Colin sat forward chuckling and waved his hand towards her as he focussed back on the screen. 'Go on, get out of here before I change my mind. We're bending the rules that much today they're starting to look like horseshoes!'

Grabbing her gear and the keys to the undamaged Freelander, she made her way out into the car park. The snow continued its assault on the building as she walked to the back of the station, noting that it was significantly deeper than when they had returned with Adams. She would have to be careful on the road, keep it in four-wheel drive the whole way. She opened the door and jumped in, taking off her cap and replacing it with the black woollen hat from her pocket. Turning the key, the vehicle started first time and the vents poured warm air into the cab. She engaged the four-wheel drive and set off, noting how dark the day was already.

Driving out of the station and onto the road she could see that the snow was covering the entire surface, very few cars having ventured out. *Good.* So far not a single call from a stranded motorist, people actually listening to the weather advice for a change. Turning right down towards Tangleha' she saw movement and a couple of dark, indistinct shapes, one of whom waved. Waving back, she turned at the junction and continued over the bridge, pleased that the vehicle's traction was holding well. The car was warm now and she turned the fan down to moderate the temperature.

With only the sound of the windscreen wipers for company she turned on the radio, the default *Northsound One* station booming from the speakers. She started and turned the volume down. *Bloody Mitch*! He must have been listening to the radio on the way in this morning. She tapped her fingers to the beat of a Foo Fighters' track that was half way through and began humming the melody under her breath.

Tess was happy. This was *actual* police work, what she had joined the force to do. Well aware that she hadn't achieved much more than the gaining of background information, she still felt a sense of pride in her researching abilities. Before she knew it, she found herself at the gate of Adams' property, their previous tracks already covered by the snow. Driving along the wooded track she made her way into the courtyard at the back and parked behind the black truck, now a study in monochrome with its heavy mantle of snow covering much of the vehicle. She turned off the engine and alighted from the car, pulling her woollen cap down over her ears then locking the vehicle with the key fob, the confirmatory beep loud in the hushed stillness of the courtyard.

Bypassing the buildings that they had already looked at, she walked directly to the spot where they had first encountered Adams. *What was he doing and where was he coming from?* She stopped and shielded her eyes with her hand to keep the snow from landing on them. Seeing nothing obvious she continued to walk in the direction Adams had come from, her feet crunching into the snow beneath her.

After some time, a dark building loomed out of the blizzard, similar in size and design as the outbuildings they had discovered on their earlier visit. As she approached, she saw that it was in good condition, a strong PVC door instead of the rough wooden ones she had seen on the other buildings. Turning the handle and pulling the door towards her she stepped inside.

In the absence of the wind, the silence was absolute. Waiting for several moments she listened but heard nothing to indicate anyone was present. The floor was simple stone flags but clean and dry and she looked down a narrow hall of sorts, noting several openings leading from it. Walking slowly forward she arrived at the first entrance and strained to see any details in the gloomy interior. Running her gloved hand up the wall inside she found the switch and flicked it on. A long fluorescent bulb buzzed and flickered into life, illuminating the room within. She raised her eyebrows at the sight of the contents. Climbing ropes, harnesses, ice-axes, crampons, skis, rucksacks, scuba gear and air tanks, oars and paddles, boots and climbing shoes, kayaks and canoes. Probably better stocked than half the outdoor shops she'd been in. This was a seriously well-equipped outdoors enthusiast, the kit running into tens of thousands of pounds at least. Two large doors at the back of the room were bolted closed but clearly provided the access for the equipment to be loaded into vehicles. She turned off the light and moved to the next room. The gear was interesting but no more than that. It didn't provide her with any further information that would assist in their enquiry.

The next room she checked was small and empty, lit only by a forlorn bulb hanging from a beam above the chamber. She turned the light off and continued to the final doorway, this one containing an actual door rather than being open to the hallway. She turned the heavy metal handle and pushed the door inwards, grimacing at the loud squeal as the hinges protested her intrusion. *Well if anyone is inside, they certainly know I'm coming now.* She found the light switch quickly and turned it on taking in the room before her. It was mostly empty, save for a large, heavy wardrobe on the far wall. The wall here must have been repaired at some point in the past as she noted the plasterboard facing, different from the remainder which were natural stone. This room, like the first, had large double doors to the rear, again, allowing access for loading. She walked towards the doors; something having caught her eye. The doors had several bolts, emplaced for securing to floor, lintels and each other and secured with a heavy padlock.

Looking around she saw nothing more of interest and made her way over to the large wardrobe. It was a dark, heavy, old-fashioned affair that stood flush against the wall. She opened the door and saw a typical empty compartment, save for a couple of old wool sweaters swinging on wire hangers from a clothes rail. She sighed and closed the door, turning to leave. Stopping mid-stride, she stared at the stone floor beside her. She was looking at the remnants of a wet footprint in front of the wardrobe. It wasn't hers, as she easily identified her own trail within the room. She pulled out her torch and shone the beam on to the stone floor. With the better illumination she could now see a very faint trail leading from the door to the wardrobe, crossed occasionally by the darker, wetter prints she had left. Glancing back at the double doors she attempted to reconstruct the movements from the trail. Someone had obviously come from outside, taken something from the wardrobe and left again, locking the double door behind them. Adams wasn't carrying anything when they encountered him and wasn't even dressed for the weather. The truck was still there, hadn't moved since her first visit. *What then?*

There was something nagging at her and she closed her eyes as she concentrated. Something wasn't right. There was something…off about this room. Opening her eyes, she pulled the wardrobe door and looked inside again. *That was it!* It was the sweaters. In all the other areas of the property she'd seen it was a case of 'everything has its place and there's a place for everything' as her mother used to say. Yes, this man was tidy and organised, old sweaters would have been thrown out, cut up for rags or stored where he used them. *And what else was in here?* Someone had been in here recently and taken or moved something. *Adams? A friend?*

She sighed and leaned on the door. She was probably reading too much into it. Adams could have had any number of things in the wardrobe that he used regularly and the sweaters were just that; old sweaters kept for some future use. She smiled at the thought of radioing back to the Sarge with her important finding of moth-eaten jumpers. Straightening up, she was turning to leave when she realised that the whole time she had been stood looking into the wardrobe she had felt a small draught on her face. She hadn't taken much notice as the room was an old one and bound to have a few gaps in the walls and windows. But now that she thought about it this draught seemed to be coming from *inside* the wardrobe. Frowning, she shone her torch on the back wooden panelling and ran the beam slowly up and down the facings. Half-way down the edge where the back of the wardrobe was joined to the side, she held the beam steady on a small thread of dark material snagged on the fibres of the wood. The tiny pennant, all but invisible to the naked eye, fluttered in an unseen breeze. Leaning in, Tess pushed at the back panel with a firm shove and gave an involuntary start as the entire panel swung backwards, revealing the opening to a dark space behind. The torch shook a little as she focussed the beam into the space beyond and highlighted a set of stone stairs descending from the back of the wardrobe and disappearing into the darkness beyond.

She reached for her radio but thought the better of it. It could still be that she found nothing of interest and in that case, she would look like an idiot when she called it in. She *knew* though, that this was definitely something of interest, every fibre in her body screaming the fact at her. But she wouldn't call it in until she had determined exactly what it was. Taking a careful step, she climbed into the wardrobe and ducked her head, stooping to enter the stairwell beyond.

17

Mitch struggled to close the door behind him against the force of the wind, heeding Elspeth's warning not to let the warmth out of the shop. He hadn't even needed to ask for his order, so accustomed was she to his habits; two scotch pies, a packet of cheese and onion crisps and a can of diet coke. He could feel the heat from the warm pies seeping through the bags they were wrapped in and hurried along the pavement towards the station, skidding occasionally in the deepening snow.

Entering the hallway, he felt the immediate contrast of the warm air and sighed with contentment. There were worse places to be today instead of in a quiet, warm nick with a couple of pies to tuck into. After removing his coat, he took his food into the kitchen, placing the pies on a large plate and squeezing a generous covering of tomato sauce over their tops. He put the condiments back in the cupboard and carried his late lunch back to his desk, the smell of the treat to come making him salivate.

Colin could smell the greasy aroma of Mitch's food in his office. *How the hell can he eat that rubbish day in, day out? Be a miracle if he lives to be my age.* He locked his workstation and stood, stretching to ease the tightness of his back. Glancing at the clock on the wall he realised that he needed to look in on their arrestee. He made his way out of his office, picking up his mug along the way and walked down to the custody suite. He unlatched the viewing aperture and watched the man inside the cell for several moments. The man was lying down, arms behind his head, staring at the ceiling, to all intents and purposes with not a care in the world. *Relaxed.* Colin thought, *that's the word. Relaxed.*

'Mr Adams, just checking to see you're okay. How are you doing?' Nothing. The man did not even acknowledge Colin's presence. The policeman sighed. 'Mr Adams, I'm pretty sure you'll tire of the silent treatment before I do but in the meantime is there anything I can get for you? Some water perhaps? Food?' Again, there was absolutely no reaction. Colin closed the small hatch and walked around the desk to the computer where he spent several minutes updating the log to show he had checked on the detainee. Picking up his mug he wandered back to the kitchen, looking forward to a fresh coffee.

Mitch wiped the warm grease dribbling down his chin with a piece of kitchen roll and gave a small moan of pleasure. *Scotch pies; food of the gods!* He was reaching for his second when the phone buzzed in his pocket and he took out the device and looked at the screen. *Cathy.* Opening the message, he stared dumbfounded for a moment before the anger set in. Looking away, he took a deep breath then read it again. *Oh, yeah, very mature Mitch! THIS is why we split up.*

You're a child Mitch, a bloody CHILD! You're vain, selfish, unfaithful and just a wee boy in a man's body. Yeah, don't think I didn't know about those other women you were messaging. He flushed at this, completely unaware that Cathy had even suspected him of being in touch with other women. *The best day of our relationship was today when it ended. So goodbye and good luck and I don't want to hear from you again. Oh, and BTW, the sex was crap x*

Mitch was furious, his rage robbing him of his appetite. He tossed the phone on to his desk and grabbed the plate, sweeping the remainder of his meal into the pedestal bin beside him. *Fuck!* There had been no need for that from Cathy. Okay, he had called her a cow but that wasn't nearly half as bad as the shit she'd vented back at him. As before, self-doubt began creeping in as he dissected each element of her message. *Was* he a child? Granted, he liked a good laugh and a joke, beer and football, but that was what all blokes were like wasn't it? He certainly wasn't vain, just took pride in his appearance, and that was a good thing wasn't it? Other women? Well…guilty as charged but he hadn't actually *done anything*…yet. The last line was the most hurtful to him. He saw himself as being particularly good in bed, not afraid to experiment a little, happy to give the woman a bit of foreplay. *Nah, no way the sex was bad.* She'd just said that to hurt him. *Cow.* Looking at the phone he thought of sending something equally hurtful back but knew he would only be playing to her accusations of childishness. *Fuck it. Her loss.* Picking up his plate he went into the kitchen and squeezed past Colin who was pouring some milk into a mug.

'You okay PC Logan? You look like a man who's lost a pound and found a penny.'

Mitch sighed and looked at his sergeant for a moment before replying. 'Well, not great Sarge. Me and Cathy just split up.'

Colin put the mug down and regarded the younger policeman. 'I'm sorry to hear that Mitch, I thought you two were quite serious.'

'So did I Sarge, so did I. But apparently we weren't.'

'Have you had a fight? You know a lot of the time these things are just a storm in a teacup.'

Mitch laughed sarcastically. 'Nah, nothing temporary about this Sarge. Definitely *el finito*.'

'Mitch look, if you want a wee bit of time why don't you just head off home? It's quiet, and myself and PC Cameron can cover anything that comes in.'

Mitch considered the proposal for a moment, an image of him sinking pints in the Inverbervie Inn mid-afternoon not a completely unappealing one. 'No, but thanks anyway Sarge, I'd rather just keep myself busy.'

Colin watched the constable for a moment. He was definitely upset, clearly Cathy had been the instigator of their parting. 'Okay, no problem but let me know if you change your mind, alright?'

'Yeah, I will.' As the sergeant turned to leave Mitch reached out and caught his elbow. 'Sarge, you wouldn't say I was…childish, would you?'

Colin placed his hand on Mitch's shoulder. 'You know PC Logan, when we part or split from someone we've been close to, the natural thing is to look for blame. Usually this will be to hold one person in the relationship responsible for the breakdown of it. In that instance, people will say a lot of hurtful things that they don't mean and might not even be true. So, don't take too much of what Cathy says to heart, okay? You'll tie yourself in knots if you do. Take it on the chin, remember the good times and move on son, that would be my advice.'

Mitch nodded, and turned quickly away, surprised to feel the sting of tears in his eyes. The old man's words had touched some emotion in him and he busied himself washing and drying his plate while Colin returned to his office. Mitch sniffed and wiped his eyes and nose before returning to his desk. It only occurred to him as he was logging back on that, as wise and comforting as the Duffer's words had been, he hadn't *really* answered the question. Shrugging the matter off he delved back into his accumulating emails. His attention was diverted by the sound of the intercom being buzzed and he walked over to the entry system and looked at the small screen. His eyes widened in surprise as he recognised the faces and allowed them entry. The Sarge had come out of his office when the buzzer had sounded and was looking to Mitch for an explanation when the footfalls in the hallway reached the office door and the mystery was solved. Colin raised his eyebrows in surprise at the two shivering, snow-covered officers standing in the doorway. As he watched, the Firearms sergeant dropped his heavy load to the ground and stretched upright catching Colin's eye. He wiped the melting snow from his face and gave a wry smile.

'Houston, we have a problem.'

18

Shining the torch around the top of the stairs, Tess was surprised to see a light switch and turned it on, gratified to see the stairwell below her now illuminated. It was an old stone staircase and while she had expected it to be cold, the temperature was actually pleasant. She pushed the back of the wardrobe closed behind her and examined the covert doorway she had stumbled upon, nodding in appreciation. This was not a case of an item of furniture plugging a hole, she could clearly see where the wall had been built around the rear of the wardrobe and the hinges on which the rear panel pivoted upon.

She could feel her pulse racing as she knew instinctively that she had stumbled upon something very important. Nobody went to such lengths to create a completely secret doorway without good reason. Turning the torch off she descended the stairs as quiet as she could, ears straining for any sound that might indicate someone was home. At the bottom of the stairs she stopped, looking at a heavy wooden door in front of her. Grabbing the round wrought-iron handle, she twisted the knob and pushed the door open slowly. A larger foyer lay beyond with several doors leading from it. She found the light switch and turned it on, bathing the area in light. The door nearest her was ajar and she made her way towards it, pushing it gently until it opened and walked inside, pausing just after she crossed the threshold.

A bedroom. The room was a large one with two single beds at either side, a couple of chests of drawers and two wardrobes. Unlike the house upstairs, this room was definitely lived in with towels hanging over the bottom of the bedsteads and wash bags sitting each side of a long alcove. There was nothing else of interest that was obvious in the room and she decided to move on. She could always return and have a look through the drawers and wardrobes if she found nothing else. Closing the door behind her, she left the room and entered the next one along, again, the door ajar and opening without protest. Another bedroom, similar in size to the first but with only one bed in the centre of the room. It also had a set of drawers and a large wardrobe and again, was definitely in use. She could make out several pairs of boots and shoes hidden in the shadows beneath the bed and again, a towel and opened wash bag casually hung by an alcove on the far wall. *So at least three people use this place then.* Turning on her heel she walked back out into the foyer and opened another door. A bathroom this time. Plain, white simple fittings with a shower, bathtub, toilet and sink and like the other rooms, clean and tidy. She closed the door and moved on to the next room, opening the door and entering the dark space.

This room was much larger than the other two and she turned on the light to help her see beyond that offered by the ambient illumination from the hallway. A double bed dominated the centre of the room and a couple of small wardrobes and a tall set of drawers were placed against a wall. Tess wrinkled her nose as she picked up a faint trace of deodorant. This room had been used recently. Walking over to the bed she ran her fingers through a large towel that was draped over the metal bedstead. *Still a little bit damp.* Looking around, she spotted a desk and chair in the corner that had been obscured by the other furniture. There was a folder and some stationery on the desk and she made her way over to investigate.

She flicked the folder open and saw that it was a collection of news cuttings printed from the internet. Curiosity aroused, she pulled out the chair and sat, leafing through the articles that had been carefully collated. They all seemed to be related to MoD or Government scandals relating to Iraq, Afghanistan or the poor treatment of veterans. The articles went back years and she paused at one in particular until the relevance of it hit her and she pursed her lips in recognition. The cutting was from The Daily Telegraph's website and gave a very vague report on a British Special Forces' veteran being disciplined for an undisclosed incident in Afghanistan. The article mentioned a breakdown in relations with the Afghans and the soldier's disregard for the Rules of Engagement under which they operated. *Adams.* The article was referring to Adams. Tess wasn't surprised it was so lacking in detail as all Special Forces' operations were covered by strict classifications that the press had to adhere to.

Closing the folder, she looked around the room but again, saw nothing else that was of immediate interest and stood, pushing the chair back under the desk. She turned out the light and re-entered the foyer, making her way to the last door. The handle turned easily and she found herself in a small office-style room. A large desk against the far wall contained several laptops, printers, reams of paper and a couple of serious digital cameras with large lenses. The object next to the desk caught her eye and she approached it, confirming she had identified it correctly. A shredder, and a good one at that. The same type she'd used herself in the military when they were destroying classified documents. *Why the hell would someone need one of those here?* She knew that you could buy a decent shredder for everyday use for less than the cost of a pub meal these days. Maybe Adams was one of these privacy nuts; shredding everything just to be safe.

The laptops were all MacBooks like her own personal one back at the cottage. She rubbed her finger on the trackpad and brought the screen to life on the first one. It was locked and password protected so she moved to the second and found it exactly the same. The third one however opened straight on to the desktop and she was rewarded with the sight of several folders stacked neatly on the left side of the screen. She opened the one labelled

'Plans' and saw a further set of folders. These were named in a series called Juno and numbered one to five, but what caught her eye was the last folder labelled 'St Cyrus'. She double clicked the folder and saw a mix of JPEG and Word document icons appear. Starting from left to right she opened each one, surprised and curious at what she was looking at. The whole folder seemed to contain pictures, Google map screenshots and land registry diagrams of the village. *What would someone want all these for? Property development?*

She closed this folder and opened a second, named 'Juno 1'. This too was split into a series of sub-folders and she opened the 'Photos' folder. Again, rows of JPEG icons filled the folder and she started clicking through them. Frowning in concentration, she tried to find a connection between the images. They seemed to be pictures of a town and streets that she wasn't familiar with as well as road junctions and roundabouts. Curiosity aroused even further she opened up 'Juno 2' and accessed the 'Photos' folder. She was looking at a similar series of images but of another town or city. *What the hell are these for?* Juno 3 and 4 followed the pattern of their predecessors but an image in 'Juno 4' made her pause. Zooming in on a photo of a roundabout she could see a road sign obscured by a bush on the grass verge that adjoined the road. Even though highly pixelated she recognised the styling and design as the standard 'You are now leaving' sign that councils up and down the country placed at the city or town limits and she could clearly make out the last five letters of the town beneath the platitude; ...lisle. *Carlisle.* You are now leaving Carlisle.

Tess leaned back and stared at the wall above the laptop, eyes unfocussed as she analysed the information she had been looking at. The way the folders were named, numbered and arranged were very military or police in style. Harking back to her Army days she remembered the operational name given to the Afghan deployments had been Herrick 1 to 14. *But what the hell is Juno 1 – 5?* Her police officer's mind knew that it was unlikely to be a simple explanation and as she mulled over the possibilities a flash of inspiration came to her. She right-clicked on the Carlisle image and chose the 'Get Info' option from the menu. The information relating to the image came up and she noted the date on which the image was taken. She then selected the Safari option to access the internet and waited while the Yahoo home page loaded. In the search bar she quickly typed a series of words and the month that the image had been taken. The screen refreshed with her new information and she saw immediately what she was looking for in the third result from the top. She clicked on this item and was directed to a historic report from the Daily Mail detailing an armed robbery of a G4S truck carrying money between bank branches in Carlisle.

Tess could feel her heartbeat thumping in her chest and minimised the website page while she opened up the images in the 'Juno 2' folder. Trawling through these photographs she found no place names to suggest where they had been taken and had almost given up when another idea occurred to her. In several of the street shots, telephone numbers were visible above the premises. Zooming in on these she identified the dialling code and entered it into the search bar. 01670: Morpeth. She repeated the process of getting the date of the image and entered the same series of words that she had on her first effort, replacing Carlisle with Morpeth. Another hit. First result on the list; two betting shops robbed of takings on Grand National day.

Tess stood up feeling a little shaky. This was big. *Very* big. Westley Adams was involved in armed robberies. Which meant Westley Adams had access to weapons. She remembered suddenly the smell of gun oil and the gun cleaning cloth in the outbuildings. *Shit, are they planning another robbery now?* She reached for her radio but stopped short of using it. Yes, she had more than enough to get back to the Sarge with but she might as well continue with her search just in case anything else turned up. In her mind she allowed a small fantasy of finding a cupboard full of guns and money to play out before shaking her head and returning to reality. *Right; search the rest of this building then straight on to the Sarge, get him up to speed with this info.*

She closed down all the folders and the browser, returning the laptop to the state she had found it in. Turning her attention to the remainder of the room she saw another door and walked over, turned the handle and pushed it open. *More stairs.* This surprised her a little but she now saw that the laptop room was in fact just a large landing or mezzanine. She identified the light switch and turned it on, descending the stone staircase and noting the two doors at the bottom. On reaching these she chose the left option first and saw with dismay the five-button security lock, soft brushed metal reflecting the light back at her. *Shit.* Optimistically she turned the handle and pushed but there was no movement. She wasn't surprised; you didn't fit a lock like this on a door and leave it insecure.

Her curiosity was aroused. This type of lock was serious overkill in a private residence. *What the hell were they keeping in there?* Sighing, she was turning to check out the other room when a thought came to her. She turned on the torch and pointed the beam directly back at the lock and its buttons. Her heart leapt as she saw her hunch had been right. Buttons 1, 3 and 5 were all a shade brighter than the others and this is what she'd been hoping for. Not many people would have been aware of it but the manufacturers of these locks provided to the Armed Forces and Civil Services and supplied them with a default code that the buyer was directed to change to one of their own choosing. Tess had entered several locations during her military career by identifying that many departments didn't bother changing the manufacturer's code. Holding her breath, she pressed buttons 1 and 5 together then 3 on its own. She turned the handle and gave an involuntary yell of triumph as the door opened, giving her access to the room. *Thank goodness for lazy people!*

The room was dark and she fumbled for the switch on the wall beside her, finding it and flicking it on. She stood, mouth agape and was stunned by the contents of the room before her and for the first time since she'd started investigating this case, PC Tess Cameron felt an altogether new sensation that replaced her curiosity and excitement: Fear

19

Bravo could feel the sweat trickling down his back and the weight of his lactic-heavy legs as he struggled up the final rise towards the woods. Ahead of him Charlie and Delta were plodding through the thick snow and although he couldn't see their faces, he knew they would be suffering as much as him. He lowered his head and continued to drive his legs, propelling himself up the last bit of the hill.

A glance at his watch showed him that they'd taken just under ten minutes to get here from the road junction they had destroyed earlier. *Not bad. Not bad at all.* Looking up, he saw that he had reached the woods and entered the gloomy interior. Ahead of him Delta picked up the path and followed it towards their second objective. Within a minute of walking they stood beside each other, breathing heavily after the exertion of the journey, looking at the chain link fence that secured the mast and antennae. All three removed their snowshoes and stacked them against a nearby tree before returning to the fenced enclosure. Delta pulled the small pair of wire-cutters from his combat vest and made a series of rapid snips along the fence. Bravo and Charlie watched the area around them while Delta concluded his action. The sound of the fence being pulled to one side told them Delta had finished and Bravo turned to see Delta holding back a large triangle of the mesh that he had peeled away. As briefed in their plan, Bravo alone scuttled under the fence and into the enclosure. Delta dropped the end of the mesh he was holding and knelt, weapon up and facing the opposite direction from Charlie, giving Bravo complete all-round cover while he was on task.

Bravo dropped to his knees and removed his pack. He unfastened the clips and dug deep inside, pulling out several items and laying them on the snow in front of him. Unzipping the top pouch of the backpack he removed a clump of detonators held together with an elastic band. He slipped one of the slim brass cylinders out of the group and laid it alongside the other components of the charge. With skill born of practice, he assembled his charge within seconds, the disparate items now a singular explosive entity. Picking his device up from the floor, he stood and walked over to the base of the mast. He clipped the charge onto a karabiner attached to his combat vest and gave a small tug on the charge to confirm it was secure. He looked up the mast through the swirling snow for a moment then reached for the ladder and began to climb.

The wind was not as strong as he had thought it might be and he remembered that the mast was sheltered by the trees around it. The metal rungs were treacherous with ice however and he took his time, taking care with each foot placement. The space for his body was getting narrower and he looked up and saw he was reaching the top and with it, his target. His head was now level with an array of dishes, antennae, and domes, the apparatus of mobile communications. Testing his foot holds he nodded, content that he was stable then unclipped the charge from his vest. He fastened the two zip ties from the rear of the charge on to the metal structure of the mast and again, gave a small tug on the explosive device to test it was secure.

Removing his glove, he wired the detonator to the improvised timing device and set it for three minutes. He knew that this would be enough time to be clear of the mast before the explosion was initiated. The clockwork dial began ticking as the device started counting down. Bravo replaced his glove, took a last look at the device and scrambled back down the ladder as fast as he dared while taking care on the icy rungs. On reaching the ground he retrieved his rifle and backpack and ran to the fence where Delta already had the opening ready for him. All three sprinted across the track, grabbing their snowshoes as they passed and into the cover of the woods where they stood and waited. The only sound was that of the trees around them groaning in protest at the wind buffeting their tops. Bravo was calculating how much time was left when a loud crack split the air. Motioning the others to stay, Bravo jogged back to the fence line and bringing his rifle up, took aim at the top of the mast. Using the magnification of his sight system he conducted a damage survey of his action. He could see that the top third of the mast had been destroyed completely, twisted, charred and smoking in the aftermath. *Good job.* All radio and mobile communications in the village were now dead.

He ran back to the others and nodded to show the task was complete and the three re-attached their snowshoes and stood, waiting for Bravo to take the lead. Walking the group to the edge of the woods, he set off with long, fluid strides, the snow kicking up around him as his snowshoes cleared the ground. He was pleased with their progress. Timings were still on track and they'd had no setbacks. He thought about Alpha, locked away in a cell in a shitty little village jail and imagined he could send him a SITREP, a Situation Report, to let him know they were on their way. Giving a quick glance back at the others he saw they were, as expected, maintaining the pace while keeping a tactical gap between them. They were a good team and they had Alpha to thank for that. His training and mentoring had made them the unit that they were today. Facing to his front once again, he constructed his mental SITREP for Alpha as he powered down the snowy slope.

Alpha, Bravo. Objectives one and two of Phase One complete. Proceeding to Objective Three.

20

There was a moment's silence in the room as Fletch finished his recounting of their crash. Colin cleared his throat.

'Well, I'm not too sure we can get anybody out to it for recovery in this weather. I'm more concerned about the road to be honest. You say it looks like it's collapsed or exploded or something?'

Fletch looked at Mark as he spoke. 'Yes Colin. I mean, I don't know how PC Armstrong would describe it but the ground was all brown earth; no snow cover at all, so it could only just have happened before we got there.' Mark nodded his agreement, sipping at his coffee with both hands around the mug as he tried to warm up.

Colin stood. 'To be honest, I couldn't tell you what runs under that junction in terms of gas or whatever else. But the whole junction is impassable you say?'

'Absolutely. It's a giant hole basically. We put out warning triangles each side of it and our 'Road Closed' on the northern side as our car is blocking this end anyway.'

'Good thinking Fletch. I was just about to send PC Logan here out to do just that. I take it you're both okay, medically I mean?'

Fletch grinned. 'Other than a severe case of injured pride I think we're okay. Just preparing for months of torture once this gets out.'

Colin chuckled. 'Ach, we've all been there man. There are only two types of coppers who have accidents Fletch; those who have them and those who are going to have them. In this case there is absolutely nothing that you could have done.'

'I know that Colin but that's not going to make a blind bit of difference to the lads back at the nick!'

'True, very true. Why let the facts get in the way of a good story eh?'

'Exactly.' Fletch finished his coffee and sighed. 'Well, no point putting it off any longer, I better give the duty officer a phone and give him the good news.' He pulled out his phone and scrolled through the contacts list, finding the Aberdeen Station's duty officer's number. He selected the contact but the call didn't go through. Frowning, he looked at the signal status and saw that he had no bars showing. 'PC Armstrong, I've still got no signal here, have you got any to call the duty officer with?'

Mark put his mug down and pulled out his phone, checking the small screen. 'Nope, not a bar. Who are you with Sarge?'

'EE, and they're usually quite good. What about you?'

'Vodafone, and again, they're usually alright up this way.'

Fletch stood and made his way to the landline beside Tess's desk. 'Not to worry, we'll do it old school style.' He picked up the handset and put it to his ear as he prepared to dial. Frowning, he hung up then picked the handset up again and listened once more. He looked at the display screen and his eyebrows rose in surprise at the text he read there. *No Connection.* He walked across the room to the other landline and saw the same message when he lifted the handset on this one.

'Colin, don't suppose your landline, or mobile for that matter, has got a signal?'

In his office, Colin reached for the handset of his landline and saw the *No Connection* message. He hung up and tried it several times before admitting defeat. Pulling his two mobile telephones towards him, he peered down at the small display screens. No signal on either. *Strange.* Snow must have brought down a mast somewhere. Mobile communications were still a black art to Colin, something he embraced the use of without understanding even the basics of how they worked.

'Sorry Fletch, I've got nothing either. Looks like this storm has damaged a link somewhere.' He heard Fletch's muffled curse.

'Shit. No worries, I'll fire them an email and fill them in on the situation that way.'

Colin grinned at the Sergeant's suggestion. 'Erm… Fletch? Not to be a smart arse or anything but if there's no landline, there'll be no internet mate.'

Fletch's curse was not muffled this time.

21

The white phosphorous grenade had destroyed the junction box and its contents, leaving a melted, smoking mass of plastic and metal. Bravo continued to monitor it through his rifle sight, noting that the smoke had dissipated to the point where it was almost indistinguishable among the whirling clouds of snow. Not that he expected anyone to see it; they had not encountered a single soul since leaving their home, the blizzard keeping everyone indoors. He lowered his rifle and looked at Charlie and Delta behind him, making eye contact before giving them the thumbs-up signal. *Objective 3 complete.* The village was now without landline and internet communications. In military speak it was now *Comms Dark*.

The team withdrew further along the narrow lane and into the open fields of the village park. They crossed a fence and some paddocks, shuffling through the drifts of snow. Another series of fences slowed their progress until finally they had reached the southern outskirts of the village. Again, they had not encountered anyone and in the poor visibility and their camouflage whites, no one could have seen them. They entered a small copse of trees and Bravo walked to a stand of sycamores near the road. He circled around the tallest, estimating its height and width. *Perfect.*

Taking a length of detonating cord from his pack he put together the new charge and laid the assembled device on the floor. He pulled a thick roll of insulating tape and stood, picking the charge up in his free hand. Charlie joined him and took the offered tape. Bravo placed the charge low against the body of the tree and held it in place while Charlie lashed it securely against the trunk with the insulating tape, tearing the end of the tape off with his teeth and handing the roll back to Bravo. With his other hand Bravo tested the stability of the charge and was happy that it was held fast.

Grabbing all his gear, he waited until Charlie and Delta had passed him and made their way across the snow-covered road and over the wall on the other side. Turning his attention back to the charge he attached the detonator to the timer and dialled the small clockwork mechanism. *One minute.* As soon as he released it the mechanism began its shrill whirring noise as it counted down to detonation. Bravo turned and shuffled across the road, his snowshoes keeping him from dropping through the deep drifts. He reached the stone wall and rolled over the top, landing on the soft snow near Delta, who gave him a wide grin.

Bravo remained in the prone position waiting for the bang but he still jumped when the explosion shattered the air and a loud crash followed seconds after. He gave it a further few seconds before he stood, followed by the others, and returned to the road.

139

Bravo was pleased with his handiwork. The tree blocked the entire road and with deep drainage ditches either side, nobody could drive around the obstacle either. Alpha had taught them well, practicing these techniques in the privacy of their own land, honing them to perfection. Catching Charlie and Delta's eyes he smiled as they nodded their approval. The village now had no communications with the outside world and both road entrances and exits were impassable. Bravo felt the thrill of anticipation in his chest. Phase One was now complete. The preparation was done and it was now time to embark on the crux of the mission. Phase Two: The extraction of Alpha.

Bravo opened his mouth to say as much to the rest of the team when he was shocked into silence by a voice behind them.

'What the *hell* do you think you're doing?'

22

Tess took her mobile phone out and began taking pictures of the room's contents, knowing it would be difficult for anyone who hadn't seen it for themselves to think she wasn't exaggerating. Panning the room and taking a series of snaps she conducted a mental inventory of the contents. Two weapon racks and a series of hooks on the wall with stencilled pistol shapes indicating where the absent items would be stored. Boxes of ammunition stacked neatly in two piles, one of 5.56mm and one of 9mm. *Rifle and pistol ammo, and lots of it.* Four wooden crucifix-style stands, one of which held a compact set of body armour draped over it. Two larger metal containers marked as explosives and a smaller one beside it labelled with 'Grenades HE'. Tess knew the HE stood for High Explosive. These people were not messing around. This was serious kit meant for killing. She hurried her photo taking, keen to get on to the Sarge right away and get the forensics out here to secure and search the place.

A tall set of three metal lockers was stacked against the far wall and she walked across to it when something on the floor caught her eye and she stopped to examine it.

Holyshitholyshitholyshitholyshit....Her breath hitched and chest heaved as she came to terms with what she was looking at: A trip wire. A fine filament almost invisible to the naked eye that stretched across the floor at foot level. Another step and she would have set it off. She closed her eyes and shivered at the thought. Turning on the torch, she pointed the beam with shaking hands at the filament. She followed it along its length to one wall where she saw that it was attached to something concealed behind an empty ammunition container. With exaggerated care and her heart still pounding she made her way to the wire's end and stared at her discovery. The end of the trip wire was attached to the ring of a Red Phosphorous grenade pin. If she'd struck the wire, the pin would have been pulled and the grenade detonated. *Red Phosphorous. What the hell?* She retraced her steps and followed the filament to its other end and found an identical set up. *Two red phosphorous grenades. Go large or go home as they say.* She stood still for several minutes, willing her breathing and heart rate to calm down. Red phosphorous was a terrifying weapon; the sheer destructive power able to burn through anything with its intense heat.

She recalled the only time she had ever seen it in use. When she was a Corporal in Basra, she had been deployed out as a member of the Quick Reaction Force to assist a trapped soldier. As their armoured vehicle was leaving the compound a muscular, bearded guy with non-conventional weapons jumped in the back alongside Tess and her team. 'I'm Jake from the Task Force and it's one of my guys we're going to help.' Jake had explained that one of his men operating in civilian profile had been identified and was now cornered in a street with hundreds of Iraqis rushing to the scene. Jake needed the muscle of the QRF's armour to punch through the crowds and extract his trapped soldier. The plan had worked and Tess remembered watching as a wounded man, dressed like a local, staggered from the car clutching a pistol and a carbine, into Jake's arms. Jake had propelled the man into the back of the Mastiff then ran back to the car, pulling something from his combat vest and throwing it into the vehicle. He'd sprinted back to them, grinning and yelling 'Fire in the hole'. The car had gone up in a fierce blaze, the like of which she had never seen before. Jake had caught her eye as they reversed out of the vicinity and winked. 'Red phos' he'd said 'the equal opportunities weapon. Burns EVERYTHING!'

Looking at the room around her, Tess guessed that rather than overkill, the Red Phosphorous grenades would kill any intruder while destroying the entire room and its contents. *Smart*. Biting her lower lip as she thought the possibilities through, she came to a decision: She would disarm the trip-wire. It was a relatively easy procedure but it had been years since she'd actually done it but she couldn't take the risk that someone else could enter the room and initiate the trap. She took a deep breath and walked over to the nearest grenade, kneeling slowly beside it, ensuring her legs remained well away from the wire filament. The grenade was secured to a small metal post, again, a familiar sight to her. Reaching forward with a shaking hand, she disconnected the pull ring of the wire from the grenade pin. Placing the wire end on the floor she pushed the grenade's pin fully home and splayed the ends to hold it secure in its hole. She crossed the room and repeated the process on the other grenade, taking the same exaggerated care. *Done.* Standing once again, she felt the trickle of sweat run down the hollow of her spine and into her underwear. *Nice, but that's it done now.* She looked at the set of lockers again but wondered if she might be pushing her luck. If they'd booby trapped the room, there was always the possibility that the lockers could be rigged as well and she couldn't really tell what they might have rigged it with without opening them or at least, getting closer. *No.* She'd seen enough.

Turning on her heel she walked out of the room on legs that were still shaky. As she was passing the door, she noted another military container and stopped in her tracks as she read the yellow writing on the side. *For crying out loud! Light anti-tank weapons; what could they possibly want these for?* M72A9s were small extendable launchers, designed as a personal weapon to fire at armoured vehicles and tanks. She had to get all this to the Sarge. Quickly.

Tess pulled the door closed and opened the one facing her. Turning on the light she found herself in some kind of communal area with a sofa, chairs, a TV, DVD player and a kitchen leading off. On the wall above the sink she saw a large wall-planner with a lot of writing over the calendar dates. Examining the floor before her she moved warily over to it and stood observing the contents. It was a basic calendar month with the dates before today crossed out and information written in pen on various days. She tilted her head to one side as she concentrated on deciphering the scrawled handwriting. *Shit! These guys are doing some serious training out here.* Acronyms and abbreviations she'd all but forgotten from her military days leapt out at her from the days promulgated on the planner. *CQC*; Close Quarter Combat. *Jap-Slapping*; Unarmed Combat. *Cam and Con*; Camouflage and Concealment. *E and E*; Escape and Evasion. *R to I*; Resistance to Interrogation. *Dems*; Demolitions and Explosives.

There were other abbreviations that she could not understand but she knew they would be of a similar ilk. She was looking at a comprehensive training program, the like of which she remembered receiving in the Army, preparing them for imminent deployments. This was a very aggressive training regime and she wondered for a moment of perhaps she'd stumbled upon a clandestine Special Forces operation, similar to some of the ones conducted in the bad old days of the conflict in Northern Ireland. *No.* For a start, Adams would have called his superiors to deal with the local police, he wouldn't just sit in a cell and wait. Secondly, this place would not have been left unguarded. That *never* happened in the military when there were weapons and ammunition involved. *So, where the hell had they got this arsenal from?* And although they had Adams in custody, where were

145

the other occupants who'd been conducting offensive training techniques? From everything she had seen on the property there were another 2-3 heavily armed, well-trained men out among the general public presenting a very dangerous situation. *Shit.*

After a while she stopped and took out her phone, turning on the flash and taking several shots of the calendar. Putting her phone away she pressed on her radio handset to speak to the Sarge but got nothing. She checked the handset and saw that the battery power was good and so tried again. Nothing. Taking out her mobile once again she attempted to call the station but saw she had no signal. *Come ON!* She hadn't seen a landline but an idea came to her. She turned off the light and left the room, climbed back up the stairs and made her way over to the laptop again. She logged on to Facebook and gave Mitch a private message, knowing he would pick up his phone when he heard the notification. She waited for several moments then sent the message again. *Still at Adams house. Urgent that I speak with Sarge. Waiting for response as no comms here!!!* Again, she waited for another two minutes and sent it again. *Come on Mitch!*

An idea struck her as she was waiting and she brought up the browsing history. The laptop had last been accessed that morning and the plans that she had seen of St Cyrus were among the most recent items listed. Going back further down the list she found a lot of what seemed to be general browsing until a cluster of items caught her eye and she selected them one at a time, opening the links and reading the content before moving on to the next. They were all concerned with a forthcoming visit of the Minister for Defence to Leuchars Air Base where a Scottish Army regiment was now billeted. There was a lot of browsing on the Minister, historic articles on him and the town of St Andrews. Someone had also been accessing Google maps of the area and she clicked on the downloads icon and found that a lot of mapping had been downloaded.

A cold, heavy knot sat in her stomach as she digested this information and its possible outcomes. Three or four people lived in this house, well-trained and well-equipped and funded by well-planned, armed robberies. The owner of the place was a Special Forces veteran with a grudge against the Army, his wife and, it appeared, life in general. And now the Minister for Defence was visiting just down the coast and these people had been building a dossier of information relating to the visit. She brushed a strand of hair from her face and gave a grim smile. As Mitch would say, *it doesn't take a genius to work this out.* Tess looked again at the Facebook page on her phone and was surprised to see that there was now no internet or telephone connection. *Strange.* She'd had access to the property's unsecured Wi-Fi since arriving and she usually picked up 3G around the area but there was absolutely nothing now.

Standing, she turned to go but noticed a USB flash drive sitting in one of the small compartments on the front of the desk. She picked it up and placed it into one of the available ports on the computer. An icon appeared on the desktop screen labelled as 'Training 2'. She was about to access its contents when she thought about the time she had already spent in the buildings. Coming to a decision, she ejected the small device and put it in her pocket. She had to get back and warn the Sarge to get this information up the chain ASAP. Her mind made up, she closed down the computer and reversed her entry procedure, ensuring that she turned out the lights as she went.

23

'I said, what the hell do you think you're doing?'

Bravo squinted hard to make out the man's details through the driving snow as he recovered from the initial shock of being confronted by a witness. He took a step towards the man and saw that the individual was dressed for the weather and wearing a set of cross-country skis. Bravo could feel Charlie and Delta waiting for his direction, silent but ready.

Kenny Dickson put his hand above his brow to shield the worst of the snow from his vision. He'd stopped dead as soon as he'd heard the bang just in front of him, then watched as the giant tree had crashed to the ground, followed by the sight of three armed individuals appearing in front of him. Their arctic camouflage uniforms made him wonder if perhaps they were Marines from the base at Arbroath. Not quite what he'd expected as he'd strapped on his skis earlier, keen to check on some of the older people in the village, make sure they were coping okay with the bad weather. It was apparent to him that these three had brought the tree down but for the life of him, couldn't understand why. What the hell were they looking to

149

achieve? As he watched, the one nearest took a step towards him and mimicked Kenny's posture with his hand, obviously struggling to make out enough detail.

Kenny started to feel a little uneasy. He's spent some time in the Engineers many years ago and could now tell by looking at these guys that they weren't conventional forces. The one nearest him had some kind of M16 variant; definitely not standard issue to British troops. The silence was not natural either. Surely if this was a military exercise or assistance to civil authorities, they would be reassuring him now rather than...*assessing* him? *Yes, that's exactly what he's doing, he's assessing me.* Kenny was starting to regret confronting them and listened to the internal voice screaming its advice to him: *Run.*

Pivoting as quick as he dared, and with his back now turned to the men, Kenny punched his poles into the snow and propelled himself forward, pushing with his skis to build up momentum. A zipping noise beside his ear was immediately followed by the crack of something splitting the air. *Fuck me, they're shooting!* He ducked his head and continued with his erratic dash forward through the snow, driving arms and legs as the adrenaline surged through his body. His left ski caught on something under the snow and for a brief moment he found himself balanced only on one ski, arms flailing until he regained his footing and reclaimed his momentum. The coppery taste of fear flooded his mouth as he was all too aware that falling now meant death. The skis underneath him soon required less driving from his legs and he realised that he had crested the small hill on the main road and that it was now a downhill slope into the village. He risked a quick, wide-eyed glance over his shoulder but saw nothing beyond the frigid static of the blizzard. Facing forward as he continued with his rhythmic exertions, he thrust the poles hard into the snow, schussing to exploit the momentum as the base of his skis cut through the dry crystals. He had to warn someone about this. *The Police Station. Get to the Police Station and let Colin know.* Let the authorities deal with, well, whatever the hell was going on back there.

Bravo didn't think he'd hit the man, the sudden movement catching him unawares and his sight picture completely compromised by the relentless snow. He'd cursed then waded through the drifts, staring down at the ground looking for a blood trail. *Nothing.* Charlie and Delta came alongside him and he pointed to the parallel tracks in the snow.

'I didn't get him so he's probably on his way to the Police Station now.' He pointed to Charlie. 'You know what to do so head off now and re-org with us at the rear of the garage as soon as it's done okay?'

Charlie gave a quick nod and began his long-gaited jog, snow shoes kicking up small plumes of frigid dust and was soon invisible in the darkening storm. Bravo glanced at Delta and pointed in the direction of the skier's tracks. Not waiting for an answer, he began powering his way along the snow-covered thoroughfare. He needed to get to the disused garage where they could monitor the comings and goings from the Police Station, ready for the start of Phase 3. *Fucking skier! Everything was going so well until he showed up.*

With a sigh he put the incident to the back of his mind, hearing Alpha's voice of reason from many of the training evolutions they'd endured. *No plan survives contact with the enemy so never expect it to. Be prepared to improvise, adapt and overcome. This should be second nature to you by now.* While not quite second nature, Bravo had to admit that he felt no panic or undue pressure, just a sense of urgency to regain some control.

The streetlights flickered on as Kenny continued his gliding descent along the main street, the orange sodium emitting soft halos through the falling snow. His breathing was ragged but he didn't care, could now see the Police Station ahead of him, the small blue sign above the wall also illuminated. With a final glance over his shoulder to confirm he was alone, Kenny slowed his progress and changed direction, skating his way into the open driveway of the station. He stopped at the base of the steps and unclipped his bindings, throwing his poles on the ground before reaching up and pressing hard on the intercom. Panting in the cold air, he listened as the buzzer sounded inside. *Come on, come on…* After what seemed like an age, he heard young Mitch Logan's voice boom from the speaker.

'Hello Kenny, what's up?'

'An emergency Mitch and a bloody big one, you need to let me in.' There was a brief pause then he heard the mechanism of the door release and he climbed the steps, turned the handle and entered the warmth of the station. He slammed the door behind him and rested his back against it for several moments, slowing his breath and regaining some composure. Pulling off his hat, goggles and gloves he made his way to the main reception area where alongside Mitch and Colin were another two policemen that he didn't know. Colin gave a small grin and pointed at his clothes.

'Been out on the skis again Kenny? Probably the only person in the village who looks forward to this weather.' The grin dropped as Colin saw the expression on Kenny's face. 'Okay mate, what's the problem?'

Kenny took a deep breath and looked the Police Sergeant in the eye.

'The problem is there's three armed men just blocked the road to Montrose and then tried to shoot me when I confronted them. *That's* the problem.'

24

Tess felt the rear of the Freelander sliding out from under her and eased back on the acceleration. Even with the four-wheel drive engaged, the heavy snow was challenging her driving ability. *Take it easy, better to get there slowly than having to bloody walk it!* She glanced at her mobile again and noted she still had no reception at all and concluded that the storm must have brought down a mast somewhere. She had the headlights on as it had gotten dark while she was searching the house and she concentrated on the road ahead.

Cresting the bridge just before the junction she could see the dim sodium glow in the air above her and realised that the street lighting had come on and with it, the realisation that it was getting late.

A small spark of worry flickered at the thought of the Sarge moving Adams up to Stonehaven but she was sure that the weather would have convinced Colin otherwise. She turned at the junction, creeping along a road she would normally have driven at sixty miles an hour. There were no other tracks illuminated by her headlights. *People with more sense.* Passing the Village Inn, she noticed the lights still on and was surprised they'd stayed open as she couldn't imagine there would have been much custom today.

Turning right into the station she breathed a small sigh of relief. *Finally, I'm here.* She abandoned the car and turned the engine off, grabbing her phone as she exited the vehicle. Leaning against the buffeting winds she made her way to the door and punched in the combination. Once inside she jogged down the corridor and burst into the main office, speechless for a moment at the unexpected sight of so many people. She recognised them all but hadn't expected anyone other than the Sarge and Mitch to be present. The Sarge was in a deep discussion with the Firearms Sergeant and Kenny Dickson but looked up as she approached.

'I'm assuming from the look on your face this isn't great news either?'

She waited for a few moments to allow her racing thoughts to coalesce into something that would at least resemble a logical statement that she could deliver.

'No Sarge, it's not. It's actually really bad.' She glanced at the station's visitors before continuing. 'Do you want me to brief you in your office?'

Colin Duffy looked at the people around him and knew instinctively that he was going to need their help. He could feel it as strongly as anything he could remember: Bad things were coming. He nodded at Tess. 'No. Brief us all here PC Cameron. I've got a feeling we're all going to be caught up in whatever's coming.'

Tess raised her eyebrows in surprise but walked over to the large-scale map and pointed to the location of Adams' property. 'As you know, we arrested an individual known to be Westley Adams at his home address *here* earlier today. Acting upon further information, I returned to the property to ensure there were no pets or animals dependent on Mr Adams for their welfare.' She saw the firearm's Sergeant give a wry grin of recognition at Colin's subterfuge. 'I'll now give you a run down on what I found and then show some of the footage I took at the scene.'

She briefed, without questions for nearly fifteen minutes, noting as she continued the stunned expressions of the other policemen. Once she'd delivered the last of her information, she flicked on the large screen on the opposite wall and worked the remote control alongside her telephone, projecting her phone's contents onto the screen.

'This is a room within a secret building that is accessed through the wardrobe of an upstairs outbuilding. This room is key-pad controlled and if I zoom in, you'll see why.' The quiet gasps behind her confirmed her colleague's shock at the sight of the weapon racks and explosive containers. 'As I'm sure you've noticed it would appear that the weapons that should be stored are not there. I'd also like to draw your attention to this part of the photo,' she highlighted a part of the screen with the remote's laser pointer, 'which, although hard to see, is a trip wire; a booby trap.'

Colin walked closer to the screen; eyes narrowed as he studied the image. 'What was the wire attached to PC Cameron?'

Even though she was just briefing the incident, Tess struggled to keep the small tremors from her voice as the memory flooded back. 'Two red phosphorous grenades Sarge. I only spotted the wire by luck, was an inch from tripping it.'

Colin put his hand on her shoulder. 'Well, you didn't trip it lass. You made it back here safe and sound, okay?'

She felt a lump in her throat and a warmth behind her eyes at the sympathetic words. Taking a deep breath, she swallowed her emotions and was about to carry on when Kenny spoke.

'Red phos? That is *mental* stuff. Why the hell would anybody have that in their homes?' He turned to the SFOs. 'Sorry guys, I should explain, I'm an ex-Army Engineer so I know a wee bit about these things.' He looked over at Colin. 'I take it this must be a terrorist thing?'

Tess spoke before her superior could answer. 'No. Not quite. I'll show you the rest of what I found and it will explain what I think they're up to.' With a nod from Colin, she turned back to the screen and continued her brief, bringing up other images and pointing out specific areas of interest. There was a moment's silence when she had finished which was eventually broken by the Firearms sergeant who pointed towards the custody suite.

'Can someone please tell me who the fuck this guy is you've got sitting in the cell back there?'

Again, Tess took the lead, going over everything she had learned from her own research and Donna's help. PC Armstrong cleared his throat.

'So, he's an ex-SAS man with a grudge against the world and its brother who is planning to kill the Minister for Defence. There's another three or four of these goons running around armed to the teeth that's already blocked a road and shot at a member of the public. The next question has to be what are they doing? Why block the road instead of escaping?' He looked at Colin and his own Sergeant. 'C'mon, you know the drill; as soon as any major player in a gang is lifted, the rest disappear off the face of the earth to avoid their own arrest.'

Colin stroked his chin as the group awaited his response. He turned to Tess, nodding towards Kenny as he spoke. 'PC Armstrong has a point but I'm thinking that maybe the ex-military aspect is important here? Would you two agree?'

Kenny nodded. 'To be honest, I've been out the mob a good while now and I was only ever in a supporting role to the fighting troops but in answer to your question, yeah; these Special Ops guys keep looking out for one another even after they've left.'

Fletch raised his hand. 'Okay, I get that, but didn't you say that this guy had been dishonourably discharged? A disgrace to his regiment? Why would anyone support him after that?'

All eyes turned back to Tess. 'This is only a theory but I think it's fairly sound. Adams' charges and termination of service were *official* actions, initiated and sanctioned at Defence, not Regimental level. What he was originally disciplined for was probably well-supported by his colleagues at the time. In my opinion, he was probably well thought of in the SAS but once he crossed the line and affected political relations in Afghanistan, he was made an example of. So, it follows that he may actually have had the sympathy of his fellow soldiers.'

Colin rubbed his hands over his face and sighed. He already felt exhausted and was struggling to put the situation into any kind of manageable event. 'Right, salient points: We've arrested an individual who assaulted people trespassing on his land. He resisted arrest until Tasered and claimed to be alone at his residence. We now know he is a former SAS soldier who was booted out and holds a serious grudge against the establishment. He and his colleagues have secured a serious arsenal of weapons and explosives and have conducted a series of armed robberies. From what PC Cameron found, it appears that they are attempting to kill or kidnap the Minister for Defence when he visits RAF Leuchars. Today, there are three of these armed men in our village who have blocked the Montrose road and shot at Kenny when he questioned them.' He stopped for a moment as something nagged at the back of his mind. Mitch opened his mouth to speak but Colin silenced him with a curse. 'Shit!' He turned to the Firearms' team.

'Thinking back to the description of the area where you lost your car, would you say, knowing what we know now, that it could have been the result of a deliberate explosion?'

Fletch nodded, his face grim. 'I was just coming to the same conclusion myself Colin; this *cannot* be a coincidence. Think about it, that's the village now effectively cut off from the north and south. Is there another road out of here?'

'Yes, there's the back road to Marykirk and Laurencekirk but we closed that yesterday morning because of the conditions so it will be completely impassable now.'

Mitch stood up. 'Come on guys. I think we're getting ahead of ourselves a bit here. Aye, we've found an arsenal of serious weapons and explosives and aye, Kenny's been shot at by a few boys playing Army, but I think you're giving them too much credit. Cutting the village off by blowing up and blocking roads? Why? What would they gain?' He turned to Colin, his voice rising slightly as he proposed his arguments. 'We're starting to see things that aren't there. *I* think that the road collapse at the northern junction is just that; a natural collapse as a result of the weather.' He turned to Kenny, pointing at him with the pen in his hand. 'And I think that you disturbed them maybe trying to *clear* the road so that they could escape and that's why they fired at you; they thought you were trying to catch them.'

There was a moment's pause as the others digested his arguments then several people started talking at once, voices raised in completion as each sought to rebut or refute

Mitch's points. They were silenced by a loud handclap from Colin.

'At this juncture, it doesn't really matter what we *think* is happening. The problem we have is that we can't let anyone *know* what is happening. We have no radio, landline, mobile or internet connections with which we can share the information and ask for help. For all intents and purposes, until these things come back on line, we are alone.' There was silence as the gravity of his statement sunk in. As each person grappled with the significance of the situation a thought came to Tess. She considered keeping it to herself at first but realised that she needed it to be voiced, for better or worse.

'You're not going to like this either Sarge but what if the phones, radio and internet are not down because of the storm? What if the rest of Adams' cronies took them out deliberately?'

Mitch laughed aloud, attracting the attention of the group. 'Aw come on Tess! Really? So, they cut the village off from the rest of the world by blowing up and blocking roads and now somehow shutting down all comms? Now I *know* you're giving them way too much credit!'

Kenny wagged a finger in the young policeman's direction. 'Not so fast there, Mitch. She might have a point. The reason I came out today to check on the old ones was because the internet crashed and a lot of their home alert systems depend on that to trigger a response. The phones were already down by then so even I could see there would be no communicating with anybody outside the village.'

'Aye, alright Kenny, I'm well aware that the comms are down, we all are. But there's nothing to say that it's anything other than weather related.'

Kenny shook his head. 'I've lived here nearly twenty years and we've *never* lost all means of communication before.'

'There's always a first time for everything Kenny.' Mitch held up a placatory hand as he saw anger begin to cloud the older man's face. 'Look, I take your point, I really do but we're getting our knickers in a knot here and blaming the boogeymen for everything, turning normal events into conspiracies.'

Tess jumped into the brief silence before it became dominated by further arguments. 'No. The lack of comms is deliberate. This is no coincidence Mitch. Think about it; since we lifted Adams there is now no way in or out of the village by road and no way to ask for help from outside it. This is *tactical* Mitch. This is what these guys did all over the world before they left the SAS.'

Mitch continued to shake his head; arms folded across his chest. 'Nope. No way. And for what possible reason? Their mate is arrested and, in a cell, awaiting questioning. Use your police head, not your Army one! These guys are criminals and will be long gone by now, wanting to be in bloody Spain or somewhere we can't find them by the time their mate starts spilling the beans.'

Even though she felt a flush of anger course through her at her colleague's jibes she kept her tone moderate. 'I'll tell you what the possible reason is using *both* my Army head and my Police head: They're a unit. A tight team who rely on each other to carry out high-risk armed robberies and trust each other more than their own families. They live together, train together, work together and you think that just stops when one of them is arrested?' She looked around the room, meeting the eyes of each man and stopped when she reached Colin. 'They are not going to leave this village as anything other than the complete unit that they are. They are going to take Adams with them. And they're coming here to get him.'

Colin held up his hand to silence Mitch's inevitable response and was about to ask a question of his own when the room was plunged into darkness. The power had gone.

25

It had taken Charlie almost twenty minutes to return to the team after blowing the sub-station. He had been confident taking a quicker route back, cutting between houses and through lanes, the utter lack of lighting and the heavy snow rendering him all but invisible to any casual observers. On reaching the rear of the garage complex he slowed his walk and approached the location with arms wide open, rifle held far from his body in a position of supplication should Bravo or Delta have problems identifying him in the darkness and driving snow. He heard a faint noise and followed its source where he saw Delta leant against a wall, beckoning him. He lowered his arms and made his way to the rest of the team.

Bravo glanced up and caught Charlie's eye then turned his attention back to the door he was knelt alongside. There was a small metallic snap and the padlock he had been forcing broke and fell, disappearing into the snow. He stood and slid the large wooden door open to enable him to slip inside. Each team member followed, with Charlie pulling it closed behind him. The three stood for several moments listening to confirm that they were alone and allowing their eyes to adjust to the dark. Other than the sound of the wind playing on the edges of the building outside it was utterly silent inside the disused garage area. Bravo made his way over to a large bench and removed his pack, placing it and his rifle on the surface. He stretched and walked over to a dark corner where he undid his cam whites, unzipped himself and urinated noisily into the dark recess.

Charlie and Delta placed their equipment alongside Charlie's and attended to their own needs, donning head torches and turning them on, the muted red light from each providing enough illumination to see without highlighting their presence. Delta retrieved a power bar from his pack and began eating it while Charlie took on some water, rehydrating after his quick sprint back to the team. Bravo returned to the bench and put on his own head torch. He was also hungry and wanted to make sure he kept his energy levels up. Like Delta, he grabbed a power bar from within his own pack and devoured the thick slab within seconds. Washing it down with some water, before securing the fastenings of his pack once again. He turned to the rest of the team, their masked faces bathed in the soft red glow of their head torches.

'Okay. Phase One complete. They now have no ingress and egress routes open to them and are comms dark; they're alone. We're now Phase two; the Extraction.' He reached into a pocket on his combat vest and pulled out a small notebook and pencil. Opening it up to a pre-folded page, he splayed the notebook out on the bench and beckoned the team forward. Shining his own light down on the pages he used the pencil as a pointer to highlight his directions.

'This is us, rear of the garage complex - Romeo 1. *This* is Avondale house, right next to the Police Station – Romeo 2 and finally, *this* is the Police Station – Target. Plan is we move as a team from Romeo 1 to Romeo 2. Secure Romeo 2 as Forming Up Position and launch assault on Target in order to secure the release and extraction of Alpha. Success code-word is JACKPOT' He paused and looked up seeing the small lights on his team-mates' heads bobbing up and down as they nodded their understandings.

'On JACKPOT my intention is to secure a vehicle from Target and utilise this to get back on track with the exfil plan. This will take a bit of coordination while on Target but Alpha will probably have resumed command at this point so we will be taking his lead from there. Happy?' Again, the moving circles of light indicated assent.

'Okay, details. Moving from Romeo 1 to Romeo 2, this is what I want to happen.' He continued to brief the team on the specifics of their next leg of the operation, ensuring he described every action he required them to take. From his research that morning he knew that Romeo 2, the house called Avondale, was occupied by an elderly couple and was confident that they could be subdued very quickly. It offered them the perfect launch-pad from which to assault the Target as the Police station had no houses to its front or rear. The plan was simple; knock on Romeo 2, force their way in as soon as the door was opened, isolate and secure the occupants then prep their assault.

He knew the Target had a controlled entry system at the front but also a back door, and that both entrances were of sturdy wood construction. The windows were double-glazed and opaque with no visibility in or out. There was also a skylight window on the roof but he had no real use for that in his plan at this point. He knew that at any given time there could be as many as three Police officers in the building but that they had no weapons other than Tasers. Bravo continued to brief the team on the details of the next phase.

On securing Romeo 2, Bravo would detach and take up a position at the rear door of the Target. He would wait for Charlie and Delta to take up their position by the front door. Delta would cover while Charlie placed a charge on the entrance and radio Bravo when complete. Bravo would then place his own charge on the back door and let the remainder of the team know it was done. Charlie would detonate the charge on the front door and wait. The police inside would rush to investigate the devastation and once at the scene Charlie would relay this to Bravo. Bravo would then detonate his own charge and enter through the breach. Charlie and Delta would simultaneously overpower the Police officers and secure them in the building. Bravo would locate Alpha and force his captors to release him and the whole team could then extract and carry out their exfiltration plan. Simple.

167

Bravo pulled his sleeve back and looked at the dim fluorescent glow from his watch dial. He raised his head and saw that Charlie and Delta were securing their packs. 'Two minutes.' Both men gave him a thumbs-up to confirm their understanding then continued readying themselves. Bravo shrugged on his pack and picked up his carbine. He reached up and flicked his head torch off, stowing the light in his leg pocket, and stood still, eyes closed while he waited for his sight to re-adjust to the darkness. His team mates carried out the same procedure before following him to the door and waiting while he eased it open and took a cautious look outside. Bravo stepped out into the gusting blizzard and pulled his goggles down, taking long steps to gain some distance from the building.

He led them at a steady pace along the deep drifts of the main road, the dark thoroughfare unrecognisable from its usually illuminated form. Visibility was limited to no more than a few feet and Bravo knew they could not have wished for better conditions. Someone would practically have to walk into them to see them. This reminded him of the skier and he pondered briefly on the impact that he could have. *Very little.* He had to assume that the man had gone directly to the Police station and reported the incident. No matter. The comms were already out by the time he'd seen them so there was no way that the Police could have informed anyone or requested help.

He altered course a little and looked back to see that Delta had noticed. Even though his team mate was only a few feet behind him, the dark and the snow combined to mask Delta, absorbing him into the storm. But Delta had noticed and turned back towards Charlie to indicate the change of direction to him. Bravo was now walking parallel to snow-covered walls that separated the houses from the pavement and main street. Working from memory he passed three openings in the walls that he knew were driveways and then stopped at the fourth. Two dark stone pillars supported a wrought iron gate decorated with clinging snow and small icicles. Bravo noticed a rounded lip protruding from the surface of one of the pillars and rubbed the snow from it with his gloved hand. He nodded with satisfaction as he read the house name displayed on the ornamental plaque. *Avondale*. They had reached Romeo 2.

26

Colin recovered first. 'It's okay, the generator will kick in soon and the lights will be back on, just give it a second.' He had just finished speaking when the lights returned, flickering in protest as the room filled with various beeps and whirring noises as computers, radios and other technology coming back to life after their brief respite.

Colin looked over at the Firearms officers. 'Fletch, I agree with PC Cameron here. I think these boys are going to come for their pal at some point and I don't think that power cut was a coincidence either. That would say to me that they're probably coming sooner rather than later.'

Fletch considered his response. 'I'm still not too sure Colin. I mean yes, based on all the evidence PC Cameron has shown us there are some serious individuals out there but coming to take him out of a Police station? I just can't see it.'

Tess held up her hand. 'Wait, listen. What's that?' After several moments had passed, they all heard the muffled voice. Colin stood and walked out of the room.

'It's our guest in the custody suite. It appears that he finally has something to say.'

Tess followed Colin along the corridor and stood beside him as the Sergeant opened the viewing hatch and looked in.

'Mr Adams. Something I can help you with?'

As Colin watched, Adams pushed himself from where he was leaning against the far wall and approached the door until he was eye to eye with the policeman. Colin noted that the dark eyes seemed to carry a hint of amusement.

'Sergeant Duffy. Thank you for coming.'

Yes, amusement in the voice too. 'What do you want Mr Adams?'

'Actually, it's not what I want Sergeant Duffy, it's more a case of what you want.'

Colin shook his head wearily. 'Look, I don't have time for riddles man. Speak plainly or I'll leave you until you do.'

The prisoner's expression remained unaltered. 'What *you* want, Sergeant Duffy, is for this night to end with you and all of your officers going home safe and sound to their beds tonight. What *you* want is to be the man who makes the correct decision that ensures all of his people are alive and coming into work tomorrow.'

'Oh aye, and I suppose that letting you go will be the reason that I manage that will it?'

Adams smiled and leaned back. 'I've been stuck back here since I was brought in with no way of knowing what's going on but let me guess. Your roads in and out of the village are blocked or destroyed, you have no communications with the outside world and the power has just been cut. All correct so far?'

Colin felt his mouth dry up as everything that they had suspected to be happening was now confirmed. He tried to give nothing away as the prisoner continued with his smug delivery.

'See, that's my *team*. My *unit*. Trained and mentored by me. And they're coming for me. And they will not stop until they have me. Will do *whatever* is necessary to achieve that aim. So, I'm telling you again. *You* want to end this without the deaths of your people on your conscience. Because my guys will cut through you like a hot knife through butter. Anything that stands between them and me will destroyed. This is what they do Sergeant and they do it very well.'

Colin could feel his anger rise. 'Listen here soldier boy, just because you've done a wee bit of time in the Special Forces doesn't cut any ice with me. You were discharged in disgrace and are nothing other than a common criminal now.' He saw something flicker in the prisoner's eyes briefly before the smug amusement returned.

'I see you've been checking up on me Sergeant but you're wrong on one major point there'. He moved back to the door and placed his hands on the doorframe, staring hard at Colin through the viewing aperture. 'I am *not* a common criminal. I am an *exceptional* criminal. But we digress. *You* need to release me now and let me be on my way. This isn't worth you and your people dying for.'

Colin slammed the aperture closed. 'Thanks for the advice Mr Adams but as I'm sure you are aware the Police have a strange tradition of keeping criminals locked up for the good of the general public. So relax, enjoy the peace and quiet and we'll talk again later.' He turned and motioned for Tess to walk ahead of him back towards the main office. As their footsteps echoed along the corridor, they both heard the prisoner's parting remark.

'You won't get this chance again Sergeant, no matter how hard you're going to wish you did.'

Mitch saw the look on the Sarge's face and wondered what had gone on back in the custody suite. Whatever it was, he'd never seen the Duffer's face like this before, struggled to find a suitable word to describe it but the phrase he would have used would be 'don't fuck with me'. Mitch could see some of the steel that the young Colin Duffy must have had as a policeman in Aberdeen.

With all eyes upon him Colin spoke. 'Right, I think we could be in a wee bit of bother here. Adams's confirmed that his team are on their way to free him. That coupled with the fact that we know they will be heavily armed means we need to come up with a plan to defend ourselves. I'm open to suggestions here.'

Fletch cleared his throat. 'Look, *if* they are coming, you've got me and PC Armstrong here armed with enough firepower to see off a small army. What I suggest we do is make sure the doors are locked and secure and we'll cover each one with a weapon. You keep trying the comms and see if you can let someone know what's going on here.'

Colin nodded. 'Sounds good. If you cover the doors, we'll keep on the phones and radios and try to get something out.'

Tess held up her hand. 'Wait. Look, I saw what these guys are armed with and I'm not sure just covering the doors is going to keep them out. They've got explosives that they've shown no hesitation in using and automatic weapons that they're highly trained and experienced in the use of.'

Mark Armstrong interrupted her, the harsh rack of the bolt slamming forward on his SIG Carbine. 'So are we.' He slapped the stock of the weapon. 'They come between me and the door this is the last thing they'll see.'

'Mark, I think you're underestimating them. They're used to being under fire, probably even like it. These aren't wannabe gangsters from Glasgow, these guys are serious.'

'Yeah, well, no offence Tess, but we've been up against our fair share of hard bastards and these bozos are no different. Excuse me.' She moved aside to let him pass and watched as the two armed officers spoke briefly in the corridor before going their separate ways. She felt Colin's hand on her shoulder.

'Come on PC Cameron, let's have another crack at the phones and leave the experts to get on with it eh?'

Shaking her head, she remained silent as she made her way back to her desk and sat down, pulling the two landlines over to her. She checked the displays as she picked up the receivers. *Nothing.* No dial tone, no connection status, nothing. She reached into her pocket and retrieved her mobile phone but again, the status remained the same; no signal. She clicked her mouse and waited while her desktop came to life then checked the internet connectivity. Nothing. Leaning back, she watched as Mitch tried his own telephone before he threw it down on his own desk in disgust. He caught her eye and she could see the gleam of excitement in them.

'This is mental, eh? Nobody will believe us that this happened in St Cyrus!' He paused as he noted her expression. 'What's wrong? There's nothing to be worried about you know, the SFOs will handle it.'

Tess shook her head. 'I'm not worried Mitch. I'm absolutely fucking bricking it! I *know* what these guys are capable of and trust me, a couple of armed policemen are no match for them.'

Mitch laughed and picked up his phone again. 'I'll remind you of this when we're laughing about it over a beer tomorrow night.'

Tess felt a coiling tension in her stomach and a dryness in her mouth, the anticipation of violence to come. She looked at Mitch and hoped he was right, that they would be laughing about it in the pub tomorrow night. But she didn't believe it.

27

Doug Neillands and his wife Liza struggled to calm their breathing. Since opening the front door earlier, their existence had been a whirlwind of terror. Doug struggled to process what had happened; three wraiths exploding into his hallway as if born from the blizzard itself, knocking him down and throwing Liza alongside him. Now, bound and gagged, the elderly couple tried to slow their breathing down, their blood rushing in their ears, chests heaving. Their young grandson, Jason, had not been brought into the room with them and Doug's rage remained in check only because of his concern for the child.

Delta stood watching the pensioners from the doorway. They'd restrained the husband and wife with zip-ties then sat them on their bed, secured against the wooden headboard. Delta could see that they were still experiencing the shock of capture and it would be some time before it wore off. They would also be out of their minds with worry at the fact that they couldn't see their grand-child but this gave the team leverage to control them with. The kid was similarly secured in the smaller bedroom at the other end of the house and other than wetting his pants in fear, had caused no problems. The bedroom was lit by a kerosene lamp, similar to the one that illuminated the small living-room and another in the kid's room and hallway which allowed them to see pretty well considering the power was out. A sound caught his attention and he turned to see Bravo beckon him. He took one last glance at the couple then walked into the living room where they were joined by Charlie who had just checked on the kid.

Bravo and Charlie retrieved the shaped charges from their packs and assembled the various components. They would detonate these by hand and each man ensured his clacker was secured. Removing their snowshoes and donning their packs they moved to the back door of the property, walking slowly through a darkened kitchen. Bravo unlocked the door and pushed it open, admitting a flurry of snow and the sound of the wind. They made their way quickly through the exit with Delta closing the door behind him as the last man. Keeping close to the side of the building the three made their way to the end of the house and stopped. Bravo took a look around before he set of at a jog, covering the open ground then stepping over the ornamental fence and disappearing into the snow drifts on the other side. Charlie moved next and repeated the actions, followed by Delta who, on crossing the fence, tapped each individual's leg to let them know he was in. They were now in the Police Station grounds and the team could see that despite them cutting the power earlier, the station still had lighting, inside and out. Bravo chewed his lip for a brief moment before rising to his feet. *No matter. The plan stands.*

The three jogged towards the station building, practically invisible in their white camouflage suits, each one holding their weapon ready for use. They reached the gable end and knelt down, leaning against the cold stone of the dwelling. Bravo turned and indicated with his hand towards the front of the Police station. Charlie and Delta nodded and turned, Delta leading with his rifle in the shoulder, and made their way to the front doors of the station.

Bravo waited a second then moved off to take up his position at the back door. He noted with satisfaction that the exterior lights were more or less useless, penetrating only a few feet into the swirling snow. He stopped slightly short of the back door and observed it for several moments. Taking his charge, he smoothly slung the rifle onto his back and crept forward on all fours. Peeling the paper from the adhesive pads, he decided to place the charge directly over the main lock, breach the door through the security mechanism. He placed the charge onto the wooden door and pressed firmly down. A small tug on the charge convinced him that it was secure and he spooled the cable from the loop in his hand and retreated several feet away, back hard against the wall. *Ready.*

Delta felt the tap on his shoulder and lowered his weapon. He dropped to his knees and followed Charlie at a crawl, taking care not to foul the trailing wire that led back to the explosive charge. He sat beside Charlie, back against the wall and allowed his weapon to rest on his legs. He looked at Charlie and saw him nod. Delta put his hands over his ears and opened his mouth. The explosion wouldn't be huge but he wasn't taking any chances, he needed to be ready as soon as the diversion went off. He heard the clacking of Charlie's initiation and a brief moment later a loud bang and a flash of light emitted from within the blizzard. Leaping up, Delta ran towards the door, rifle at the ready with Charlie close behind him.

On reaching the doorway, Delta stopped and felt Charlie stack up behind him, shoulders and thighs in contact ready for the assault. He could see the door hanging at an awkward angle where it had been blown from its mountings. The lock was gone, a ragged mouth of fibrous wood teeth all that remained. Delta aimed his weapon into the dimly-lit hallway while keeping most of his body behind the stone entranceway.

He heard another bang and felt a small concussion wave gust out from the hallway and puff out his hood. He could hear shouts and cries from within and smiled as he imagined the shock and confusion inside. A burst of gunfire sounded, shocking and loud in the enclosed confines. *Bravo's in.* He was just about to move forward when there was a further burst and a frantic voice in his ear.

Delta Delta, this is Bravo. Require covering fire for extraction to Romeo 2 now, I say again NOW!

Without hesitation Delta stepped out, dropped to one knee and fired three bursts into the corridor, blinding himself briefly as the flames burst out the end of his muzzle. Through the dim lighting a dark figure dashed across the hall and Delta ducked involuntarily as he saw the muzzle flashes coming from the moving shadow. *Shit, they're armed.* He stood and leapt back behind the cover of the entranceway and glanced at Charlie who nodded to show he'd heard Bravo's message. With a final look behind, Delta led the pair back through the open ground, crossed the fence and reunited with Bravo at the back door of Romeo 2. Bravo held the door open and allowed Delta and Charlie to jog straight inside before he followed them, closing the door behind.

Standing in the dark kitchen, Delta wiped the snow from his goggles and pushed them up to rest on his forehead. He looked at Bravo and was about to ask for a SITREP when he noticed the blood seeping through the white cloth around Bravo's neck.

'Shit Bravo, you're hit.'

Bravo shook his head. 'No it's okay, I've checked it. I think it's just frag from the door when that fucking copper shot at me.'

Delta nodded. 'How come they've got guns? I thought the Police weren't armed?'

Bravo laughed sarcastically. 'They're not as a rule and I have no idea why this lot are but it was definitely a carbine or automatic rifle of some sort.' He caught Delta's eye and held the gaze. 'That was pretty close though.'

Charlie threw him a tea towel he'd taken from the oven door handle and Bravo began dabbing at the wounds on his neck. He was thinking hard. The plan had gone to rat shit in minute one of the execution and they had now lost the element of surprise. *And* these bastards had guns. *Shit.*

'What's the play Bravo?'

Bravo tossed the towel into the sink and looked at his team mates. 'We need a whole new entry plan. They'll be waiting for us next time so it will have to be something that gets us really close so we can neutralise their shooters immediately. Or something that draws the shooters out so we can slot them before we even gain entry.' His mind raced as he considered and discarded scenario after scenario. After a few moments a seed of an idea began to take hold and he explored the concept for some time before a small smile crept up on him.

'I've got it. It's a bit risky but it will definitely work.' He nodded towards the rear of the house. 'And it all comes down to the grandkid.'

28

Tess removed her hands from where they had been covering her ringing ears and stared at them as they shook violently in front of her. She coughed as the smoke caught the back of her throat, the sound dulled and muted to her hearing. The side of her face felt strange and she raised her left hand and explored her cheek, recoiling as she registered the sensation of liquid under her palm. She drew the hand back sharply and looked at the blood sticking to it. Her hearing was returning and the shouts of the others began permeating through the whining in her ears. Raising her hand again she probed her cheek with her fingers, wincing at the pain. From what she could feel it seemed as though she had a big abrasion, not deep but sore. Looking around her through the thinning smoke, she saw Mitch on all fours trying to stand on shaking legs. One of the Firearms' officers stumbled into the room, weapon dangling from his hand and his face a crimson mask as blood flowed freely from a massive gash on his forehead.

'TESS. TESS. ARE YOU OKAY?'

She shook her head and followed the sound of the Colin's shouting. She saw him in the corridor applying a dressing to the other Firearms officer's arm with Kenny helping him. Pulling herself up by grabbing the edge of the desk, she stood on wobbly legs and staggered over towards the bleeding Firearms officer.

'Colin, I'm okay. I'm going to help Mark here.' She saw Colin look up and nod his acknowledgement before he yelled again.

'MITCH. MITCH. HOW YOU DOING MATE?'

Tess heard Mitch's reply that he was also okay just as she reached the Firearms officer and gently took the rifle from his unresisting grip. She placed the weapon on a desk and settled him in a chair.

'Mark, you're going to be fine. It looks like it's just a big cut but it's bleeding a lot because it's the scalp. Don't open your eyes till I've cleaned you up or you'll get blood in them okay?'

She watched as he nodded and then she grabbed some sterile wipes and a dressing from the medical pack that was open beside her monitor. Working quickly, she cleaned the constable's face and wound, making soothing noises when she saw him wince with the pain. As she applied the dressing, she heard Mark chuckle before he spoke.

'Glad I didn't make a bet with you on this. You were bang on the money Tess. They came for him and they came just the way you said they would.'

'No Mark. Even I didn't think they'd come like that. That was fucking awful. I'm not even sure exactly what they did.'

The Firearms' officer cleared his throat. 'Looks like they used two explosive breaches, one as a diversion and the other as the entry to get their guy. When it didn't go as planned, they opened up with automatic weapons.'

Tess nodded as she checked the dressing. 'That makes sense I suppose. Look, we're all okay but what about them? Do you know if you hit any of them? Oh, you can open your eyes now, I'm done.'

Mark Armstrong opened his eyes and leaned forward in the chair running his hand gently over the dressing. 'I definitely either hit one or got very close but couldn't say for sure which.' He looked into her eyes and swallowed. 'They're going to come back aren't they?'

Laying her hand on his shoulder she returned the gaze. 'I would have to say yes Mark. They don't have what they want and these guys just do not give up.' A voice behind her caught her attention and she turned to see Mitch stood shaking his head.

'Fuck me Tess, please don't give us any more motivational pep talks. Not sure I could cope with all that positivity and enthusiasm!'

She gave a wan smile. 'You okay?'

'Yeah, just knocked about by the blast and my ears are ringing. Nasty graze on your cheek there though.'

'Yeah, well I'll live. I think we need to work out what we're going to do next 'cos you can bet your arse that's exactly what those bastards outside are doing right now.'

She nodded towards the corridor and the three of them moved on unsteady legs towards the two sergeants and Kenny. Colin heard their approach and stood, assessing their conditions.

'All walking wounded? Nobody got anything more serious?' Taking their shaking heads as answers he pointed to the shattered front door. 'Good. Come up with something to block that with then do the same for the back. Right now, they could practically walk back in.'

Fletch stood up and examined the dressing that Colin had applied to his arm. He clapped Colin and Kenny on their shoulders. 'Good job guys, thanks for that.' He turned his gaze on the remainder. 'Right, we're in some serious shit here as I'm sure you've noticed. That was as good a breach entry as I've ever seen. Even their extraction was impressive; once they saw their plan had failed there was still no panic, they just reacted with slick drills and were gone in an instant.' He turned his attention back to Colin. 'We need to find a way either to hold this place until help arrives or come up with an escape plan.'

Colin nodded. 'Okay, you lot get going with barricading the doors. Me and Fletch will try and come up with a plan here. Kenny, see if you can find some way, *any* way, of getting through to someone.' Kenny nodded and crossed the floor towards the telephones and computers as Tess and the two constables made their way to the front door.

Colin looked at his colleague for a moment before speaking. 'You know, initially I just thought we could give

Adams back to his people. This shit isn't worth dying for but then it struck me; we know about their plans for the minister, they won't just let that go.'

'Nope. I completely agree. I think the minute they put this rescue into action we were designated as dead.'

Colin sighed and coughed, the lingering smoke aggravating his throat. 'What the hell are we going to do Fletch?'

Sergeant Fletcher ran his hand over his face and looked at the activity further up the corridor. 'Let's keep going with the barricades and sorting communications out in the short term. I do think though, that we need to think about getting someone out of here to go and raise the alarm.'

'Yes, I'm with you on that but have a bad feeling that Adams' goons will be watching this place for just that very thing.'

'Definitely. But if we don't get any comms up and running, we can only hold these guys off for so long.'

Colin sighed and sat heavily on one of the few chairs that remained upright. 'I think we should have a wee chat with our guest back there, see if there is any chance we could let him out of here and have him and his squaddie mates just make good their escape.' He raised his hand at his colleague's shaking head. 'I know, I know. He'll probably tell us what he thinks we want to hear but we *have* to at least try it Fletch.'

'Look, we can't let him go; we would be giving up the only leverage we have for staying alive. And what do you think will happen when he re-joins his band of merry men? He'll assume command, grab a weapon and they'll come at us harder and faster than before.'

'Hell's teeth Fletch! Don't you think I know that? We're damned if we do and damned if we don't: We let him go and he comes back just like you said. We keep him here and they keep hitting us until they get him. I just want to see what he has to say face to face, gauge his reaction.' He pointed a shaking finger towards the working figures in the dissipating smoke of the corridor. 'I owe it to them to explore every opportunity, no matter how slim, that I have to keep them alive.'

The Firearms' sergeant rubbed his eyes then met Colin's and gave a brief nod. 'You're right. We've got to try anything we can.' He broke Colin's gaze and looked towards the custody suite. 'Come on then, no point hanging back. Let's go check on your guest.'

Colin rose from the chair and led his colleague down the corridor, pausing to kick pieces of the shattered back door out into the yard. Fletch stopped and tapped his fellow sergeant on the shoulder.

'I'm going to stay here and cover this entrance just in case they come back quicker than we thought.'

Colin nodded and watched as Fletch turned off the corridor light and positioned himself to the side of the door, keeping his body from being exposed but with a good view of the yard outside. As Fletch brought the assault rifle up into his shoulder Colin turned and continued in the semi-darkness to the custody suite. Without preamble he jerked down on the aperture cover and looked inside the brightly-lit cell. Anger flooded him as he saw that, to all intents and purposes, Adams hadn't moved a muscle since his last visit, still reclined on the mattress, hands clasped behind his head. Colin opened his mouth but caught himself in time. *Easy lad, this is exactly what Mr Adams wants.* He took a breath, steadied himself and addressed his prisoner as calmly as he could.

'Sorry about the racket Mr Adams, had a surprise visit from some undesirables who got a bit carried away. Hope it didn't disturb you too much? If so, I can provide you with a complaint form to fill in.'

There was no immediate reaction from within the cell and he was about to say something when Adams stretched out, arms above his head, yawned and slowly raised himself until he was sat on the edge of the bed, feet on the floor, staring back at Colin with those dark eyes.

'Why, Sergeant Duffy. What a nice surprise. How are you tonight? Everything okay?'

Colin's knuckles tightened on the handles of the door as he fought back the urge to open the door and beat ten bells out Adams' smug face. 'Alright; enough of the dancing. Let's get down to it shall we? Your men blew up my station and shot at my officers with automatic weapons. When we get them, and I emphasise *when*, they will be spending an awfully long time in wee boxes just like the one you are in now.'

Adams' laughter echoed around the small cell and he raised himself to his feet in one fluid movement, approaching the door and locking his unsettling gaze upon Colin's. 'Sergeant Duffy, do you *really* think a country plod and a couple of constables have even the remotest chance of taking on my unit and surviving? From what I heard back here, you're only lucky that you're not dead already.'

As Colin watched, Adams leaned into the door and cocked his head to one side, trying to see further along the corridor.

'Although…I could swear I heard the sound of rounds being returned. I wasn't aware a little *bumfuck* outpost like this held any weapons Sergeant Duffy?'

Colin let the question hang, unanswered as he stared into the prisoner's unblinking eyes. 'Well see, that's the thing Mr Adams; it's never what you know that catches you out and lands you in the shit. It's what you *don't* know that does it every time.' For the briefest of moments, Colin saw a small flicker pass across Adams's face before his customary cool smugness returned.

'Look Sergeant Duffy, this isn't worth you and your people getting hurt or killed over. That's why you're here, we both know it. Do the right thing; open the door, let me walk out of here, grab my guys and we'll be on our way.'

Colin broke eye contact and looked beyond Adams and into the cell, allowing the silence to extend beyond comfort before clearing his throat. 'Were you a good soldier Mr

Adams?' He looked up to see the prisoner's eyebrows raised in surprise.

'Yes, I was Sergeant Duffy. One of the best in the world as a matter of fact.'

'And would you say you're a good criminal?'

A wry smile from Adams. 'I would say I'm an exceptional criminal Sergeant Duffy. Why do you ask?'

Colin allowed a wry smile of his own as he suddenly stepped back and slammed the aperture closed, the crash of the metal echoing around the rooms.

'Because you're a bloody terrible liar.'

29

Bravo picked up the photo frame and studied it for a few moments before replacing it on the dressing table. He turned to the bed and looked at the couple leant against the headboard, bound and gagged; their wide eyes visible even in the gloom of the barely-lit room. He pointed back at the photo.

'Grandkid?'

A barely perceptible nod from the old lady confirmed his suspicion.

'Good. You have something to live for. Do as I say and you and your grandkid have nothing to worry about. Try to fuck me up and I will destroy your entire family in front of you. Understand?'

Both heads were nodding now and unintelligible noises were coming through the gags. Bravo brought his finger slowly to his lips, held it there for a moment and the noises dissipated to become quiet sobs. He looked at Charlie who was leaning against the wall, his carbine resting loosely across his arms. 'Keep an eye on them while I see if Delta is ready.' Charlie gave a slow nod of assent and straightened a little, giving his full attention to the restrained couple.

Bravo left the room and walked through the gloomy house to the small bedroom at the back. A warm glow came from the lamp within and he pushed the door open to see Delta rummaging through a small pile of clothing on the bed while the kid looked up at him, bound and gagged, eyes wild and body trembling. Delta turned at Bravo's entry.

'Hey. I think I've got what we need here. Found all this in the bottom drawer. Spare clothes for the kid.' He gave a smirk. 'Need to make sure it's appropriate clothing, after all.'

Bravo took in the bundle of clothes, separated into two piles, the relevant one being the light summer clothes that Delta had segregated. Bravo picked up a small t-shirt with an image of a beach-ball and umbrella on the chest. He dropped it and lifted a pair of thin trousers, nodding his agreement. 'These are perfect, exactly what we need. I've told the grandparents what will happen if they don't step up and we won't have any trouble.' He paused for a moment and caught Delta's eye. They were winging this: Sure, they were all experienced in tactical stuff but *this*, this was very different. He placed his hand on Delta's shoulder. 'You good for this? We could find another way.'

Delta shook his head. 'No. I'm good. It's a solid plan and as long as the old farts play their part, it'll work.'

Bravo nodded and clapped Delta on the back. 'I know. Just wanted to make sure one last time. Okay then, be ready in ten. Me and Charlie will get the oldies prepped and good to go.' He turned to the kid and knelt beside the bed so that their faces were level. 'It's almost over little man then you can go back to your gran and grandad. Just one last thing to do then we're done, okay?' There was no reaction from the child and Bravo could see he was in deep shock. Sighing he stood and patted Delta's shoulder as he passed him. Delta nodded and picked up the clothing as Bravo left the room and returned to Charlie and the old couple.

Leaning into the room, Bravo caught Charlie's attention and beckoned him to step out into the hallway. In a soft voice he briefed Charlie on the plan and what was required. Charlie remained silent, only nodding occasionally to show he understood. When Bravo stopped talking, both of them walked back into the room, Charlie remaining on one side with his weapon aimed at the couple while Bravo walked around the bed to the other side and sat beside the old woman. Her moan carried through the gag and Bravo placed his hand on her shoulder making shushing noises.

'Listen to me. I'll say this once and once only. I'm going to tell you what we're going to do now and what I need you to do for me. Do not fuck this up. I told you before, one mistake from you and I will kill that grandkid of yours in your own fucking kitchen while you watch. All you need to do is follow my instructions and we'll be out of your way in no time at all, leaving you with nothing more than a cool story to tell your friends and neighbours, okay?' He patted the old woman's knee and was rewarded with a flinch and a controlled sob. The old man was watching him with utter hate in his eyes but more importantly, his breathing was

193

settled. *Have to keep an eye on him.* Bravo stood and addressed them both.

'We only need one of you for this. The other will stay here with one of my guys to make sure,' he turned his attention to the old man, 'that nobody tries to play the hero. Mrs Old Lady, you'll be coming with me and Mr, you're staying home.' The old man began struggling, throwing himself forward and trying to shout through the gag. Charlie stepped forward raising the rifle but the old lady placed her head on her husband's shoulder and he ceased his struggles, chest heaving and eyes wide with fear as looked at his wife. She gave a soft shake of her head and Bravo nodded in approval.

'Good. I'll let you have that one old man. I know that this must be a bit hard for you to put up with but pull that shit again and I'll carry out my promise and leave you to die last so you can fully appreciate the impact of your actions.' Without waiting for any reaction, he stepped forward and cupped his hand under the old woman's armpit, assisting her to her feet. She adjusted to standing after such a long period of sitting then, maintaining his grip, Bravo escorted her in small, shuffling steps out of the room.

He led his diminutive captive into the hallway by the front door and stopped, looking at the floor. Kicking at a pair of slippers with his feet, he indicated with his head towards them. 'Put them on.' The old woman slid her feet into the worn footwear and waited. Bravo lifted his hands with exaggerated slowness and reached around her head, untying the gag and peeling it softly from her, taking care not to pull it too hard from between her dry lips. He heard her take a deep breath through her mouth and listened to her ragged breathing for a several moments before speaking.

'Good. That's all I'm asking for here, a little cooperation, nothing more. Okay, I'm going to untie you now, let the blood flow back into your arms again. But let's not ruin what we've achieved so far with any stupid ideas.' A brief nod gave him his answer and he stepped behind her and with a flick of his knife sliced the flexi-cuffs from her hands and allowed the plastic filaments to drop to the floor. He heard a small exclamation of either pain or shock but the old woman supressed it before it became anything else. *Good girl.*

'Okay, rub your arms slowly, get the blood circulating again. Roll your shoulders a little, you'll be quite stiff after sitting around all that time.' She followed his instructions and after several minutes he could see the improvements in her mobility.

'Okay, okay, you're good now.' As she met his gaze, he could see the fear in her eyes but also the determination to do exactly what he was telling her. 'Right grandma, I know this is going to sound a little weird but I need you to take your cardigan off.' As she opened her mouth to protest, he raised an eyebrow and whatever she had been thinking of saying remained in thought only and with shaking fingers she undone the buttons of the garment and shrugged it off, letting it fall to the floor behind her.

'Good. Almost there now.' He placed his hands on her shoulders and brought his face close to hers. 'Liza. It *is* Liza isn't it?' A small, terrified nod of assent. 'Good. Liza, you're going to go for a walk now. A walk and that's all. Nothing else. Yes, it's cold and I've taken your cardigan but it's not for long and you'll be back here with your husband before you know it.' He paused, gripping her thin shoulders for emphasis. 'You will hear a lot of noise behind you as you walk but that's just me trying to get someone's attention. You just ignore that and keep walking down the road until the noise stops then you get back here and untie your husband and get on with your life okay?' He could feel her shaking and he removed one of his hands and used it to gently lift her chin until she met his eyes. 'As far as you are concerned, this is just you and your grandkid walking down the street towards the shop and once the noise stops, this is all over for you and your family. You're nearly there Liza, this is it, the last bit. You can do this.' As he watched, he saw the tears streaming down her face but she nodded vigorously and he patted her shoulders. 'Good Liza, good. In no time at all you'll be sitting in the pub telling this story for the next ten years.'

Looking behind her, he saw that the kid was ready. Hearing the sound of movement, the old lady turned, eyes widening and raising her hands to her mouth but Bravo cupped her chin with his hand and moved his face closer to hers.

'I told you; just do as you're told and you'll all be back here playing happy families before you know it. Mess this up and your last moments will be the worst of your life. Got it?'

Again, the silent nod with the rheumy eyes streaming tears that flowed unchecked down the old woman's cheeks. Without waiting for anything further, Bravo turned the stiff key in the lock and opened the door several inches, staring intently in all directions for several moments before he opened it fully. With his free hand he guided Liza out, his hand in the small of her back and felt her shiver as the wind and snow assailed her. Her small feet were swallowed immediately in the drifts and she shuffled uncomfortably in the inadequate footwear. Increasing the pressure on her back, Bravo pushed her forwards, whispering as she shuffled past him. 'Remember; you and the kid walk towards the shop. Don't stop for the noise, keep walking till you reach the shop and your job is done. Now *go*.' She didn't even look back, terror and shock combining to motivate her, in jilted steps, through the snow-covered driveway and onto the main road. The child beside her in the thinnest of summer clothing, hunched over and already clutching his arms around him in a forlorn attempt to retain some heat. Within moments the pair were lost to the dark and the snow and Bravo spun on his heels and leapt back into the house, closing and locking the door behind him.

He jogged through the hallway, into the kitchen and let himself out of the back door pulling it closed behind him. Wading through the snow drifts he sacrificed caution for speed, essential that he made it to his next position without delay. *Everything* depended on that.

30

Tess looked at Mitch and both nodded in agreement. The barricades were about as good as they could be, given the limited equipment they had at hand. The metal lockers from the store rooms had proved invaluable as had some of the filing cabinets and spare desks. Both entrances were now as secure as they could be under the circumstances. Looking around the station, Tess felt a surge of anger well up inside her. *How dare they! Who did they think they were? This is a police station for crying out loud.* All the main lights had been turned out and some of the battery powered lanterns had been set up in corners to provide enough illumination without providing anyone outside with a clear view in.

Fletch was covering the back door, his SIG assault rifle resting on a chair back but aimed in readiness at the assembly of lockers and office furniture. They'd left the exterior lights on for what it was worth so from his position he could see the snow swirling around the sodium halos.

PC Armstrong had taken the front entrance and was in a similar position, ready for any indication that another attack was on the way. His head throbbed and he'd been grateful for the painkillers that Tess had found for him earlier. He still felt a little shaky, nervy even, hating the thought that all he could do was wait for these thugs to come again. Taking a deep breath, he attempted to calm himself, recalling other close calls he had been exposed to during his career. *Yeah, this is nothing mate. You've been here before, maybe not against such well-trained bastards but just bastards all the same.* Feeling slightly better he returned his full attention to keeping watch, squinting his eyes in a vain attempt to discern any details beyond the small pool of illumination and swirling snow beyond the doorway.

His mind turned towards the options available to them. While it went against the grain of his professional police ethos, he was all for releasing Adams and getting them all out of this situation alive. They could then hoof it out of the village on foot and get help from either Montrose or Inverbervie, but...*What the hell?*

Heart beating faster, he raised his rifle into his shoulder and stared hard along the length of the barrel and into the falling snow beyond, striving to confirm the movement he believed he had just seen. *Nothing.* Just the snow. He waited several moments and was just lowering the rifle when he saw it again: People. Walking, no, *staggering*, through the storm. He turned his head and yelled back at his colleagues.

'Heads up! We've got movement out here!'

Almost immediately he heard the someone behind him and the pressure of a hand on his shoulder and Tess's voice.

'What have we got Mark?'

'There's people out there Tess, at least two from what I can make out.'

'Is it Adams' guys?' She could hear the nerves in her voice and the hitching of her breath and attempted to slow her breathing down.

'I don't know…I can't quite make out enough detail yet.'

There was silence save for the howling of the wind around the corners of the building as they both strained to see into the maelstrom beyond their refuge. Tess gasped as between the clouds of driving snow she saw what had caught Mark's attention.

'Shit! It's a woman and a kid!'

Mark shook his head in disbelief. 'Are you kidding me? A *kid*? Out in this?'

Tess shushed him and pointed into the snow. 'Mark, it's an old woman and a kid and they're only wearing indoor clothes. They must be freezing.'

'What the hell are they doing out here?'

Tess didn't answer immediately, focussing her attention on the people who she saw now were staggering against the wind. 'Shit Mark, the kid has only got a t-shirt on. We need to get to them or they're going to freeze to death.'

'Tess wait. Let's think about this. They must be going somewhere. Let's watch them for a bit and…' He was cut short by the sight of the woman pitching forward onto her face and the boy kneeling beside her. Before he could interpret what was happening fully, he felt Tess barge past him and burst out of the doorway. 'Shit!'

Getting to his feet he stepped over the barricade and followed his colleague into the storm, Tess now just a dark shape among the swirling flakes. The wind and snow whipped his exposed face and he shielded his eyes with his hand to keep his vision clear as he went after her. He saw Tess drop to her knees and reached her as she was checking the woman on the ground. The boy was crying loudly and calling out for his Grandma, trying to push Tess away. As Mark watched, Tess grabbed the child and pulled him hard against her, holding his face into her chest while she looked at Mark and shook her head. He cocked his head to one side as he attempted to work out what she meant. Stepping closer to the prone woman he saw the dark pool expanding from the side of her head and understood instantly that she had been shot. Cold fear ran through him and he spun on his heel, bringing the rifle into his shoulder and aiming into the dark street before him.

'Mark, let's go, we have to get out of here!'

He shook his head and turned, following Tess as she ran pulling the crying child behind her. As he ran, he threw regular glances over his shoulder, anticipating gunshots coming for them at any moment. He gave a shaky sigh as they reached the improvised barricade and waited while Tess helped the wailing child over the blockade. Once they had cleared it, he scrambled over the lockers and filing cabinets and threw himself on the floor behind them, breathing heavily as the adrenaline coursed through his body. *Fuck*! Those animals had killed an old woman. *Why*?

What possible threat could she have been to them? He rubbed his face with a trembling hand and rose to his knees, taking up a position behind the metal furniture and keeping his rifle aimed at the space beyond the door. Adams' thugs had just demonstrated that they would kill anyone who got in their way and Mark Armstrong was no longer in any doubt that every police officer in this building was now a prime target.

<u>**31**</u>

Bravo pushed the door closed behind him and shook the snow from his clothes. He made his way into the kitchen and pulled his hood down, exposing his white balaclava. He sighed and shook his head gently, touching the wound on his neck to assess if it had worsened and was pleased to find no change whatsoever.

He had only just made the shot, the old woman and kid making far quicker progress than he would have expected. It had taken two shots to achieve it but the second one had hit the old lady on the side of the head, dropping her instantly. He'd pulled back a little, taking cover behind a snow-mantled wall. As he'd anticipated, the police officers had arrived within seconds, grabbing the kid and running back to the station. *Perfect.* He walked through the kitchen and into the hallway nodding to Charlie as he made eye contact. Charlie shook his head and nodded in the direction of the room behind him.

'We have a problem here Bravo.'

Bravo walked towards his team-mate. 'What's up?'

'See for yourself.' Charlie stood aside to allow Bravo to enter. He heard Bravo's muffled curse as he took in the sight before him.

'What the fuck happened?'

Charlie sighed and shook his head again. 'Best I can figure was either a heart attack or an aneurism or something like that. He was okay one minute, then when I checked again, I found him like this.'

Bravo looked at the old man, head collapsed on to his chest and no rise and fall of his torso to indicate any breathing. He heard Charlie come closer to the bed.

'I checked his pulse a few times but there's nothing Bravo.'

Bravo stood and made his way out of the room, followed by Charlie and made their way back into the kitchen. Bravo laid his carbine down on the worktop and was silent for several seconds before speaking.

'No matter. Nothing we can do about it. Chances are he would have crumbled anyway when he learned about his old lady.'

'Okay, go do a final check then meet me at the back door when you're done.' As Charlie left, Bravo poured a glass of water, drinking deeply, surprised at how thirsty he had been.

Bravo watched as Charlie returned, picked his own rifle up and walked towards the kitchen door. Opening the door, he struggled to hold it, the howling wind and snow driving it hard against him. He waited till Charlie grabbed the doorframe from behind and then stepped out, feeling the gale buffeting his body. He pulled up his hood and placed his goggles over his eyes. Charlie tapped his shoulder and the pair set off into the maelstrom, practically invisible to anyone who may have been watching.

They kept the pace brisk, kicking through the snow drifts that tried to slow their progress. Following the route they had taken to the Target previously, they crossed the fence and approached the Police Station from the side. Without a word each man went their separate ways as they reached the gable of the house, Bravo towards the back and Charlie to the front. Bravo was pleased that the weather had deteriorated even further. The small pools of light emitting from the station's external lights were practically useless now, showing nothing more than a few feet of swirling snow before the darkness dominated once again. Crouching against the wall, he crawled slowly towards the back door and stopped as soon as the damaged entrance was in sight. He assessed his position for several moments before moving back a couple of feet and carrying out the same procedure. *Better.* He wanted to be able to see the back door but without the risk of being discovered by any of the policemen who might pop their head outside.

At the front of the building Charlie mimicked Bravo's actions, also taking care to secure a good view of the main entrance but without exposing his position to any of the policemen within. A short message came through his earpiece and he cocked his head to one side then nodded at

Bravo's transmission. He spoke softly into his radio mic, giving Bravo the reply that he was in place.

'Ready. On Target now.'

32

Tess shook her head as she watched the kid shivering under the blanket they had provided. He remained curled up in a ball on the big chair, face buried in the blanket, only the top of his head showing. She felt rage well up inside her as she thought again about the brutal way in which the old lady had been cut down in front of her grandson. *Who the hell are these animals? Would they have killed the boy as well, given time? And why? What possible reason could there have been to kill the old lady?*

She crouched and patted blanket covering the child's form. She felt him flinch underneath but he did not withdraw. She stroked the area and spoke in a calm quiet voice.

'Hey, you're okay now. You're safe. My name is Tess and I'm a police officer. You're in my Police Station now and you're safe. No one can hurt you in here. We're all here to make sure you're safe okay?' Seeing no reaction, she spoke again. 'What's your name darling? I'm Tess, like I said, so what do I call you?' Nothing. *Probably still in deep shock.* She sighed and stood upright. 'All right, look, I'm here and I'm not going anywhere. There's some water there beside you if you need a drink hon, and anything else you need, you just ask, okay?' Still no movement. She walked over to the hall and motioned for Colin to come to her. As he reached her he nodded his head towards the huddled figure in the chair.

'How's he holding up Tess?'

Running her fingers through her hair she sighed and met the Sergeant's eyes.

'Still in shock I think Sarge. Not a peep out of him, just completely withdrawn.'

'Poor wee mite. Can't imagine what he's going through and how he's going to come through it. I don't even remember the kid's name, only heard Doug and Liza mention him a few times over the years.'

'I know. I still can't believe that they killed Liza. What possible reason could they have for doing something like that? An old lady for fuck's sake!'

Colin placed his hand on the PC's shoulder. 'I know, I know. I have no idea but they must have felt she presented some threat to them or knew their identities or something. Or perhaps they are just indiscriminate murderers. Might be we'll never know.'

He felt her shoulders drop and he gripped them with both hands, forcing her to meet his gaze. 'Look, we can do this. *They* have to come to *us*. We are the ones in a position of strength. All we have to do is hold the fort until help comes or they give up.'

'You really think that they'll give up? I don't. And I think the old woman they just killed kinda shows us that, don't you?'

Colin could see the anger apparent in Tess's face even in the gloomy light. 'Look, I'm not saying they're not determined but there has to come a point where they accept the fact that they're not going to achieve their goal and will make the decision to cut and run. Adams or no Adams.'

Tess returned a rueful smile. 'I wish I had your confidence Sarge. I can't see them giving up on their colleague for anything.'

Colin dropped his hands to his side for a moment before he pointed at the huddled figure in the room. 'Well, whatever happens we've got this wee fella to look after now. So come what may, they're not getting in here and putting a child's life at risk. *Again.*'

Tess nodded her agreement. 'I'm with you there Sarge. There's no way I'll let them anywhere near that kid after everything he's been through.' She had just turned back to face Colin when the kid spoke in a small, shaky voice.

'*I need the toilet.*'

Tess caught Colin's eye. 'I'll take him Sarge.' She turned back into the room and made her way to the small figure still swathed in his blanket. She could see one eye watching her as she approached. 'Hey there. Come on, I'll show you where it is.'

The boy shuffled off the chair keeping the blanket around him and walked slowly, still hunched over and

210

completely withdrawn. He looked back at Tess as he reached the hallway and she pointed to his left to show him the way. She followed close behind and watched as he entered the door and closed it behind him. She sighed and crossed her arms, feeling the chill in the air as it blew in through the broken doors. She wondered how old the kid was. *Ten? Eleven?* She couldn't imagine how he would get over this, watching his grandmother die at his feet. *Unbelievable.* And she still didn't even know the poor mite's name.

She was starting to feel a little concerned at the amount of time he was taking when the door opened and the kid stepped back out, shuffling towards her in his hunched-over, introverted manner. She let him pass and laid a hand on his shoulder as she accompanied him back into the room. He gave a brief flinch, a tensing of the shoulder under her hand but allowed her to keep it there and she gave him a gentle rub of reassurance. He sunk back into the chair and covered himself up once again, shunning any further contact. Tess watched him for a moment before turning and heading back out into the hall. She walked into Colin's office and saw he was still trying the mobile and landline for a signal but by the expression on his face she could tell there was no good news.

'No joy Sarge?'

Colin looked up and shook his head. 'Nah, no change. How's the kid?'

'Back in the room keeping to himself.'

'Okay.' He stood and stretched, running a hand across his tired face. 'I'm going to check on the rest of the troops, make sure they're doing all right.'

Tess nodded and made her way back into the main office, passing the kid as she walked to her desk and sat down. She mentally ran through everything that had happened that day, trying in vain to find some sliver of knowledge that could help them out of their current situation but there was nothing. She leaned back and let out a long sigh, disappointed with her lack of success. Her eyes alighted on a small object by the side of her monitor and she remembered that she had not yet had time to investigate the contents of the thumb drive she had taken from Adams's place. Rolling forward on her chair she picked up the small device and inserted it into one of the USB ports on the computer tower. She toggled the mouse and clicked on the new hardware icon when it appeared on her screen. Leaning forward, she devoted her full attention to the glowing monitor in front of her.

Colin patted Kenny on the back, the former Engineer now sat behind the Firearms' Sergeant, offering some support. 'Kenny, Fletch. How we holding up?'

Fletch gave a brief turn towards him and smiled. 'Oh, just bloody brilliant Colin. Nothing I like more than waiting for a team of madmen to assault an undermanned and poorly defended location.'

Colin smiled back at the sarcastic statement. 'Now, now Fletch. Let's keep it upbeat shall we, you'll scare the women and children!'

Fletch and Kenny both laughed, a moment of levity grasped at. Kenny looked up at Colin.

'I take it there's no improvement on the communication front?'

'Wish I could tell you otherwise Kenny but no, no change my friend.'

Fletch maintained his watch out through the broken doorway and spoke over his shoulder.

'So, we just hold here until they get sick of trying or until the cavalry arrives. That about the size of it?'

Colin sighed. 'Unless you've got a better plan Fletch then yes, that's about the size of it.'

'No mate, I don't have a better plan. Been sitting here running through scenarios in my head but I don't have anything new to bring to the party I'm afraid.'

'The way I see it Fletch, is that if we give them Adams, we're as good as dead. They can't leave us alive now that we know who they are and what they've been up to. The killing of old Liza kind of underlined that point. Right, going to check on Mitch and PC Armstrong now so I'll see you guys in a wee while okay?' Walking up the hallway Colin wondered if he was right. *Was there any way that they could perhaps send someone for help? Tess or Mitch perhaps?* No. He needed every able body here to fight off Adams's goons and protect Liza and Doug's grandson. Plus, there was the risk that whoever he sent would be either captured or killed by Adams' gang and it would all have been for nothing.

Mitch turned as he heard the footsteps and nodded to his superior. 'Hi Sarge. Got any good news?'

'Actually yes, I do Constable Mitchell. It's very unlikely, due to current circumstances that you'll get your horrible, greasy pie tomorrow so you've probably extended your lifespan by about five years. See; not all doom and gloom is it?'

Mitch smiled and shook his head. 'I could actually murder a pie right now.'

'How you two holding up?'

Mark Armstrong turned around and taking one hand off his rifle, gave Colin a thumbs up gesture. 'Not bad Sarge but a bit cold now. Oh, and bricking it waiting for these lunatics to come at us again.'

Colin squatted down on his haunches beside the men. 'I know, I know. But think about this for a minute; they didn't know we had guns and extra people here. Surprised the hell out of them, I could see it on Adams's face. So whatever plan they had has gone to shit now and they will be nowhere near as confident of their success as they were at first. My guess is they might try once more then disappear before our help arrives and it's too late for them.'

Mitch shifted position and touched the bandage on his head. 'Well, I hope you're right Sarge. I didn't have much going on up here before so I can't really afford to be losing any more brain cells to these bozos.'

Colin stood and placed a sympathetic hand on his colleague's shoulder. 'Very true Mitch, very true. You *definitely* didn't have much going on up there before!' He turned and began walking back down the hall before he could see their response but he was heartened by the gentle laughter he could hear behind him. A lump came to his throat as he was struck by how well his people were holding up. None of them were trained for this, not even the Firearms guys. For them a tough day might mean a bold criminal taking them on with a few shots, not a dedicated, battle-hardened special forces team intent on killing them all. Once again, he pondered the decision not to let Adams go and take the chance that he and his gang would just flee. *No. You know what will happen as soon as you set him free.* He sighed, well aware that all they could do was wait and react to whatever was coming their way. Walking into the main office he noted that the kid remained curled up under his blanket and that PC Cameron was looking at something on her computer.

'You watching old movies PC Cameron? You're definitely not that worried by our current predicament, are you?'

Tess turned but did not return Colin's smile. 'Check this out Sarge, think you'll find it pretty interesting.'

Colin joined her and stood, crouching slightly to see the screen better, hand on the back of her chair. 'What am I looking at?'

'I took this from Adams' place when I was trying to get comms with you guys. I thought it might give us an insight into who we were dealing with.' She turned her face and looked up at Colin, the green illumination of the screen casting her features in an eerie glow. 'I know, I know. Shouldn't take evidence from the scene and all that but we didn't have anything much to go on back then.' Seeing Colin's nod of assent, she continued. 'Anyway, this wee pen drive was marked up as 'training' so I'm going to fire it up and see if we can learn anything from it that might help us against these creeps.'

Colin patted her shoulder. 'That's good thinking. Well done. Let's open it up and see what we've got, shall we?'

With a few clicks of the mouse the static screen came alive with camera footage of men firing guns from various positions. The men were all dressed in full white camouflage and carried a variety of weapons. Tess indicated with her finger on the screen. 'Three of them by the looks of it and one filming. This is CQC; Close Quarter Combat, training for engaging enemies at close range.' She watched in silence for a moment longer. 'They're actually very good; look at their movement, nobody is moving without another one providing covering fire. Very slick.'

The footage changed to a scene where two of the white-clad figures practiced disarming each other with flurries of strikes and blows. Colin whistled softly.

'They don't muck about do they. You can see a lot of those blows are landing with a bit of power.'

Tess nodded in silent agreement and the pair watched the remainder of the footage without a word. The screen changed once again, this time displaying the inside of a building that seemed familiar to Tess. 'I know what this is. It's the training gym we found, look.' She pointed at the screen as an individual began attacking a punch-bag with a rapid combination of punches, kicks and elbow strikes. The camera moved out and they could see another two individuals in the gym training on other pieces of equipment with similar intensity. The voice behind the camera made them both jump as it yelled out *'Thirty seconds!'* Tess could see now that it was circuit training as the individuals in the gym increased their work rate in response to the time being shouted.

She felt there was something she was missing but couldn't quite put her finger on. *What the hell is it?* The lighting wasn't great and the camera jerked up and down a lot but there was definitely something…she caught her breath and with a click of the mouse, paused the footage and leaned forward to stare at the frozen image on the screen. She felt Colin also lean in and heard his intake of breath when he saw what had caught her attention. The camera had zoomed into the individual on the punch-bag and he was now revealed in full detail on the full screen in front of them. The silence remained until Tess cleared her throat and spoke.

'Shit, Sarge. He's just a kid. Fifteen, sixteen if he's a day.'

Colin nodded slowly, coming to terms with what he was seeing. 'Play the rest PC Cameron.'

Tess clicked the mouse again and the footage resumed, following the other individuals as they swapped positions in the gym. As the camera focussed on the new individual behind the punch-bag, Tess felt her heart race and mouth go dry as she recognised the person immediately. The significance of what they were watching dawned on the two of them at the same time and as Tess lifted her face to look at Colin, a determined voice behind them spoke.

'Both of you lay your hands flat on the desk in front of you or I'll kill you right now.'

33

Tess turned her head slowly towards the voice, ensuring her hands remained firmly anchored to the desk. She took in the small pistol held at arm's length and pointing directly at her forehead. Looking beyond the weapon, she directed her gaze up along the bare forearm, the cords of muscle apparent even in the dim light. Finally, she made eye contact with the gunman and felt her stomach sink as her fears were confirmed beyond doubt. *The kid. The fucking kid.* Except…he looked a whole lot older now, standing upright and staring back at her with an amused smile sitting on his lips.

'Sorry…Tess, was it? You look a bit shocked. Oldest trick in the book; the Trojan Horse. I wasn't even sure you'd fall for it but Bravo was adamant and well, have to say he was absolutely right.'

Tess felt tears of anger and frustration well up in her eyes as she took in the confident teenager in front of her. She could see how they, *she,* had been fooled. With the kid hunched over and in poor light beneath a blanket he had passed for a nine or ten-year old but she could see now that he was older, more in the range of the early teens. The kid

219

also looked strong and athletic and she remembered the footage she had been watching only moments ago. She swallowed and tried to find some moisture in her mouth before speaking.

'Who are you and what do you want?'

The kid smiled and walked slowly backwards to the door, giving a quick glance down the corridor before replying.

'It's not important who I am. But I'll tell you what I want. Sorry, what *we* want. We want Alpha. You took Alpha and we want him back and that's what I'm here to do.'

Colin cleared his throat and addressed their captor.

'Alpha? You mean Adams? The detainee?'

The kid nodded. 'Yes, Mr Policeman, I mean Adams. He's Alpha to us and that's how I'll speak about him okay?'

Colin nodded and lifted his hands from the desk to emphasise his point. He didn't get the opportunity to say a word before the kid had crossed the room in two strides and rammed the muzzle of the pistol against Tess's temple.

'You fucking try that again old man and her death will be the last thing you see. Get your hands back on the desk. NOW.'

Colin responded instantly to the command, heart hammering in his chest. The kid took a moment before he backed off a little and stood by the chair he had previously been sitting in.

'Okay, now that's settled I want to know where Alpha is. I know he's not in any of the rooms between the front door and the toilet so he has to be further down the corridor. Where is he?'

Colin sighed. 'Look kid, you fooled us once but there's no way we're just going to hand over Adams, sorry, *Alpha*, to you. We're as good as dead as soon as we do.'

The kid laughed quietly and gave a quick glance over his shoulder to check that no one would be surprising him. 'Look old man, I thought you'd have got it by now. We are not leaving until we have Alpha. And we'll do anything, *anything*, to get him back. If I have to shoot every one of your officers in front of you until you tell me then that's what I'll do.' He paused and moved closer and Tess shivered as she saw the deadness behind the eyes.

'So, let's stop wasting fucking time and get this over with.'

Colin's head was spinning as he tried to identify a way out of their predicament. He would not give up Adams, but neither could he accept the toll of his officers being killed in cold blood just to make him give the prisoner up. He couldn't even rush the kid. Whether through accident or design, he was keeping enough distance between himself and the police officers to render such a plan unworthy of consideration. *Shit*.

Tess watched the kid intently as he and Colin spoke. The kid was calm and that was what concerned her. She could see that beneath the thin t-shirt he was wearing that his breathing remained slow and even, no hint of an increase in rate despite the nature of the situation. He was also very

221

confident with the weapon which she could see now was a Sig 230, a small-bodied pistol that fired 9mm bullets. *Makes sense.* A normal 9mm like a Glock or a Beretta would be pretty big and cumbersome in the kid's hand but a 230 would be ideal. It was also a lot easier to conceal which explained why none of them had seen it when they'd taken the kid in. She felt anger flush her face and was speaking before she considered her words.

'So, you just killed that old lady in cold blood. Cut her down like she was nothing just so you could get in here? What the hell is wrong with you people?'

Delta stared hard at the female police officer, wondering if she had any further value or if he should just kill her now to motivate the old man to move things along. He decided to hold on to her a little longer. Maybe Alpha would have a use for her if their exfil had been compromised.

'There's nothing *wrong* with us Miss Piggy. You took Alpha, we're here to get him back. Simple. You should have left us alone and minded your own business. But no, you had to stick your fucking oar in and cause all of this.' He looked around the room and his gaze was drawn to an object on the desk. Keeping the gun trained on the pair, he moved to the desk and picked the object up. A torch. Pointing the light to the floor he turned the device on and nodded, happy that it was in working order before ramming the tubular end into the waistband of his trousers.

Tess stared at the boy in front of her, struggling to process that a child, a *child*, was capable of being part of a murderous gang. Her instincts fought the evidence for possession of her assessment, the nurturing woman versus the logical, reasoning police officer. Yet she could see it in his eyes. A deadness that lent a maturity well beyond his years. And the familiarity with the weapon, still as a stone, unwavering or shaking. She shook her head to gather her thoughts. 'What do you think you can achieve here? There's six of us in this nick. Whatever plan you had you must realise by now won't possibly work.'

Her statement was met by a wry smile from the boy. 'Oh, don't worry. Our plan will work. *Is* working.' He moved closer and gestured with the gun, waving it in the direction of the door. 'So, moving on with our plan, you're going to take me to Alpha now. No sudden moves, no shouting or warning your friends or I'll shoot you in the face.'

Tess glanced quickly at Colin, met his eye and registered his almost imperceptible nod indicating that they should comply with the boy's demands. She stood, looking for any opportunity that she could exploit to get the gun away from the child but he remained just far enough out of reach to make it impossible. As they made their way towards the door the boy ushered them out into the corridor before him and Tess gasped in surprise as she felt the pistol barrel rammed hard against her spine and the warm breath in her ear.

'Like I said, no funny stuff or you'll get it first.'

Tess nodded her understanding and regained her breathing. Just ahead of her, Colin glanced back and frowned when he saw the boy's position. *This is getting harder by the minute.* Colin tried to stop thinking about the gunman as a kid. This was a killer in a child's body and there would be no reasoning or negotiation with someone like this. The police sergeant's mind was racing as he attempted to identify how the hell he was going to get them out of this new mess without getting someone killed. He knew one thing for sure; he could not let Adams out of that cell. The boy had seen the training footage and would know that Tess had been to their secret location. *No.* He had seconds to come up with a plan to stop this in its tracks right here. His thoughts were interrupted by the boy hissing to catch his attention. Looking back, Colin met the boy's eyes and saw the threat implicit. They were about to pass the back door where Fletch and Kenny were guarding and the boy was clearly aware of the opportunity for one of them to spot his actions. Colin continued to walk and glanced to his right as he passed the doorway leading to the pair. He saw that both men had their backs to the station, their attention focussed on the threat outside, ignorant to the danger within. He looked over his shoulder and nodded at the boy who pushed Tess ahead of him and beyond the doorway.

Delta stole a quick glance backwards and was happy to see the empty corridor behind. The plan was working well so far. The woman and the older policeman would lead him to Alpha and release him. Delta would signal Bravo with the torch from one of the windows and Alpha could then take charge. He assumed that they would kill all the police, especially since the woman had been to the location and discovered a lot of their planning and operational materiel. That would be Alpha's decision though. Delta turned his attention back to his captives as they proceeded along the corridor and into a smaller sub-section of the station. He watched warily as the older policeman stopped and indicated with his head to a door.

'Your *Alpha* is in there.'

Delta motioned with the barrel of the pistol and the officers followed his direction, moving beyond the door and up against the wall. Delta studied the door and with his free hand pulled down the view-hole cover. Seeing no sign of movement, he called out. 'Alpha?'

He heard a faint noise from within and grinned widely as a face filled the aperture, returning his smile.

'You took your time.'

Delta laughed at Alpha's deadpan statement. 'Yeah, well we got a little surprise at the firepower plod had on scene. Wasn't expecting that.'

Alpha nodded and looked sideways through the viewing aperture, taking in the police officers stood to one side of the door. 'You'll need the key from them to get me out.'

Delta turned to Colin. 'You, old man. Get over here and open the door. Any sudden moves and I'll shoot the woman first.'

Alpha stepped back, nodding his approval. He heard the older policeman's footsteps approaching the door. Colin unclipped a bunch of keys from the lanyard on his belt and began sorting through them.

Delta raised the pistol and aimed it at Tess's head. 'I warned you, don't fuck with me old man. Last chance, unlock that door now or she dies.'

Colin sighed and raised a shaking hand to the lock having achieved nothing more than a slight delay in whatever was going to happen to them. He had run out of options and with the certainty that the boy would not hesitate to kill PC Cameron he had no choice. He turned the key and the door unlocked with a definitive click.

34

Alpha took a theatrical deep breath as the door was opened and he was face to face with the police officers who had arrested him. 'Well, well, well. I did tell you Sergeant Duffy, that this was not going to end well for you.'

Colin swallowed, mouth and throat dry as he struggled to speak. 'Okay Adams, you've done it. You're a free man now. No need to do anything stupid. Just get the hell out of my station.'

Alpha cocked his head to one side, the corners of his mouth lifting in wry amusement. 'For your information Sergeant Duffy, I've never done anything stupid in my life.' The smile disappeared and his eyes hardened as he stepped out into the corridor. 'But you have.' He turned his attention to Delta who was keeping his gun covering the police officers. Alpha looked him up and down and raised an eyebrow. 'Nice clothes. Couldn't you have found something a little smaller?'

Delta laughed at the sarcasm. 'Had to play a little grandson to get plod here to bring me in.'

Alpha nodded his approval. 'Good thinking. How's the rest of the team?'

'All good. Bravo is covering rear and Charlie front. We've brought a spare weapon and ammo along for you but I couldn't sneak it inside in these clothes.'

Alpha grasped Delta's shoulder and squeezed. 'Good job Delta. Good job. I knew you guys would smash this.' He turned to address the police sergeant when Delta interrupted.

'Alpha, just so you know, they've been to the location and gone through the computers.'

Colin watched Adams' reaction to the news; a tightening of the muscles around the jaw and a slight frown. The former SAS man folded his arms and regarded Colin and Tess with a cold, reptilian stare.

'Had to go poking your noses in, didn't you? Couldn't just leave it alone. Well, what is that biblical quote? *As ye sow, so shall ye reap*? That sound about right?'

Tess felt her mind spin as the utter certainty that she was about to live her final moments assailed her. She felt her breathing quicken and her pulse race. *No! Come on, think of something. Anything!* Forcing herself to take deep breaths she attempted to calm down, well aware that a panicked mind could not think logically. She lifted her eyes as Alpha turned back to Delta.

'How many more are we dealing with here?'

Delta indicated with his head to the corridor behind him. 'Two at the back door and two at the front with longs and shorts.'

Longs and shorts. Rifles and pistols. The boy's casual use of military jargon showed Tess just how indoctrinated into Adams' world he was.

Alpha pondered the statement for a moment. 'What's the plan?'

Delta tapped the torch stuck into his waistband. 'I'll signal Bravo from a window, he'll let Charlie know, we wait thirty seconds then they open up on the entrances to create the distraction. We'll use this to cover us to the back entrance, slot the plods there and RV with Bravo and extract.'

Tess shook her head at the boy's offhand reference to killing Fletch and Kenny. There had to be a way to stop this, they couldn't just let this happen. Her thoughts were interrupted by Alpha.

'How many rounds have you got?'

Delta replied. 'Three full mags'

Alpha seemed happy with this and gave a glance towards her and Colin. For a brief second, Tess thought little of it until the full meaning of his question and look came to her with crystal clarity: Adams was checking that the kid had enough ammunition to kill them all.

Alpha took charge once again. 'Okay Delta, give me the torch and you make sure these two don't try anything funny. I'll signal Bravo and get the ball rolling. Happy?'

229

Delta nodded his agreement and focussed his attention back to the police officers, the pistol aimed directly at Tess. With his free hand he took the torch from his waistband and handed it to Alpha who turned it to face the floor and flicked it on, checking that it worked. Content with this he spoke to Delta. 'Nearest window?'

'About ten feet along on your left, just above head height. Signal three long, three short.'

Alpha nodded and strode off down the corridor. Tess felt her desperation increasing as the inevitable bloodbath approached. *What the hell am I going to do?* A quick glance around her showed nothing of any use. The booking-in computer, the log-book, the armoury cage. Her eyes widened as an idea dawned on her. She would have to quick and it relied upon her captors being as disciplined as she thought they were. *But it just might work.* Risking a glance at the kid she allowed her knees to buckle and staggered off-balance clutching at the counter edge to regain stability. Colin moved towards her to help but was warned off by a loud hiss from the boy. He froze but as Tess snuck a look from the corner of her eye, she could see that she had achieved her aim. Colin was now between her and the boy, blocking his view of Tess. Without hesitation she reached quickly over the counter and grabbed an object, ramming it into her belt and covering it with the hem of her sweater. She was just in time as Delta pushed Colin roughly to one side and brought the pistol up and placed the muzzle against her temple, the cold metal in contrast to her warm flesh.

She closed her eyes and held her breath, heart pounding, waiting for him to fire. But he spoke instead.

'What the fuck are you up to?'

Opening her eyes, Tess forced herself to meet the young killer's gaze and feigned dizziness. 'I…don't…I think…sick…feel…funny…' Her back made a muted thump as she fell back against the wall, allowing her head to droop on to her chest.

Delta swore. He wanted badly to pull the trigger on this troublesome plod but couldn't risk alerting her colleagues until Bravo and Charlie were ready. He lowered the pistol and took a step back motioning to Colin. 'You, help her stand up straight before I change my mind and slot you both.'

Colin hurried to her side and placing a hand under her armpit, lifted her up, allowing the wall to support the bulk of her weight.

'Tess are you okay?'

She met his eyes with what she hoped was as meaningful a look as she could manage without attracting the kid's attention. 'I'm fine Sarge. Just had a bit of a….*shock*…You understand? Quite a *shock*.'

Colin frowned and opened his mouth to question her further but closed it rapidly as the weight of her meaning became clear. 'Ah yes, I completely understand. Is the shock wearing off?'

Tess shook her head. 'No Colin. The shock is very strong.'

Colin nodded to show he had understood: Tess had retrieved the unused Taser from the morning's arrest. What he didn't know was how she intended to use it. His thoughts were interrupted by the kid.

'Right. Stop making a meal of it and step away from her where I can keep an eye on both of you.'

Colin looked at him and saw that the kid was suspicious but obviously couldn't put his finger on anything tangible. *Good.* He acquiesced to the demand and moved several feet away from Tess, leaning back against the wall. He could feel his pulse quicken as he anticipated what was to come. He closed his eyes to concentrate. Whatever they were going to do, it had to be done before Adams and the kid reached the back door and killed Fletch and Kenny. Thinking it through, Colin didn't think Adams would risk killing him and Tess before his colleagues outside provided the distraction. It would make too much noise. *Unless he uses a knife.* Colin shook his head to rid himself of the insidious notion. *No.* Adams would use them as leverage right up until the moment he didn't need them anymore. And that moment would be just before he killed Fletch and Kenny.

Tess risked a glance at Colin and saw that he was relaxed against the wall, eyes closed and deep in thought. She wondered if he was, like her, running through their options. She knew that they had until the distraction kicked in to do something. *Anything.* But whatever it was it would absolutely depend on the element of surprise. There would be no second chance with Adams and the kid.

232

A few moments later, Adams appeared from the gloom and gave a quick glance towards her before turning his attention to Delta. 'How long till distraction?'

'Figures one, Alpha.'

One minute. Tess bit on her lip as her mind raced. They had one minute until Adams's team outside opened up and their plan was put in motion. She caught Colin's eye and motioned gently with her head, indicating further down the corridor. He raised an eyebrow in response and she hoped that he understood her intention to allow them to be taken down the corridor by the two criminals. Her thoughts were interrupted by Adams striding towards her.

'Right, we're moving. It's going to get noisy and scary but hold yourselves together and you'll get out of this. We just want to get out of here and back with my team. Okay?'

Tess knew the words were a mere charade to allow Adams and the kid to get to the door. She had no doubt whatsoever that at the first opportunity she and Colin would receive a bullet to the temple along with Fletch and Kenny. But she needed Adams to believe that she had swallowed the lie.

Nodding jerkily, she gushed out her gratitude. 'Thank you, thank you. We will be good. We won't do anything to try to stop you.' She allowed her eyes to fill with tears. 'Thank you so much.'

Adams took her arm in a firm grip and pulled her away from the wall, directing her to stand in front of him. He motioned to Colin to do the same. The police sergeant stood and joined his colleague, his mouth dry and temples throbbing with stress. Colin snuck a look at Tess and took in the pale skin and clammy forehead. He knew he would have to be ready as soon as she produced the Taser from wherever she was hiding it.

'Let's go. Small steps and stay just in front of me. This is nearly over for you so don't fuck it up now.' Adams gave Colin a firm push on his lower back and he moved forward on shaky legs, Tess matching his stride as they made their way down the corridor.

In the dim light, Tess moved the hand she had been holding at her front up her sweater and took hold of the Taser. Moving in step with Colin she oriented the device in her hand and located the 'on' switch and trigger. Her hand was shaking badly and she took deep breaths in an attempt to calm herself. She knew she had to wait until the last moment to use the device but if she left it too late, she knew that someone would die. Too early and they all would. *C'mon, you can do this.*

A sudden burst of gunfire made her jump and a series of red sparks ricocheted off the walls ahead of them as the bullets struck the stone and metalwork of the corridor. A loud curse from Fletch was followed by louder gunfire as the policeman returned fire. She felt Adams's hand on her shoulder and she looked around. He nodded in the direction of the back door and she followed his direction, moving towards the gunfire. She had seen that Delta was still holding the gun, pointing it at Colin's back and she knew that this was the main threat. A strange sense of calm enveloped her as her thoughts became actions and she slowly pulled the Taser out, keeping the device close to her body and out of view of her captors. Out of the corner of her eye she saw that Colin had seen her and would know to be ready. Her ears were ringing with the shock of the gunfire that was echoing down the corridor. They were now mere yards from the back door and she had to act.

As Colin reached the doorway a large burst of gunfire came from outside, shredding the walls and causing them all to crouch in reaction. *Now.* Tess pushed the on button and heard the whine as the charge kicked in. Feeling Adams's hand on her shoulder again she didn't dare look but stepped back into him as she screamed at Colin 'DOWN!' With her free arm she smashed her elbow into Adams's throat and felt the satisfaction of a solid connection and his hand fall from her shoulder. She registered his choking sounds and his hands on his own throat as she spun and confronted the kid. The gun was turning towards her and away from Colin who was now crouched on the floor and looking up at her with wide eyes. Everything seemed to slow down for Tess; Adams collapsing to his knees clawing at his throat and gasping for air, Colin now trying to get to his feet, the sound of Fletch returning gunfire and the kid's gun almost pointing directly at her. *Almost.*

The two projectiles were in his chest before Tess even registered having pressed the trigger and the kid went into an immediate spasm, his arms jerking and knotting with convulsions, the gun spinning away from him and back towards the cell. Tess didn't hesitate. Dropping the Taser, she propelled herself towards the gun. Adams was directly in front of her, still on his knees desperately trying to suck air down his damaged windpipe. Ignoring the distraction, she barged past him and ran to the gun, dropping to her knees and screaming with relief as her fingers clasped around the handgrip. She stood, wild eyed with adrenalin and turned back to her captors. Something struck her full on the face causing her to scream in pain. Looking up, she watched as the Taser body bounced off her head and clattered against the wall. She felt the blood flow immediately and wiped it from her eyes as she raised the gun. Through blurred vision she saw Adams had picked up the kid and was carrying him past Colin. The policeman tried to grab him but Adams kicked him hard in the stomach and again in the face as Colin collapsed. Barely breaking a stride, the former SAS man made his way towards the door and freedom. Lining up the sights as best as she could Tess fired at Adams's back and then he was gone and she couldn't hear much above the ringing in her ears. She lowered the weapon and wiped the blood away again before making her way to Colin who she could see was curled up on the floor in obvious agony.

A series of shouts and long bursts of gunfire gave her pause for a moment but she carried on and knelt by her sergeant, raising a wary eye towards the door in case Adams reappeared. 'Sarge, Sarge, it's me. Are you okay?' She could see his nose was broken and bleeding and that he was struggling to get a breath. 'Okay, okay. Just going to sit you up against the wall now, get some air back into you alright?' She manoeuvred him into a sitting position and could see that his breathing was improving. Colin groaned and opened his eyes, grimacing with pain.

'Adams?'

She patted his shoulder. 'Gone Sarge. He's gone. We did it.'

Colin tilted his head back and pulled a handkerchief from his pocket, stemming the blood flow from his nose. 'How's everyone else?'

Tess nodded. 'Not sure, I'll go check if you're okay here?'

'Yeah, I'm good. Just need a minute or two to get back on my feet. Go on, see how they're doing.'

Standing up she felt shaky and knew that it was the comedown from the earlier adrenaline rush. There were shouts now from Mitch and Mark at the front asking if everyone was okay. What concerned her was the lack of response from the door just around the corner from her. Raising the pistol before her she advanced warily, hyper-aware and ready for anything she might encounter. Turning into the doorway she first saw the boots, then the legs and uniform. *Fletch.* Moving forward she saw Kenny sat against the wall with his head in his hands and something at his feet. Tilting her head to one side she knew that there was something wrong here, something definitely off. It was

Fletch. To all intents and purposes the policeman was lying in the prone marksman's position but Tess could now see that his head was face down on the floor in a large pool of blood. She felt her eyes well with tears as she approached the body. *No, please no.* But the gaping exit wound just behind the Firearms' officer's ear told her all she needed to know.

The tears rolled down her face unchecked for several moments before she turned her attention to the survivor. Kenny still had his head in his hands and seemed to be sobbing. She moved over to him to make him aware of her presence and make sure he wasn't injured. The bundle at his feet drew her attention and she bent over to examine it before recoiling upright in shock, hands drawn up to her mouth in an involuntary gesture of horror. A moan escaped her and she shook her head, forcing herself to make sure. There was no question. The bullet had entered the right eye and exited straight out the back of the skull. Even as she was dealing with the shock of the discovery, she was grateful that the dim light of the doorway stopped her from seeing all the grisly details. Letting out a sob of frustration and anger she looked at Kenny and knew why he was in the state that he was. One thing to see a police officer killed before you. Another thing completely to see a twelve-year old kid shot in the face.

The kid, who only moments before had been their captor and potential killer, was now dead on the dirty floor of a freezing police station.

35

Tess remembered that Adams and his gang remained outside and crouched quickly behind the makeshift barricade, grabbing Kenny's knee as she did so. 'Kenny. Kenny. Look at me?'

She watched as Kenny's pale face rose from his knees and made eye contact with her, his eyes red and rheumy with sorrow and fear. 'Aw shit Tess, they killed Fletch and the kid. A poor bloody kid. What the hell are they on? Eh? What the hell are these lunatics on?'

Tightening her grip on the older man's leg she spoke firmly. 'Listen Kenny. That wasn't just a kid. He's one of Adams' goons. Had me and the sarge at gunpoint and forced us to free Adams. They were going to kill us Kenny. He wasn't a kid, Kenny. He was a cold-blooded killer. Save your tears for Fletch.' She watched as a range of emotions swept over Kenny's face. Her words had been harsh and she certainly didn't feel the confidence with which she had delivered them. One of the crucial lessons that she remembered from the Army was that of using confidence and courage to dominate fear and recover a situation, even if it was a false front. People needed and responded to strong leadership in crisis situations and if this wasn't a crisis situation nothing was. She nodded to Kenny as she saw him regarding the small corpse with a new perspective. 'That's right Kenny. He's a killer. A young one granted but a killer, nonetheless. And the rest of Adams' goons? Teenagers, little bit older than this one but still kids. It's absolutely fucking crazy but true.'

Kenny shook his head and held it in his hands again as he attempted to come to terms with the information the policewoman was telling him. *Kids? Really? A bunch of kids were doing this?*

Picking up on his thoughts, Tess moved closer to him and spoke in a quieter tone. 'My guess is that these kids are Adams' sons. Before we lost comms, I was in touch with an old Army mate who gave me some background on the family. Adams has…*had*, three sons who were supposed to have emigrated to New Zealand with their mother years ago but nothing had been heard since. I think these are his sons that he's indoctrinated and trained over the years to be his little SF cell.'

Kenny looked her in the eye again. 'What the hell for? Why go to so much trouble?'

'I found a stack of stuff back at their location that explains all that but I think it's better if I tell everyone together what I know, okay?'

Kenny looked at the small body beside his feet and then over to the cooling corpse of the SFO. 'Suppose we should put these guys somewhere a bit more respectful as I'm assuming we can expect Adams back?'

She nodded her agreement. 'Definitely. He'll want revenge for his dead son, that we can count on.'

'But *they* killed him Tess, not us. Adams surprised us from behind carrying the kid in his arms. He tripped or staggered just as he reached us and that's when one of the bullets from outside hit the kid in the face. Adams dropped him and was trying to pick him up again when Fletch turned his gun on him. Adams knocked it away and as Fletch was turned he got shot through the head. Adams just screamed and stood for a second before leaping over the barricade and escaping.'

Tess had worked out in her own mind already what had happened but she was glad to have the details confirmed. Because killer or not, for a brief few moments she had lived with the uncertainty that it been one of her bullets that had killed the kid. She looked beyond the barricade at the swirling snow and shivered. Adams would be back, that much they could count on but this time it would be extremely personal. A movement behind her caught her attention and her heart leapt but it was only Colin, making his way slowly around the corner. He stopped when he saw the corpses on the floor.

'Aw shit. I take it you've…'

Tess nodded, a lump in her throat as she replied. 'Yes, Sarge and sorry, but yes, Fletch is dead along with the kid here.'

Colin sagged against the wall and rubbed his hand over his swollen face, the bruising already starting to appear around his eyes. 'Okay, let's give them some dignity and move them into the bigger store room. Give me a hand Kenny. Constable Cameron, take Fletch's rifle and ammunition and keep watch in case these bastards try to surprise us.'

Tess picked up the carbine, deliberately avoiding looking at the head area of the body. She racked the cocking lever back and a round spun out of the breech, tumbling through the air. Looking inside she could see that there were still rounds in the magazine and she released the catch and removed it, nodding with satisfaction as she felt the weight and knew it was nearly full. Seating the magazine back on the weapon, she hit the cocking lever and the working parts of the rifle slammed forward with a harsh metallic rasping, taking a new bullet into the chamber. Carrying out a second confirmation that the safety catch was applied, she put the sling over her shoulder and let the carbine hang by her side. She noted that Colin had opted to take charge of Fletch's body at the head, sparing Kenny from having to deal with any more trauma than was absolutely necessary. Holding her hand up to pause them in their actions, she removed the black webbing vest the dead policeman was wearing. Her brow wrinkled with distaste at her actions but she was pleased to feel that the vest was heavier than expected, a good sign that there was plenty of ammunition in the remaining magazines. She stepped back, vest hanging from

242

her hand and allowed the men to continue with their macabre duty. Taking the carbine off, she leaned it against the wall as she fitted the vest, adjusting the straps and the buckles to suit her smaller frame. Content with the fit, Tess began an inventory of the contents of the pouches. Seven full magazines for the carbine, two smoke grenades, two flash-bangs for distraction, and a small trauma pack. She also remembered that Kenny had a Glock and a couple of magazines but couldn't be sure how many.

Colin and Kenny returned to take the second body and Tess noted again how Colin took responsibility for the trauma end, shielding Kenny from the worst. A welling of emotion rose within her at this demonstration of consideration from her sergeant. She had always held him in high esteem and now, when it mattered most, he still held himself to the highest standard. Shaking her head, she moved back slightly to allow them to pass with their funereal load. The floor of the doorway was empty now but for the large pools of blood thickening in the frigid air. Giving a quick glance outside before moving, she dashed back into the corridor and into the smaller store room, emerging with two large, thick luminous jackets. She placed one over each pool and felt the better for it, not having to confront the evidence of her colleague's death every time her eyes wandered. Lowering herself to the ground, she took up as comfortable a position as she could, watching over the top of the barricade into the maelstrom beyond.

A sound behind her caught her attention and she saw Kenny returning. He stopped and nodded with approval at the jackets before he too took up a position on the floor, back against the wall and the Glock loosely held in his right hand. 'Colin's gone up to Mitch and Mark to fill them in on what's happened Tess.'

'Yeah, I thought that's what he would do. Mark will take this hard.'

Kenny nodded and sighed. 'When the hell is this going to end Tess? Surely at some point they're going to give up and make their escape?'

Tess thought for a moment before replying, not wanting to spook him but unwilling to give him false hope either. 'I think we'll see them one more time Kenny. Adams will be raging and determined to kill us all for getting his kid killed but I think if we can hold them off that will be it. He knows it's only a matter of time before the storm dies or we get comms back, he's not stupid. So that's my theory. They'll try once more and then they'll go.' She could see Kenny close his eyes as he digested her information. He nodded and looked at her.

'Let's hope you're right Tess. Let's hope your right. 'Cos I think I've probably only got one fight against these monsters left in me.'

Although she smiled at his statement, Tess knew that deep down inside, she felt exactly the same way.

36

Bravo watched as Alpha remained hunched over the kitchen worktop, head in his hands. He'd hardly moved since Bravo had led him back to the house. Bravo still couldn't believe that Delta was dead. Delta. His brother. The youngest on the team. When he'd seen Alpha exploding out of the police house, he had almost killed him by reflex. He'd screamed over the wind and Alpha had heard him, sprinted through the snow and dropped on one knee beside him. He'd gripped the back of Bravo's head and pulled him close before yelling the awful words. *'Delta's dead Bravo. I say again, Delta's dead. Extract, extract, extract.'* Bravo had frozen only for a moment before the training kicked in and he was standing, relaying the order to Charlie as he led Alpha back to the old people's house.

Charlie came into the kitchen and clapped Bravo on the back. 'House clear. Kid still secure. I gave him some water and then gagged him again so he's all good. He was asking about his grandparents so I told him they would be back soon to keep him calm.' Bravo nodded, pleased that Charlie had carried out the drill of making sure no-one had entered the house in their absence. He looked at Alpha, still lost in his rage and grief.

'Alpha? Alpha, what's the plan?'

At first there was no reaction and he was about to repeat himself when Alpha rose slowly and turned to face him. Bravo took in the cold, dark eyes and the rage emanating from Alpha's stare.

'The plan? The plan is simple Bravo. We go back in there and slaughter every one of these pigs for killing your brother.' He nodded to Charlie. 'Enough of this fucking time wasting, where's my gear?'

Charlie walked back into the hallway and retrieved the larger backpack. As he made his way back to the others, he could feel the shock and emotion kicking in at the realisation of the loss of his brother. Shaking his head to deny the tears that were starting he cleared his throat and took a deep breath. *Emotions can come later. We've got work to do here.* Entering the kitchen once more he heaved the pack onto the bunker and undone the buckles. He pulled out the carbine first, the weapon camouflaged with white tape as their own had been. He extended the folding stock, cocked and cleared the weapon, the noise echoing in the silent kitchen. He handed the weapon to Alpha who took it and placed it on a kitchen top beside him. Charlie continued emptying the pack, pulling a webbing vest loaded with ammunition and grenades and then a thick, white smock. He passed these items to Alpha who donned the smock and fitted the vest before removing a magazine from the pouch and loading it on the weapon. He made the carbine ready and checked the safety was on then looked up at the remainder of his team.

'Okay, same drill as before. Charlie front, Bravo back. On my order you will give sustained covering fire into the entrances. Bravo, I'll be at the back door and post the first flash bang. I'll enter and take out the plods there. I'll signal when done then you enter and support me in clearing the station. Charlie, remain front, keeping the pigs there occupied until you get my signal to hold fire then Bravo and I will deal with them. I'll give you the all clear then you'll join us inside. We need Delta's body and to torch this fucking place to the ground. Questions so far?' He paused for a moment but there were none. 'Okay, once we're happy the fire is prepped and good to go, I'll initiate then we'll move out and carry on with the extraction. Let's move.'

Charlie led the way again and they followed the same route, their previous tracks barely visible in the deepening snow. Alpha pulled on his white balaclava and fitted his radio microphone around it as they walked. He gave a quick test and received Charlie and Bravo's replies. After they crossed the fence Charlie split to the right while Alpha and Bravo made their way to the back door. Alpha could see that despite the external lights being on they were of no use in the poor visibility, the swirling snow allowing only a couple of feet at best. In front of him Bravo crouched lower and lay down in the snow, crawling slowly towards the back door. Alpha dropped to one knee and stayed there, weapon up and covering the rear entrance in the event that someone came out and surprised Bravo.

After a couple of moments Bravo's voice came through his earpiece. '*Bravo in position.*' A brief silence before a second transmission. '*Charlie in position.*' Alpha replied. 'Alpha moving.' He rose to his feet, moving with bent knees and weapon now up in the ready position as he made his way in a long arc out past the point where he could be seen by anyone inside the station and back towards the opposite side of the door. Nearing the building, he kept his eyes on the entrance looking for any signs of movement. Slowing his approach, he reached the wall of the station and edged along until he was beside the edge of the door. Again, he remained still for some time, waiting for any indication that he had been seen, but all was still in the lee of the wind and hush of snowfall. He spoke quietly into the mic. 'Alpha in position.'

The responding clicks told him that Charlie and Bravo had heard him. He lowered the carbine and allowed it to hang from the sling around his shoulder. Slowly he lifted his hand and opened up one of the pouches on his webbing vest. He removed the small cylindrical object and raised it to his face. Checking the safety pin, he pinched the ends of the small piece of split metal, closing the ends together so that a stiff pull would be all that he needed to make it ready. He edged as close to the door as he could without exposing himself and spoke again into the radio. 'Standby, standby.'

37

Tess could see the Firearms' officer struggling to hold the tears back. PC Armstrong had taken the news of his colleague's death as she'd expected, with disbelief, grief and rage. Mitch too had been badly shaken after Colin had filled them in on the events, their situation now all too real. Leaving Kenny at the back door, she had come forward to find Colin and try and identify what the hell they were going to do to prepare for Adams' next assault.

Glancing at her sergeant's face she grimaced as she saw the swelling had now increased and the pain Colin was experiencing. Yet still he continued to take charge, putting his own misery and pain to one side while he dealt with the very immediate problem of keeping his people alive. Sensing her attention, he looked at her and gave a wan smile.

'You're wondering what the hell we're going to do to hold them off aren't you?'

'You must be psychic Sarge, that's exactly what I'm thinking.'

Colin gave a short laugh. 'Hardly psychic PC Cameron. It's the one thought on all of our minds.' He frowned as the laugh threw a jolt of pain up his injured face. 'Still, better think of something quick as I don't suppose those bastards out there will hold off for much longer.'

Tess nodded. 'Agreed. They'll be back as quick as they can and this time it's personal for them. We can expect this to be a tough one sarge.'

'Yeah, I know. The other problem we have is that they know the layout of the place now giving them another advantage.'

Tess bit on her bottom lip and shivered in the cold. 'Look, you're right; Adams has been in here and he knows the layout. So, let's take that advantage from him. Even the playing field a bit.'

'Okay...how?'

Tess nodded in the direction of the back door. 'I think they'll hit us from the rear. He spent most of his time here at that end of the station and he went out that way. I think he'll come at us from a position he's familiar with.'

Colin stroked his chin in thought. 'Makes sense I suppose. So, what do we do about that?'

'Change the layout. Get some lockers up to block corridors and doorways. Make it completely unfamiliar and put them off their game. And while we're at it maybe try to funnel them into an area where we can either control them or they can do the least amount of damage.'

Colin was now nodding with enthusiasm. 'Yes, I get it. Let *us* be the ones in control for a change!' He placed a hand on her shoulder and squeezed. 'That is some smart thinking

Tess, really smart. You'll make a brilliant detective lass, no two ways about it. Can I let you run with this deception operation?'

She smiled and clasped his hand. 'I'd be mad if you didn't.'

'Good. Get going and just tell us what you need.'

A rough plan had already formed in her head and she spun on her heel and made her way to the back door. Kenny looked up and she knelt beside him and talked him through the plan. With his engineer's experience, he provided some salient advice and she told him to let Colin take the sentry position. With the sergeant in place, Tess pulled Kenny into the corridor and watched as he did some quick calculations. She knew time was a factor so ran to the front entrance and grabbed Mitch, leaving Mark to man the barricade. When they returned to Kenny, he started giving them commands, reverting completely to his old army persona. Following his directives, she and Mitch began hauling lockers, desks, computer towers and other large objects into the corridor. Kenny showed them where to place the objects and would give them the occasional adjustment. They worked fast, sweating and breathless despite the cold of the station's corridor. They had just placed a large desk on top of a cabinet when Kenny stopped them.

'Right, that's fine. Go back to your posts. I'll put out some booby traps to slow these bastards down a bit but I'll show you where they are when I'm done.'

Tess and Mitch returned to the makeshift barricades and joined their colleagues, briefing them on Kenny's progress. Colin nodded his satisfaction and turned to face Tess.

'You know, I had my doubts earlier but there's a chance we just might survive this.'

She smiled her agreement. 'I think they'll try this one last time Sarge then they'll know they've got to go before it's too late. If we fight hard enough this time they won't come back, I'm sure of it.'

Colin turned back to face the open doorway. For all of their sakes he hoped she was right. His face ached like hell and he was exhausted and knew he couldn't deal with much more of this. There was silence for a while, save for the whistle of the wind around the building and he thought of Susan, comfortable and warm at home and wondering why the hell she couldn't reach him. She wasn't the panicky sort though and was probably thinking that he was out rescuing stranded motorists or some other mundane winter policing matter. His thoughts were interrupted by Kenny returning. Colin indicated that Tess should go with the former engineer first and she rose and followed Kenny into the corridor. Only a few moments later she returned, a small grin on her face. Colin stood and raised his eyebrows as they swapped positions, Tess now getting down on the floor beside the carbine. She shook her head at his inquisitive look. 'Better if you see for yourself Sarge.'

Colin walked behind Kenny and stopped when directed by the smaller man. Kenny pointed out his array of trips, traps and obstacles and Colin was surprised by the man's ingenuity. None of the traps were obvious but would undoubtedly be effective. The impromptu barricades that they had placed also made the internal layout of the station completely unfamiliar and had the secondary effect of funnelling the unwary into cupboards or dead ends where they would have to turn back on themselves to get out of. Colin clapped the former engineer on the back. 'Bloody brilliant Kenny, absolutely first class mate.' Kenny blushed at the praise and lowered his head.

'Well, it was Tess's idea to be fair Colin but I think this gives us a fighting chance if nothing else. Plan is simple; we hold them off at the rear entrance until I give the signal then we fall back to the office doorway and take a position there. Let them get in the back door and engage them once they hit the corridor. From there they will take the only option for cover which funnels them into that dead end. We'll drop back into the office and take cover behind the locker wall there. Whoever comes out of that dead end will follow us in and trigger the traps in here, slowing them down and giving us a chance to pick them off. We can then retreat back to the top end of the corridor and lure them into the second bunch of traps at the doorway there. Right, you're the last to see this so let's get back to our positions and be sure we're ready for these clowns when they return.'

'Wait. I'll take your position with Tess; you stay out here directing and co-ordinating us. If they come at us as hard as

I think we'll need someone to take charge in the event that we have wounded or are in danger of being overrun.'

Kenny nodded, face grim with determination. 'Good idea. You let Tess know and I'll go and make Mark and Mitch aware.'

The men parted and Colin strode back to join his colleague at the rear entrance. Hearing his approach, she turned her head. 'All good Sarge?'

Colin lowered himself and looked out into the sodium-lit snow beyond the doorway. 'Yes. I've tasked Kenny to remain inside and take control of us once the shit hits the fan. I think we can stand by for a really hard time so having someone to get a grip of us when we're running around like headless chickens made sense.'

'That's a good call Sarge. And Kenny's done some awesome work with the deceptions and the traps. This will work. We'll get through this.'

A gust of wind blew some snow flurries into the small ante-room and Colin watched as they drifted slowly on to the jumbled metal of the makeshift barricade. 'I hope you're right PC Cameron. I hope you're right. 'Cos if I get murdered out here by these bozos, Susan's going to kill me!'

38

Bravo. Charlie. Alpha waited a brief moment after his team's acknowledgement of the standby call before creeping forward, knees bent, to the edge of the doorway. Through the snow before him he saw Bravo materialise and take his position on the other side of the entrance. Bringing the flash-bang up to his chest, Alpha pulled on the circular metal loop and removed the pin, throwing it casually into the snow at his feet. Clasping the fly-off lever firmly against the body of the grenade, he took a final look at Bravo then lobbed the device into the open doorway and the interior of the station.

Tess saw an object tumble through the air and separate in two parts and just had time to cover her ears with her hands when the explosions started. The small entranceway she shared with Colin was rocked by a series of explosions and ultra-bright flashes of light. Despite the shock and fear assailing her she understood that this was a mere prelude to what was coming. Opening her eyes, she squinted against the bright flashes and aimed the carbine at the doorway. No sooner had she done so when the open frame was filled by a wraith, a spectral figure in white with no face, scrambling over the upturned lockers and tables. Her shock held her stiff with fear for a brief moment until she registered that the figure was raising its own rifle and bringing it to bear upon her. In a reflex action, she thumbed the safety lever to the fire position, looked over the top of the barrel and squeezed the trigger. The sound of the shot was dulled after the concussive effect of the flash bang but the recoil in her shoulder and the small flash at the end of the barrel confirmed that the weapon was working as intended. The figure before her staggered slightly but kept coming forward, rifle now at the ready. She could see that the figure seemed disoriented and felt a small flicker of relief that their deception plan was working.

Reaching out her hand, she pulled on Colin's foot to attract his attention. When he caught her eye, she saw immediately that he was suffering from the effects of the stun grenade. She pointed behind her and indicated with her head that he should fall back in that direction. To her relief, Colin immediately shuffled backwards and passed behind her as she supplied covering fire. Throwing herself to the floor, she wriggled backwards through a maze of upturned furniture until she bumped into Colin. Settling herself against a wall, she raised the rifle up and aimed it in the direction of the area she had just vacated.

A brief moment later a white-clad figure stumbled into view and tripped over an upturned filing cabinet, falling hard into the melee of lockers and desks. Without hesitation, Tess fired a shot at the figure but couldn't be sure that she'd hit it. The figure rose, confirming her assessment and she fired again, this time a double-tap, two rounds in quick succession designed to inflict maximum trauma over a small area. As she watched, the figure visibly sagged, dropping to one knee, their rifle hanging from a sling by their side. Tess felt a small burst of triumph and started to rise to one knee when a huge burst of automatic fire sent shredded wood from the desks and sparks from the metal lockers into the air. As she was throwing herself to the ground, she caught sight of another figure bursting through the doorway, the muzzle of his weapon a constant flash as the hail of bullets spewed forth.

Alpha had watched Bravo drop as the police bullets found their mark. Wasting no time, he flipped the carbine to full automatic and threw himself into the room, firing from the hip. Reaching Bravo, he used his free arm to scoop under his Bravo's armpit, continuing to fire his weapon in the direction of the police. Hauling on Bravo, he was relieved to feel the latter push up with his legs to assist. *Good.* He might be hurt but he was thinking clearly. Alpha began walking backward in his awkward embrace with Bravo, continuing to fire until he saw they had reached the doorway and was finally outside. He pulled Bravo with him and out of the view of the door. He spoke into his radio mic.

'Charlie, Alpha. Your location imminently. Stand by for friendlies.' He heard the acknowledgement and waded through the snow, half dragging Bravo, towards Charlie at the front of house.

In the silence that ensued after the assaulters' departure, Tess raised her head and brought the rifle back up on aim. They had gone. There was no sign of the white-clad attackers. She took a breath and could feel her chest shaking as the adrenaline was leaving her body. She thought of Colin and whipped her head around, remembering that he had seemed in shock the last time she had seen him. Her sergeant was hunched behind an overturned locker with the pistol out in front of him. He was dead still and for a brief moment she feared the worst but then as she watched she saw him lower the pistol and turn his head in her direction. She met his vacant stare and open mouth and realised that he had probably absorbed the full shock of the flash-bang's effect. Taking a quick glance in the direction of the back door, she scrambled over to her superior and grabbed him by the shoulder. 'Colin. COLIN! Look at me.'

Colin turned his head and stared at her. He raised a hand to his ear and grimaced as he touched it. She pulled his hand gently away and moved her face closer to his.

'It's okay Colin, this will pass, it's just the effect from the flash-bang, alright?'

He nodded and hyper-stretched his jaw in a vain attempt to clear his ears. '*Just?*'

Despite their predicament, she found herself laughing and hugged Colin hard, tears forming in her eyes with affection. 'I'm so glad you're okay Sarge, I really am.'

Colin hugged her back and spoke in her ear. 'Like I said PC Cameron, Susan would kill me if I got myself hurt out here.' He pushed her gently away and indicated with his head towards the open entrance. 'What do you think they're doing now?'

She exhaled. 'I think I got one of them Sarge. In fact, scratch that. I *know* I got one of them. My guess is that they'll be concentrating on keeping him alive. I think we've bought ourselves some breathing space.'

Colin could feel his head clearing and some of his hearing returning to normal. 'Good. What can we do with it PC Cameron?'

Tess had been thinking of little else but still couldn't believe what she was about to say. 'We go after them Sarge. We go out there and take the fight to them while they're vulnerable.'

Colin's eyes widened. 'Go out there after them? You mean, me and you, now, go after them?'

'Think about it Sarge, it's not as mental as it seems. Right now, they'll be tending to the wounded guy. We can follow their tracks in the snow right to them. I'll bet they're not even looking for us, so confident that we'll stay hunkered down in here shitting ourselves.'

Colin could see the merit in what she was saying but he also knew that leaving the cover and safety of the station was madness. 'How badly do you think their guy is wounded?'

259

'No idea, I just saw him stagger and drop. Depends if he was wearing body armour or not but judging from what I saw I don't think he was.'

Colin mulled it over for a few moments. 'I suppose if we're going to do this, we'd better do it now before my bottle goes completely.'

Tess gave a wan smile in return. 'Okay, I'll lead with the carbine. I'll keep it dead slow and as soon as I see them, I'll give a few busts on auto. You come around to my side and see if you can get some well-aimed shots into them while they're distracted. I'll shout for us to break contact and we'll leg it back here. Sound alright?'

Colin stood, pistol hanging by his side and met her gaze. 'That really depends on your definition of alright PC Cameron. On any other day and in any other situation it would sound bloody insane. Here and now it's actually our best course of action.'

Despite herself she gave a small grin. 'C'mon, let's do this before *my* bottle goes!' Climbing over the jumbled office furniture she raised the carbine in front of her and led them out of the safety of the station and into the blizzard and the night beyond.

<u>39</u>

In the lee of the wind Alpha could hear that Bravo's breathing had settled. Charlie continued to apply the dressing to Bravo's chest but Alpha knew that the bleeding was superficial; the rounds hadn't penetrated to any real extent. Bravo's magazines that he was carrying in his combat vest had stopped the bullets the police woman had fired. One however, had managed to punch through, but with most of its power depleted by the magazines and rounds that they held.

Alpha had been worried when he'd seen Bravo drop. His fear immediately transformed to action as he'd sprayed the police with a good rate of fire to enable him to extract Bravo. Looking at his son now, leaning against the cold wall of a half-destroyed police station, Alpha had a brief moment of doubt. He'd already lost one son to this fight and had been very close to losing this one. With his face mask removed and his features racked with pain Bravo looked like the seventeen-year old that he was. Alpha grabbed his shoulder to catch his attention.

'You good Bravo?' He watched as his son's eyes opened and met his own.

'All good Alpha. Just knocked the wind out of me for a bit.'

'Good man. It's not serious, your mags stopped most of the rounds, only one of them got through and even that had lost most of its power. You're one lucky bastard Bravo. One very lucky Bastard.'

'Doesn't really feel that lucky at the moment Alpha. Feels like shit!'

Alpha grinned and ruffled his son's hair. 'Good. If you can feel it then it's not that serious so let's quit the fucking dramatics, shall we?'

Bravo returned the smile. 'I'm good. Just need a minute to catch my breath then I'll be a hundred percent.'

Alpha looked at Charlie and watched as he removed his mask and ran a hand over his face. The stress and exhaustion added years to the young face, belying its tender fifteen years. Alpha gripped his younger son's shoulder. 'Hey Charlie, how you holding up mate?'

Charlie met his father's gaze but without the humour or warmth of his brother. 'I'm okay Alpha.'

'You sure? You don't look so good mate.'

Charlie let his head droop and sighed before raising his face to meet his father's gaze. 'Delta's dead and we just about lost Bravo. What are we still doing here?'

Alpha dropped his hand from Charlie's shoulder and pointed at the station behind him.

'They killed your brother Charlie. Those fucking pigs killed your brother. And they know who we are, what we've been doing and what we're going to do. They cannot be allowed to live. Understand me? We *cannot* and *will not* leave a single one alive.'

Charlie drew back from the fierceness in his father's delivery. He'd seen this before; the black eyes, the intense stare, the deep growl of the voice. There would be no more questions. 'Okay Alpha, got it. *Scorched Earth.*'

Alpha nodded and relaxed a little on hearing the words. Their code-word for complete destruction of life and property had never been used for real until now and he was happy that Charlie understood what they had to do. 'Good. Right, enough time-wasting. Sort yourselves out and let's get moving. I want this done and dusted ASAP.' He looked at Bravo who, although grimacing, was getting to his feet without any mobility problems. Charlie nodded and pulled on his white face mask once again. Alpha checked the magazine on his weapon and replaced it with a new one, releasing the bolt and forward-assisting the round into the chamber.

'Okay, plan; all of us into the front entrance this time. Classic three-man stack with me point, Bravo second and Charlie third. I'll deploy flash-bang and enter. Bravo watch my position and support. Charlie follow on rear and prepare to clear rooms along the axis. Questions?' His team was silent. 'Okay, check your mags, get squared away, we move in figures one.' He watched as Bravo and Charlie exchanged magazines to replace the damaged ones from where they had been struck by the policewoman's rounds. They then inspected each other's equipment, ensuring no pouches were left open or damaged from where precious magazines could be lost. Their inspections complete, they turned to Alpha and gave him the thumbs-up to indicate their readiness. He nodded and turned to the corner of the building where he nestled his side against the cold wall, weapon in the low ready position. He felt Bravo slot in close behind him, the youngster's thigh in contact with the rear of his own. A moment later he felt Bravo's hand grip his thigh once. *Team Complete.*

Knees bent and weapon now up and aiming forward, Alpha led the trio in the classic room entry format they had practiced thousands of times before, the three moving as a single, fluid entity. With no need for communication, their approach was silent and covered completely by the howling blizzard. They progressed through the snow drifts and came to the side wall that covered the front door. Alpha halted and leaned against the wall, allowing his carbine to hang from the sling as he prepared the flash-bang. With the pin out and taking a firm grasp of the device he held it above his head for several moments to ensure the team saw the intention. He felt Bravo hunch closer against him and with a smooth action lobbed the grenade into the open doorway and pulled his head back sharply to avoid becoming a collateral victim of his own grenade. The snow whirling outside of the doorway became lit by a blinding flash followed almost instantly by a loud bang which set off the series of flashes and explosions that rocked the small ante-room beyond. Counting each one in his head, Alpha waited until the penultimate bang and moved forward confidently, knowing from experience that he would arrive in the doorway only a split-second after the grenade's final detonation. Feeling Bravo move with him, he knew that Charlie would be doing the same behind Bravo. He entered the doorway just as the last explosion had gone off and with the carbine aimed before him breached the station's makeshift defences for a second time.

40

The explosions stopped Tess and Colin in their tracks. Tess turned to the older man and shouted over the shrieking wind. 'They've hit the front of the station! We need to go, now!'

Not waiting for an answer, she strode through the snow making her way round the building to the front entrance. *Shit, shit, shit.* She could hear gunfire now and knew instinctively that Adams's gang had a serious chance of breaching the barricade. Colin was close behind her and as she reached the side of the front entrance she stopped. Turning again to her superior she cupped her hand to her mouth and moved closer to speak directly into his ear.

'This is bad Sarge. We could just as easily be killed by our own people going in here. I'm hoping we've arrived in time to catch Adams between us and Mitch but we need to be really careful okay? Follow my lead and don't take any chances.' Without waiting for a response, she turned on her heel, crouched low and peered around the wall into the hallway beyond.

Head still reeling from the effects of the grenade, Mark Armstrong knew that if he didn't lay some fire down, they would be over-run in seconds. He couldn't see anything but flashing lights, his hearing was gone and he felt dizzy and nauseous but he knew he had to fire back. Keeping the carbine pointed in the general direction he knew to be towards the doorway, he clicked off the safety catch and began firing short bursts praying they would at the very least, keep Adams's head down. He yelled Mitch's name several times but couldn't even hear himself, let alone hope that the other policeman heard him.

Mitch reached out and retrieved the pistol that he had dropped when the flash-bang went off. His hearing was returning and his vision was almost back to normal. He had seen the grenade fly into the entrance and had reacted instinctively, turning away, closing his eyes and covering his ears. It had still rocked him to his core but he wasn't as badly affected as knew he could have been. His ears were ringing now as Mark continued to fire small bursts towards Adams and his gang. Hands shaking, Mitch picked up the Glock and aimed it in the same direction as Mark just as a shower of sparks and a series of concussive thuds hit an upturned locker in front of him. He dropped to the floor and lay flat, terrified and trembling. He could hear Mark yelling his name and replied but it was obvious that the other policeman couldn't hear him. The thought that Mark might be hurt or injured spurred him into action and he crawled over to his colleague, wincing as bullets whizzed past over his head and struck walls and doors with dull *thocks*. Reaching Mark's side, he slithered alongside him, put his arm around his shoulder and yelled in his ear. 'Mark, you okay?'

The Firearms' officer continued to shoot into the darkness beyond. 'Mitch, I can't really see or hear very well. You're going to have to take over mate.'

Mitch nodded, surprised to find himself actually calming down from his previous state of abject fear. Wasting no time, he placed his hand on Mark's forearm and the shooting stopped. Mark laid the carbine on the floor and slid backwards, away from the weapon, allowing Mitch to replace him in the same position. Mitch took hold of the weapon and brought it up, putting the stock into his shoulder and looking into the sight. He could feel Mark had stopped moving and was laid beside him. A shadow flitted in the darkness beyond and in pure reaction, Mitch pulled the trigger, the flash from the muzzle briefly illuminating their surroundings. A fierce volley of fire was returned and he dropped his head as the air above him was shredded by the deadly projectiles. He felt Mark tap his shoulder and looked around to see the fresh magazine his colleague was offering. Mitch took the magazine and placed it on the floor in front of him, ready for immediate use. The rate of returned fire was slowing somewhat and Mitch knew that he had to keep firing at Adams' gang until someone came to help or they would both be dead in minutes. Slowly raising his head to ready himself he prayed that Tess, Colin and Kenny would be coming to help them soon. Really soon.

Tess ducked back as another burst of automatic fire tore chunks of stone from the edge of the brickwork around the doorway. She knew that this must have come from Mitch and Mark. *Good.* They were still alive and holding off Adams and his goons. *At least for the time being.* She looked around the wall again and saw a shadow detach itself from the mound of upturned furniture. Her heart was in her mouth as she realised that this was one of Adams' gang. Instinct took over as she took control of her breathing, adjusted her eye to the sight picture, thumbed the safety catch to the fire position and gently squeezed the trigger. The sound of her shot and the flash from her muzzle were almost instantaneous but she waited for a brief moment as the rifle steadied from the recoil and she fired again, this time lowering the weapon and pulling back rapidly behind the cover of the wall. Safe behind her cover she analysed her action, reliving it piece by piece in her mind and was convinced that she had struck her target. She felt Colin's hand on her shoulder and turned into him, closing the distance until they were face to face. 'I think I got one of them sarge. Pretty sure I put two rounds into the back of him.'

Colin's grey eyes met her own as he took her by the shoulders. 'Good work Tess. Good work. Let's just hope it was that bastard Adams. Maybe if we cut the head off the snake the rest of them will turn tail.'

She didn't reply but her wish too, was that the shadow she had just fired two rounds into was Adams. Because if it wasn't, he would now be at least two men down and probably insane with rage. And as bad as things were now, she knew that an insane Adams would resort to any means to achieve his aim.

41

When Charlie's body fell across his legs, Alpha had at first
spun around in anger, thinking Charlie had tripped or fallen.
When there had been no response to his shouts and Charlie
had made no effort to raise himself, Alpha felt a sickening
sensation in his stomach. He grabbed Charlie, who was
lying face down, by the shoulder straps of his webbing and
hauled him up until he was face to face with his son.
Charlie's eyes were closed and he wasn't breathing. Even as
Alpha watched, a small trickle of blood seeped out of the
corner of Charlie's mouth and ran in a small, dark rivulet
down his chin. Alpha could hear himself moaning as he
manhandled his son, searching the body with his hands for
the source of the wound. He stopped when he felt the
warm, wet, viscous area on Charlie's back. He raised his
head and hunched over his son, staring at what he
encountered. Grabbing his knife from his own vest, he
sliced into the wet area of Charlie's clothing and gasped at
what he saw. Two rounds had gone into his son's back, right
behind the heart. Charlie would have died almost instantly.
There was nothing to done. He had lost another son. His
scream of rage was loud enough to be heard by Bravo who

271

continued to put down sustained fire towards the policemen. Bravo turned his head towards the sound but could not see anything. Turning back to his duties he knew though, that something terrible had happened.

Alpha cradled his dead son against his chest, tears rolling unchecked down his face and mapping the contours of his stubble. Two sons dead. *Two.* For some time, he was lost in his grief, the fugue of emotion removing him completely from the situation. Until a small nagging notion fought its way in through persistency. Frowning with concentration, he returned to the present, the smoke-filled entranceway, the echo of shots being fired, the thuds as bullets embedded themselves in plasterwork and walls, the whine of occasional ricochets, the dead son in his lap. *What? What the fuck is it?* Something was nagging at him that he couldn't put his finger on but knew instinctively that it was important. It was something to do with Charlie, he knew that much, so he began to replay the moments of Charlie's death and look for anything he should have seen. Closing his eyes, he relived the painful event, moment by moment, his tears continuing to flow. His eyes snapped open and took on a ferocious intensity as he realised what had been staring him in the face from the beginning. *Charlie had been shot from behind.* Turning his attention to the open doorway behind them he stared at the blizzard beyond. Charlie had been shot from behind. *The bastards have flanked us. Snuck up behind us and killed my son.* The coldness inside him returned and with it the calmness and ability to reason. Adams knew he had a gift, an ability to compartmentalise things no matter how bad, until they needed to be dealt with. The ability to prioritise issues regardless of how painful or terrible the situation was that he found himself in. It was a characteristic found among exceptional Special Forces operators. It was also a well-known character trait of psychopaths. Clear-headed and focused once again, Adams gently laid Charlie's body on the ground beside him. He went through his son's equipment and removed the full magazines, placing them into the pouches of his own vest. Picking up his carbine he leaned his back against the barricade behind him and kept a wary eye on the doorway beyond as he spoke into his mic.

'Bravo, Alpha over.' The reply was instant and he could hear the loud gunfire over the transmission.

'Alpha, Bravo, send.'

'Bravo, Charlie is KIA, I say again, Charlie is KIA. Roger so far, over?'

There was a long pause and, in the background, Alpha could hear that the firing had stopped. Eventually Bravo's voice came over the net, subdued and solemn.

'Roger. Charlie is KIA.'

'Bravo be aware we have bandits rear, I say again, Bandits rear over.'

'Bravo roger, we have bandits rear.'

Alpha could hear that Bravo had snapped back into the game with his acknowledgement that they had enemy behind them.

'Okay Bravo, new plan. You extract to my location. We will re-org here and on my command fight through bandits and commence with exfil. Roger so far, over?'

'Bravo roger. Extract to you and standby for exfil.'

'Alpha roger. I will maintain watch at our six. Move now, move now.'

Bravo began crawling backwards on his stomach, keeping his eyes focused on the threat of the policemen to his front. He was crying, silent but screaming inside at the thought of another dead brother. Navigating backwards through the jumble of upturned furniture wasn't easy but he made his way slowly, safe in the knowledge that Alpha was covering their six; the area behind them referenced to a position on a clock face where twelve was always their direction of advance. Another small burst of rounds zipped between the furniture around him but he could tell that it was more for effect than being aimed at him and he continued with his awkward progress.

Alpha's brain was racing as he planned their next series of moves. They could not, as two men, succeed in taking down the Police Station and all those in it. His losses were too heavy. They needed to focus now on the exfiltration. He knew that the nosy policewoman had no information on that as they'd never committed anything to the computers or drives. So, their exfil plan was safe, they just had to get out of here and carry it out. A small nagging voice intruded in his mental dialogue; *What about after?* He knew that as soon as these cops had some backup, there would be a national manhunt for him and Bravo. But fuck it; after was after, he needed his head in the here and now. His thoughts were distracted by Bravo's legs inching alongside him. He reached out and grasped the back of Bravo's webbing and pulled him close to him.

Bravo joined Alpha and leaned against the barricade, both now facing the entranceway of the police station. Bravo turned his head slightly to take in the heart-rending sight of his brother's body laid on the other side of Alpha. He felt his breath hitch and the tears begin again. Seeing his distress, Alpha put his arm around his surviving son's shoulder and pulled him in close.

'Listen Bravo, it's nearly over. We're going straight to exfil plan now, but don't worry; I intend to get as many as these fuckers before we go. Alright?'

Bravo nodded without really hearing what his father had said. He was numb inside. He had lost both of his brothers in one night, the two human beings he was closest to in his whole life. Alpha continued to talk to him.

'I need you to pull the attention of the shooters inside. Let me get in position then move over to that side and give them something to fire back at. I'll pin them down, get a good sight picture and slot them. Soon as I'm done, I'll grab you and we go out the front fighting, fire and manoeuvre all the way to the houses on the other side of the road. We'll break contact and rally on my call then commence with exfil. Clear?' He watched and saw that Bravo was nodding merely out of reflex. Grabbing him forcefully by both shoulders, he thrust his face against his son's. 'Listen, the time for grieving comes later. Right now, we have to finish the mission, honour the sacrifice of the men who died here. Got it? Good. Now let's fucking go, shall we?'

Without waiting for an answer Alpha slithered on his stomach over the jumbled furniture to take up his position. Mimicking the action, Bravo made his own way to the opposite side of the small ante room. As he reached the wall he reflected on his father's words. Alpha was right; there was no time at the moment for grief, they had to concentrate on the mission. But he was wrong about honouring the death of their fellow men. They weren't men. They were *boys. Young boys*. He sighed deeply and raised himself slightly to where he could see over the top of the barricade. There was little in the way of light and he couldn't really identify any potential targets. Raising the carbine, he took aim at an area behind a fairly large foot locker and fired a burst. The sound was shocking after the brief silence but he was gratified to see the flash of a weapon on the other side being fired back at him. He dropped to his stomach on the floor as the rounds being returned passed harmlessly overhead.

Alpha adjusted his rifle slightly and aimed at the area just behind the muzzle flashes. Bravo had done his job well, drawing the shooter into firing and revealing his position. Taking control of his breathing, Alpha began firing a series of deliberate, well-aimed shots into the target area. He paused after he'd fired six shots, lowering the rifle and looking and listening. Nothing. No return fire or sounds of magazines being changed. He waited a moment longer just to be certain then scrambled back down the barricade and joined Bravo. Clapping his son on the shoulder he nodded towards the open doorway. 'It's done. Let's go.'

42

Mitch shook the Firearms' officer again. 'Mark, Mark, c'mon mate say something for fuck's sake!' There was still no response. Mitch gave a quick look over the top of the barricade then pulled his colleague by the shoulder and rolled him so that he was lying on his back. Mitch gasped and felt his heart kick in his chest. A large portion of PC Mark's head was missing just above the right eye. Blood flowed and gore dangled from the bone-rimmed crater. Mark was dead. Mitch kicked his way back across the floor screaming at the horrific sight, determined to get as far away from it as possible. He felt his back slam up against a wall and stopped, drawing his knees to his chest and burying his head in them, sobbing loudly. *What the fuck? How could Mark just die? He's fucking Firearms for crying out loud!* The thought came to him that if Adams' gang could take out both Firearms' officers, there was no hope for the poor rank and file like himself, Tess and the Duffer. His head snapped up as the thought struck him; Were any of his colleagues still alive?

Tess listened intently as the second round of gunfire ended. Colin raised his eyebrows and she shrugged her shoulders to show she had no answer to his question. The silence continued from inside. She didn't like this. Didn't like it one bit. A silence like this after a gunfight usually meant someone had won. Question was, *who*?

Lifting the carbine into the shoulder she knelt and peered round the wall to look into the hallway beyond. She let out a yell of surprise and pulled on the trigger at the same time the figure in front of her barged into her, knocking her onto her back on the snow. She swung the carbine up as the figure raced past her, rolled smoothly on to her stomach and lined up the shot just as the snow around her erupted in small puffs. *SHIT*! She rolled quickly away from the bullets shredding the very spot she had just been lying in. Knowing she had the protection of the wall behind her she rose and leapt for the hard cover, crashing in a heap beside Colin who was standing with his pistol aimed towards the road. The wall above their heads exploded as a burst of rounds hit it, causing both of them to drop to their stomachs. Looking towards the threat she saw a second figure run out of the police station, exploiting the cover of the fire that was keeping her and Colin buried in the snow.

As she made to get to her knees and return fire, another burst from the darkness beyond hit the doorway and wall beside her. She saw that this time it had come from the person who she had just seen. Something seemed familiar to her and it took only a brief moment for it to click. *They're*

279

pepper-potting! Classic fire and manoeuvre, one moves while one covers. The base line of soldiers advancing under fire. Nobody moving without cover.

Her mind was racing as she sought to identify what Adams would do next. *C'mon woman. Think, think!* Then she had it: Adams was breaking contact. He was leaving the fight. And that could only mean one thing; they were going for good. Whatever it was they had planned for their escape; it was happening now. Relief washed over her as she dared to hope that their ordeal was finally coming to a close. Turning to Colin, she grabbed his arm and pulled him in close. 'Sarge, they've gone. Adams and his guys, they've broken contact. They've gone!'

Colin's head drooped and he did not answer her. She repeated her statement and became alarmed as she watched him visibly sag.

'Sarge, what the hell?' She reached out and took his weight, supporting him under the armpit.

'I'm hit Tess. Got me in the shoulder I think lass.'

Her training kicked in as she lowered her superior into a sitting position against the wall. Running her hands over his upper back, she felt the hot, wet area just below Colin's right shoulder. There was a lot of blood and she could feel him tensing as the pain began to bite. 'Right Sarge, they've caught you right enough so we need to get in and get you sorted out, stop this bleeding okay?'

Colin merely nodded and grunted as she hauled him to his feet. Although unable to conduct a proper examination, the exit wound seemed pretty big so it was likely that the round had done a lot of damage on the way out. She could feel he was heavier than before as she took his weight, allowing him to lean on her and lead him to safety.

'Okay Sarge we need to be careful. Our guys inside are liable to shoot at anything that moves.' Moving forward, she gave a last glance in the direction Adams and the other person had gone, then made her way into the doorway. Crouching down, she lowered Colin into a sitting position and then moved on her hands and knees to the front end of the barricade, stopping dead when she saw the body in front of her. It took a moment for the realisation to sink in that she was looking at one of Adams' team and she reached out a hand and rolled the body over. The two crimson blossoms on the back told her all she needed to know. This was the target she had hit. She had killed this person. With a shaking hand she gripped the white mask from under the chin and pulled the garment up and over the face, transfixed by the young, pale face beneath. Her tears fell, heavy globules racing down her cheeks and falling freely from her chin. A kid. *Another kid*. Couldn't be more than fourteen or fifteen. *FUCK!*

A hand grasped her shoulder and she looked up through blurred vision to see Colin kneeling alongside her. The Sergeant looked in bad shape and was breathing heavily but he increased the pressure of his grip on her until she met his eyes. 'Tess, this isn't your fault. It was him or us. Yeah, he's a kid in years but he's a killer by experience. If he wasn't dead another one of us would be. C'mon now, there's nothing more to be done here, let's check on our own people 'cos I've got a feeling they'll be in pretty rough shape.

She wiped a hand across her face and tried to banish the horror to the back of her mind. Colin's words made absolute sense but she still couldn't lose the gut wrenching feeling of nausea in her stomach. She helped Colin to the edge of the barricade and cupped her hands to her mouth.

'MARK. MITCH. KENNY. IT'S COLIN AND TESS. CAN YOU HEAR ME?' She paused and then when there was no response, shouted her request once again. There was still no answer and she was just about to repeat herself when he heard Mitch's voice carry across the lockers and desks.

'I'm here Tess. It's Mitch. I'm here.'

Tess looked at Colin and gave him a small smile of reassurance. 'Okay Mitch, don't shoot, we're coming in, okay?'

'Okay guys, it's safe, you can come in.'

Tess supported Colin on stilted legs, feeling slightly numbed from her experience of finding the kid's body. She staggered as she lost her footing but righted herself with a quick grab. Tumbling down the other side of the barricade, they both saw the Firearms' officer's body at the same time, the dark pool beside the head reflecting what little ambient light remained in the corridor. Colin cursed beside her and she helped him lean against the wall before going to check on Mark's condition. She crouched down and did only the briefest of examinations, but the result was immediately apparent. Standing back up, she turned to face her sergeant and shook her head with a finality that needed no further explanation. Colin turned his attention further down the hallway and saw Mitch propped against a wall staring at them.

'Mitch, how you doing mate? You injured?' Tess put her arm around Colin's back and made their way to the constable and dropped to their knees before him. Mitch met Tess's eyes with a glassy stare and was silent for several moments before speaking.

'Mark's dead Tess. They got Mark. I'm alright though.' He gave a small laugh that had no humour. 'Go figure, eh? The one guy who could make a difference and help us get out of here gets killed and the fuck up who can't even fire a gun properly is good as gold. How fucked up is that Sarge? How fucked up is that?'

Colin raised his head and spoke with obvious difficulty. 'Listen, PC Logan. Don't you bloody dare sit here feeling sorry for yourself. Good officers died here today keeping us alive. So enough of your self-pity; get a grip and do your job. Help me and Tess find Kenny and look for a way to hold this place down until help comes. Adams and his men are gone, okay? We just have to hold our nerve a wee while longer.' He saw Mitch look up at the mention of Adams' departure. 'That's right Mitch, they're gone. So, get your shit together and let's lock this place down.'

Mitch stood, feeling weak but slightly better than he had moments before. *They're gone.* They just might make it through this after all. He looked over at Colin and for the first time noted how pale and shocked he seemed and wondered what they had gone through to have affected him so much. Before he could ask, Tess addressed him.

'Right Mitch, we don't have time for this. The Sarge is wounded and we need to get him somewhere we can clean him up and stop the bleeding. Let's get to the office and get this done. I'll get him there if you go find Kenny and fill him in on what's happening.' Without waiting for an acknowledgement, she manhandled Colin along the corridor, taking care not to become entangled in any of Kenny's improvised booby traps. She shouted over her shoulder. 'Watch yourself on these traps Mitch.

Mitch took exaggerated care as he manoeuvred himself around the crazy farrago of lockers and rearranged furniture, stepping over electrical cables re-employed as trip-wires for the unwary. He gave a quick glance back to ensure Tess had made it to the office with Colin and was relieved to see them make their way into the room. Before he knew it, he had reached the turn into the rear entrance and halted his advance, shouting into the alcove.

'KENNY, IT'S MITCH MATE. I'M COMING IN SO DON'T SHOOT.'

The answer was almost immediate. 'Where the hell have you lot been? I've been here on my own for ages, shitting myself thinking you were all dead!'

Despite himself Mitch felt a smile rise on his lips as he turned the corner and caught sight of Kenny's pale face, wrinkled with tension, worry and indignation.

'No, we're good Kenny, despite Adams' efforts to have it otherwise. You okay?'

'Oh aye, I'm just fucking brilliant thanks. Don't leave me here on my own again alright? That was a shitty thing to do.'

Mitch shook his head. 'Deal. No more leaving you on your own anymore.'

Kenny stood and moved back from the entranceway and into the cover of the corridor. 'So, where's Adams and his gang now?'

Rubbing his hands through his hair, Mitch caught the former Engineer's eye. 'Well, that's actually the good news Kenny. Adams and his morons have scarpered.'

Kenny cocked his head to one side and eyed the constable with suspicion. 'Oh, aye? And what's the bad news then?'

'Mark is dead and the sarge has been wounded mate. Tess is patching him up in the office right now.'

The former engineer shook his head and sighed. 'Come on, I still remember a fair bit of first aid, let's see if I can help.'

43

Tess cut the material away from the shoulder, knowing it would be too painful for Colin to have the garment pulled over his head. Peeling the cloth away from the wound, she paused as she heard the sharp intake of breath. 'Sorry Sarge, being as gentle as I can.'

She watched as he nodded, his features now a lot paler than they had been before. He looked especially haggard in the dim light and his breathing was becoming ragged. She frowned and turned back to her work, concerned that Colin was beginning to deteriorate. With the wound exposed she could see the extent of the damage to his shoulder. The entry wound and exit wound were just over a couple of inches apart but the exit wound was very large. It was pretty much a through and through but it looked as though the round had tumbled inside Colin's body, exiting sideways and thereby leaving a much larger wound than usual.

She stretched past Colin and ripped the cover from the first-aid station, pulling the bottle of distilled water from its mount. Squirting the water on and around the wound, she washed the clotting blood and clothing fibres from the area. She retrieved the sterile wipes and bandages next and, ignoring her superior's grunts of discomfort, cleaned and dressed the wound with swift, confident movements. Pausing for a moment, she rested her hand on Colin's shoulder. 'Okay Sarge, I won't lie to you. This next bit will hurt but I've got to get the pressure on the dressing to staunch the bleeding.'

Colin let out a deep breath, inhaled and gritted his teeth. Prepared and warned though he was, his eyes widened and mouth opened in a grim rictus as the pain hit him. Tess looped the bandage around Colin's torso and chest, pulling tight on each revolution, ensuring the dressing was pressed hard against the wound. She pinned the end of the bandage, gave it a final check for security and was happy with her handiwork.

'That will stop the bleeding Sarge. It's a through and through but I think the round must have deflected off your shoulder blade as it's come out sideways. That's why there was so much bleeding. How you feeling?'

Colin raised his head, the small action taking more effort than he could have ever thought possible. 'Just exhausted PC Cameron. Absolutely exhausted. I'll be okay though, just think I need a bit of rest.'

Her brow furrowed with concern, the realisation hitting her that although the wound itself was not immediately life-threatening, Colin had lost a lot of blood and the shock to a man in his late fifties would be quite considerable. 'Yeah, I hear you Sarge. Look, let's get you settled in the big chair and keep you warm okay? Come on, sooner started, sooner

287

done.' She helped him to his feet and walked him to the larger chair, lowering him gently. His eyes closed the moment he was seated and he reclined, keeping the injured area away from the backrest of the chair. Tess looked around and found the blanket they had used earlier and draped it around Colin, taking care not to touch the wounded shoulder. She observed him for several moments then made her way out into the corridor, almost bumping into Mitch and Kenny.

'Guys, let's talk in the kitchen for a moment. Kenny, can you clear the traps please? We can move about a bit more freely now those bastards have cleared off.' Kenny nodded his assent and moved further along the corridor while she and Mitch made their way to the kitchen. Once inside she turned her back to the sink and leaned against the counter.

'Mitch, the Sarge isn't doing too great. I've stopped the bleeding but I think the shock and trauma at his age, as well as the blood loss, are having a serious effect.'

Mitch placed the black carbine on the melamine counter, the matt black of the weapon in direct contrast to the cream coloured work-top. 'The Duffer's going to be okay though isn't he?'

'I don't know Mitch. I'm not a trained medic but what little I do know tells me that he's not doing too great.' She paused and thought for a moment. 'I think he probably needs an IV line and some fluids into him. In fact, I *know* that's what he needs but we don't have any of that here and

288

it's not like there's a surgery or GP's office in the village that we could raid.'

Mitch shook his head. 'Alright, but there must be somewhere that we can get it from, surely?'

'Where Mitch? I really don't think there is anyone I know around here that…'

'That what? What is it Tess?'

She met her colleague's eyes and saw the hope and desperation in them. Shaking her head even as she said the words, unwilling to concede it was even a viable answer. 'Adams. Adams will have all that kit and more out at his place.'

Mitch's eyes widened in surprise. '*Adams*? Are you insane? We've lost half of our numbers to that crazy bastard and you're talking about just popping out to his place to pick up some medical kit? Seriously?'

She felt her anger rise as she sought to justify her suggestion. 'Alright smart arse. For better or worse, that's the best idea I've got to save Colin's life. So, let's hear yours. You're the man with all the answers at the moment so let's hear your fucking brainwave!'

Mitch held up his hands. 'Whoa Tess, whoa. Look, I didn't mean to take the piss it's just…I'm bloody terrified here. The thought of going anywhere near that madman again makes me feel sick to my stomach.'

'I get it, and I'm just as frightened as you. But what's the alternative? Let Colin deteriorate and die before help gets here?'

Mitch dropped his head into his hands and moaned loudly. He looked up again at her and gave a rueful smile. 'We're going out there aren't we?'

Tess returned his smile with one of her own even though she felt no humour to accompany it. 'We are Mitch. We have to. There's been too much death already and I will not let the sarge become another corpse.'

There was silence in the kitchen as Mitch digested her words. She watched as he wrestled with his conscience then seemed to come to a decision. He straightened up and without a word, picked up the carbine, released the magazine and checked the rounds within it before placing it back on the weapon which he then slung on to his shoulder. 'Okay boss, what's the plan?'

'Well, I wouldn't go so far as to call it a plan, but I reckon that Kenny stays here with Colin while you and I take the Rover and go get the med kit from Adams' place. I know it seems mental but I also think they'll be gone. Think about it; they've got to be away from here well before this storm breaks, otherwise they'll get caught when the roadblocks and checkpoints are put out.'

She could hear the hope apparent in his voice. 'You really think they'll be gone by the time we get there?'

'Yes Mitch, I really do. Why would they wait? They must have an extraction plan in place and they know they're against the clock on this one. Yes, they'll be wasting no time in getting the hell out of here. They've murdered two police officers and have lost two of their own. They're not going to be hanging around to answer for that, trust me.'

He let out a long sigh and bit on his lower lip. 'I hope you're right Tess. I really hope you're right.'

They were interrupted as Kenny entered the room indicating with his head to the corridor behind him. 'All clear folks. Walk wherever you want now; everything's been made safe.'

Tess nodded. 'Thanks Kenny, that's brilliant. Right, we don't have any time to waste so I'll fill you in on the next part of the plan while Mitch goes and gets the car started.' She watched as Mitch gave her the thumbs-up and left the room. Kenny turned to watch him depart then faced her again with an almost comical look of puzzlement.

'Tess, you can't seriously be thinking about going after these clowns, can you?'

She closed the distance between them and placed a hand on his shoulder before briefing him on her plan and the reasons behind it. To his credit, Kenny said nothing and allowed her to complete her brief. After a moment's silence he finally spoke.

'Yep. It's the right thing to do. If Colin doesn't get those fluids, at the very least he'll deteriorate very quickly and there's nothing we could do to stop that.' He looked up and met her eyes and she saw the determination there, a glimpse of the old soldier he once had been. 'Right Tess, get going. I'll head in and set up next to Colin. I'll keep trying the comms in there as well. Sooner or later something's got to work.'

'Thanks Kenny. We'll be as quick as we can but it's still going to take some time in this snow.'

He looked at her with a raised eyebrow. 'Well you'd better get a move on instead of loafing round here giving me your life story eh?'

Despite herself, she laughed at the older man's remark. Black humour, something she'd missed since leaving the Army. 'Alright Kenny, see you at the re-org.'

It was Kenny's turn to smile at the military term for the coming together after a firefight or battle. 'Aye, see you there lass. Move fast stay low, okay?'

Nodding her agreement, she brushed past him and left the room, walking along the corridor before picking her way over the jumbled furniture at the back entrance. Mitch had pulled the Land Rover closer to the door for her and was waiting in the vehicle with the engine running. Kicking through the small snow drifts, she made her way round the vehicle to the passenger side, opened the door and placed the carbine into the foot-well before clambering in. The fans were loud as Mitch sought to get some heat into the vehicle and she looked her colleague in the eye with what she hoped was confidence and determination.

'Right Mitch, let's get this done.'

44

Alpha's breathing was rhythmic and steady; his body acclimatised to the effort of jogging through the snow and self-regulating its systems. Beside him Bravo kept pace, matching his father's cadence, clouds of snow kicking up from his feet. Alpha looked ahead and could make out the edge of the woods that bordered his property, a darker lump in the night emerging from the curtain of snow. *Almost there.* The exfiltration plan had been in place for some time and was ready for immediate deployment. They just needed to collect a couple of items from the base before leaving. Alpha was determined that the mission would go ahead despite their losses. His team would not have sacrificed their lives in vain. This mission had taken the best part of a year to train for. A year of planning, preparation and rehearsals. A year of armed robberies to fund their escape and a life thereafter. The plan had obviously gone to rat shit with the death of half of his team, but even as he was running and feeling the burn in his thighs, he was adapting the plan in his head to suit their new circumstances. The old plan had been based upon a four-man team employing distraction and misdirection to facilitate Alpha getting the kill shot on the minister. He no longer had that option. With just him and Bravo, the plan needed a complete reworking. But it was still achievable. They could still do this.

Bravo glanced at his father running alongside him and felt a strange sensation in the pit of his stomach. It was a heavy coldness the like of which he could not remember having experienced before. A slow realisation crept over him as he became aware that he was looking at his father with an absolute void of emotion, no feelings whatsoever. He had never been like this before, had worshipped his father since he was a small boy, loving him with all of his heart. But something had changed. Looking at the man next to him Bravo could not even summon a crumb of affection with which to build upon. His brothers were dead and Alpha had failed to save them. *And for what?* They hadn't needed to go back in to the police station after they'd lost Delta, it had been completely unnecessary despite Alpha's justifications to the contrary.

Looking to his front again Bravo felt his attention drift as memories of his brothers played behind his eyes. Tears rolled down his face and were absorbed by the material of his face mask. Returning to the present he knew that the mission would continue even though their numbers were depleted. Knowing his father as he did, he knew there was no way that Alpha would abandon the mission while there remained a chance, however slim, that it could still be achieved. Bravo felt no trepidation at the prospect, merely a lack of any interest or enthusiasm for the task at hand.

Alpha slowed his pace as they approached the edge of the woods and wiped the accumulating snow from his face. Turning to Bravo he pointed into the woods at the base of a tree and they made their way towards it and took a knee. Alpha placed his hand on his son's shoulder and leaned in closer. 'Okay, we're still on track here as long as we keep moving. Let's get to the base and collect the rest of the kit and get the hell away from here before the cavalry arrives for plod back there.'

Bravo nodded, merely going through the motions, aware that Alpha would need to see some form of reaction.

'Once we've got the kit we'll get straight down to the boat. You guys checked it this morning, right?'

You guys. That would probably be the last time that Bravo heard himself included with his brothers. Again, he nodded and cleared his throat. 'Yeah Alpha, I checked it myself. Fuelled, loaded and ready to go.'

'Good man. Right, we've wasted enough time here. Let's get moving.'

Alpha stood and looked out of the woods at the thick snow falling beyond. *Good.* The longer the snow stayed heavy the longer it would take for reinforcements to arrive at the police station. He was quite confident that they had made good their escape but he never took anything for granted. Nodding to Bravo, the pair set off on a slow jog through the trees and deeper into the forest.

Even with the four-wheel drive engaged, Mitch struggled to keep the Land Rover on the road. Not that he could actually see the road, their world now reduced to a whirling vortex of snow lit by the glare of the headlights. Every change of direction provided the unwanted thrill of weightlessness as the rear end of the vehicle slid and skidded before coming back under control. Leaning forward in his seat he peered through scrunched-up eyes straining to see beyond the end of the car's bonnet. He swore under his breath and slowed the vehicle to a smooth stop, turning to look at Tess. 'Best I can tell, that's us at his gate.'

Tess looked out of her own window and could just make out the darker shadows of trees but she felt Mitch was right. This was roughly the area where the entrance to Adams' property was. She nodded, zipping her jacket all the way to her chin and pulled on her woollen hat, stretching the black wool down over her ears. 'Okay, let's pull this inside the gate and get moving, I don't like the idea of the sarge going even more downhill while we're pussyfooting around out here.'

'Fair enough Tess. If you guide me into the gate, I'll drive in and park up.'

Without a word she opened the car door, the cold immediate in the small confines of the car's interior. She slammed the door closed behind her and made her way towards the posts where she wrestled the gate from its closed position and with some difficulty moved it away from the posts, swinging it wide open. Shivering as the cold settled on her bare nose, she watched as Mitch inched the Land Rover through the gap between the posts. Once the vehicle had passed her, Tess dragged the heavy gate back to the posts and closed it. She jogged back to the car and opened the door, leaping back in to the warmth of the interior. 'That's cold out there Mitch!'

'Yeah, I could feel it when you opened the door.' He paused and looked over at her. 'I really hope you're right about this Tess; I don't want to face these maniacs again.'

She reached across and laid a hand on his arm. 'Me neither Mitch, believe me. But they'll be well on their way now. They're not going to hang around.'

They remained silent; the only noise in the vehicle the sound of the windshield wipers' rhythmic battle against the accumulating snow. Tess turned her thoughts to Colin and hoped that he was doing okay. She was sure they would find what they needed at Adams' base, stood to reason that he would keep decent medical kit on hand. Leaning forward in her seat, she strained her eyes to see beyond the headlight's reflected glare against the snow. She indicated with her hand to let Mitch know to take the right fork at the track junction and avoid the trap she and Colin had fallen into earlier. They kept their slow progress through the blizzard until she placed her hand on his arm. 'Stop here Mitch. Any closer and the headlights will show to anyone near the house.'

Mitch stopped the vehicle and turned off the ignition, plunging them into silence and blackness. For a moment there was only the ticking of the cooling engine as they quietly contemplated their next move. The stillness was broken by Tess clearing her throat.

'Okay. I'll lead as I know where we're going. We'll keep the pace slow and go together, no need for splitting up in this snow and darkness.' She turned to face her colleague. 'We've got a carbine and pistol to get us out of any bother we find ourselves in. First sign of trouble we get the hell out of there and fall back here, okay?'

'Yeah, no dramas.' He sighed and rubbed his face, registering the exhaustion for the first time. 'I'm holding you to your word though that there won't *be* any trouble!'

She leaned over and laid her hand on his arm. 'I don't think there will be Mitch, but on the off chance there is, we know what we have to do.' Without waiting for an answer, she lifted the rifle from the foot-well and clamped it against her chest. 'Let's go.' She exited the vehicle and heard Mitch's door close a second behind her own. Making her way to the front of the car, she waited a brief moment until Mitch reached her then moved off between the dark rows of trees. Sheltered from the wind by the dark forest on either side, they remained silent in the snow-muted hush of their surroundings.

Tess felt her senses on full alert as they moved towards the house. Even the sound of their footsteps as they squelched on the soft snow sounded extraordinarily loud to her. She wanted to believe her own assertion that trouble from Adams and the surviving kid was unlikely, but one

298

thing that the army had instilled in her was to always expect the worst-case scenario, that way you were always prepared. Even though in the dark she couldn't see the house, she knew from memory that they were getting close. The trees to their front widened and the wind returned as the shelter of the woods receded, buffeting her jacket. The bulk of the house loomed from the darkness and the swirling snow and she pointed towards it to ensure Mitch had seen it. His nod confirmed that he had.

Mitch felt his stomach roil with anxiety as they made their way slowly towards the building. He could hear his breathing become more ragged as they advanced. *At least there's no sign of life.* Clutching at this positive he glanced at Tess and once again was amazed at how confident his colleague appeared. *Mind you, after Afghanistan I suppose this is a walk in the park for her.* He wished he could find the same confidence, calm his jangling nerves a little at least. His eyes were drawn by a motion from Tess; a wave of her arm indicating that they were going to be changing direction.

Tess turned the corner of the building and led Mitch across the rear courtyard and towards the outbuildings where she had found Adams's secret base. The Toyota remained where it was but was now a misshapen white lump as the accumulated snow colonised the vehicle and altered it completely. When she reached the end building, she opened the door, stepping over the threshold quickly while aiming the carbine into the darkness beyond. She heard Mitch enter behind her and stop. After several moments she was happy that there was no activity in front of them and moved forward slowly, unwilling to risk switching on a light and exposing their presence. She heard the door close behind her and was glad Mitch was alert and thinking. Knees bent and weapon up in the aim, she advanced forward, all senses on high alert for the slightest sound or movement. They passed the doors to the left and right as they made their way to the room with the secret entrance. Tess led the way into the room and lowered the weapon as she approached the wardrobe. She stopped in front and turned to Mitch, leaning in and whispering in his ear.

'Right, the entrance to their location is actually through this wardrobe. You just step through it and you're at the top of a staircase. I'll go first and wait for you and we'll go down the stairs together okay?'

'Wait; we go *through* the wardrobe?'

She could hear the disbelief in his voice and was about to reply until he continued.

'What the hell is this? The Lion, the Witch and the Wardrobe?'

She smiled; her spirits lifted slightly by her colleague's sarcasm. Humour however dark, was always preferable to silent angst. 'C'mon you. Let's get this done.'

Reaching in and relying on memory, Tess found the panel at the back of the wardrobe and pushed, feeling the panel move away from her. She stepped wide over the base and into the cooler partition beyond. Opening the secret doorway wider, she took a further step to allow room for

Mitch. A small thump and a muffled curse behind her informed her that Mitch's taller frame had made contact with the top of the wardrobe. She smiled again and shuffled forward as she felt Mitch bustle in beside her. Tess whispered over her shoulder to him.

'Once we get down here, I'll use some light so we can search the place for med kit okay?'

'Sure.'

'Right, take it slow down these stairs. Last thing we need is to survive being killed by Adams and his cronies just to break our necks here.' She led them down the small staircase taking exaggerated care with her movements, determined to avoid any mishaps. When she realised that there were no more stairs, she held her hand out to the darkness in front of her and felt the smooth wood of a door. Fumbling around its edge she eventually made contact with the large iron doorknob she remembered from before and turned it as she felt Mitch at her back.

'Okay, there's an open door to your front so put your hands out to make sure you don't walk into the side of it.'

'Good advice Tess; I banged my head a good one on that bloody wardrobe back there!'

She stopped and waited for him to reach her side and she halted him with her hand on his chest. 'Right, wait here, I'll close the door then we can get some light on.'

He heard the rustle of her jacket as she moved and the closing of the door. A brief moment later he shielded his eyes from the glare of her torch as it lit up the floor at her feet. Unstrapping his own torch from his kit and turning away from it, he pointed it at the floor and clicked it on. He kept his eyes closed for several seconds, allowing them to adjust to the light before opening them fully. He could now make out a lot more detail and grinned at his colleague. 'That's better. Was beginning to think we'd be doing everything blind.'

Tess returned his smile. 'Yeah, this sure makes it easier. Right, I'll show you where a lot of their equipment is stored and see what we can find there.' Leading the way, she took Mitch down the second staircase and, ignoring the weapons room where she had disarmed the trip flares, led him into the larger communal room. She shone the torch beam into the various corners of the room. 'Right, I'll take left you go right. There's all sorts of boxes and cartons that I didn't inspect before so have a good look for IV kits and any other medical stuff you think we can use.'

Mitch followed her directive and using his torch to sweep the room in front of him, made his way to a collection of boxes and small crates stacked beside a table and chairs. He parted the cardboard flaps on the top container and shining the light inside, saw that it contained various foil-wrapped packages. Frowning, he picked one of the smaller packets up with his free hand and examined the writing on the side. *Biscuits Fruit.* Another packet yielded more information; *Lancashire hot pot.* He straightened up as he understood what he was looking at. *Rations; military rations.* Moving the box to one side, he began rummaging through the contents of a plastic container beneath.

Tess had found nothing more useful than bulk stationery among her pile and moved to the farthest corner of the room to a larger collection of boxes. Her heart quickened as her torch light illuminated the contents of the small box sat atop the others. *Gloves. Examination gloves.* Wasting no time, she placed this box by her feet and continued with her search. The next layer of cartons yielded nothing useful but as she moved one of these aside it exposed the box below and she gave a small grunt of triumph as its contents were revealed. Reaching in she retrieved the bag of saline solution, still sealed within its packaging. *Perfect.* Moving this heavier box alongside the gloves, she went back to investigating the remaining boxes in the pile. Tess saw what she was looking for almost immediately; a smaller box than the others with yellow hazard-warning stickers prominently displayed on the top and sides. Needles. She ripped the box open and studied the contents, wanting to make sure it contained exactly what she needed rather than just assuming so. Nodding to herself, she retrieved and examined several of the small packages. These were the cannulation kits; the needles and sleeves that would carry the saline solution into the body. There were mixed sizes too which she was happy to see as she wasn't sure what state Colin's veins would be in so it was good to have the choice, should they encounter problems getting a larger needle into the vein. She placed the box with her others and called to Mitch.

'Hey, let's wrap this up. I've got everything we need.'

Mitch stopped his own search and walked towards her. 'Good job. That was really quick.'

'Yeah, nice to have a bit of good luck for a change. C'mon, give me a hand with these.'

Wasting no time, they retraced their steps back up the stair case and out through the covert entrance, closing the wardrobe door behind them. Tess was feeling pleased that their search had taken so little time and that, against the odds, they had found exactly what they had needed. She led Mitch out of the building and back into the darkness and blizzard. Looking up at the sky, she squinted against the falling snow as it was driven against her face. *When the hell is this storm going to break?* She shook her head to disperse the snow and clear her face as they passed the snow-shrouded Toyota.

Alpha grabbed Bravo by the shoulder and hauled him to the ground alongside him, bringing the carbine up on aim as he dropped. *Movement.* He had definitely seen something moving beside the truck but had lost it again through the sheets of falling snow. *There!* He had it again; two dark shapes walking towards them through the knee-deep snow. His mind raced as he assimilated the information before him. He pondered the possibility that reinforcements had arrived at the station far earlier than he had anticipated but he discounted this as there had been no let-up in the storm to facilitate any support. Straining his eyes, he stared hard at the figures, noting that they were both holding objects in their arms. Whatever it was they were carrying, it had obviously been taken from here. Alpha had no doubt that they were Police officers but couldn't be sure how many there were. The dark figures began to appear clearer as they neared and his eyes widened with recognition. *The girl.* The female police officer from the station. *How the fuck did they get here before him?* He felt the rage well up from within. He'd had enough of these interfering cops and their determination to scupper his plans. He was contemplating his next decision when he felt Bravo rise up and stand behind him.

Bravo stood and raised his rifle at the approaching figures, smoothly flicking the safety lever to the fire position and resting his cheek on the stock as he sighted the targets through the driving snow. Tears rolled down his cheeks as the cocktail of sorrow and rage coursed through his system. He'd lost his brothers thanks to these fucking police officers and he wasn't going to let them away with it. The burst of flame from the muzzle and the simultaneous crack of the rounds splitting the silence startled him and dulled his senses for a moment. Turning his head away to clear the flashing from behind his eyes and the ringing in his ears, he opened his mouth in surprise as he was hauled unceremoniously to the ground. Landing hard on his backside, he glared at Alpha who grabbed him by his jacket front and snarled at him.

'What the fuck?'

Tess screamed and dropped the boxes as she ran back to Mitch, her colleague lying face down in the snow. She dropped to her knees and turned him over, leaning close and holding his head in her hands. 'Mitch, Mitch. Look at me Mitch.'

His eyelids fluttered and opened, his gaze unfocused and glassy. She slapped his face with her gloved hand. 'Mitch, c'mon. Look at me. It's Tess.' His eyes drifted towards her and she saw the recognition kick in. He coughed and a trickle of blood crept out of the corner of his mouth and ran down his chin.

'Hey Tess…I…don't feel so…good…'

Her heart sank and she heard herself moan. 'Mitch, no mate. You're fine buddy, you're going to be okay just…Mitch…MITCH!'

Mitch's eyes rolled back in their sockets and his head lolled to one side, the small river of blood now coursing across his pale face. Tess began to scramble to remove her glove but stopped when her eye was drawn to Mitch's chest. The area around the centre of his chest was darker than the material around it and she could see that it was reflecting what little light there was. Leaning in closer she now saw the holes torn into the fabric of the jacket, three small punctures oozing dark fluids. Her head dropped as she understood the significance of what she was seeing. The three rounds had all struck Mitch in the heart area, killing him almost immediately. Sobbing, she pulled her colleague's body into her chest, rocking softly until the harsh reality of the situation hit her; whoever had killed Mitch was still nearby. For a brief moment she thought about just staying where she was, holding her dead colleague and waiting for the bullet to end her own life. *Get the fucking misery over with.*

But her mood changed abruptly, the self-pity replaced with a cold rage that calmed and energised her at the same time. With care, she lowered Mitch's lifeless body on to the snow and closed his unseeing eyes with her gloved fingers. Remaining on her knees she turned to face the direction that the noise of the shots had come from and brought the rifle up on aim, looking through the telescopic sight system. The flurries of snow disturbed what little she could see and she changed her focus so that she was looking over the top of the sight itself waiting for the first view of the killers who had just taken the life of her colleague. She felt completely devoid of fear, her breathing steady and hold on the weapon firm. Her world narrowed to a few square yards of snow-covered courtyard.

Alpha lowered his weapon and turned back to Bravo, pushing his face close to that of his son. 'I can't see anything through the snow. You sure you got one of them?'

Bravo stared back, feeling no real motivation to answer. Alpha grabbed his shoulders in a rough grip and shook him.

'What the fuck's wrong with you? Answer me. Did you get one of them?'

Bravo nodded. 'Yes. Definitely. I shot the taller of the two and watched him drop.' He could see that Alpha was watching him intently, puzzled as to his son's lack of motivation. Eventually, Alpha released his grip, took hold of his weapon and stood, ensuring the corner of the wall afforded him cover from the police officers' line of sight.

'Okay. So that leaves one of them. Here's the plan; We move forward covering each other till we get to the building. We'll clear our way to the wardrobe then I'll enter while you cover. I'll go down and grab the bag and come back up and meet you. Any resistance we encounter, deal with as individuals, break contact, then RV at the jetty. Roger so far?' He watched Bravo nod his assertion, again however, without much enthusiasm. 'Good. Actions on one of us not showing, the other waits a max of ten minutes then goes. Understood?'

Bravo stood and ran a gloved hand across his face-mask before replying. 'Got it. Wait ten then go.'

There was a moment's silence as Alpha continued to scrutinise him, broken only by the gruff command. 'Let's move.'

Alpha led the way around the building, keeping the dwelling between them and the police officers. They jogged through the knee-deep snow drifts, breaths puffing in the frigid air, small clouds punctured by the relentless falling snow. When they reached the other side of the house, Alpha crouched at the corner of the gable and raised his rifle up as he cleared the area in front. A brief moment later he motioned for Bravo to keep moving and the pair covered the open ground and entered the doorway of the large outbuilding.

Tess stood up and keeping the weapon on aim, advanced towards the corner of the building where the shots had originated. Despite the obvious risk to her life she felt no fear, only a clear sense of purpose: She was going to kill these bastards if it was the last thing she did. Closing the distance rapidly, she reached the corner and dropped suddenly on one knee, leaning around the edge of the wall, finger on the trigger in readiness. *Nothing.* She scanned the area around her, convinced that the gunman couldn't be far when her eye was drawn towards the ground in front of her. The snow cover was disturbed, large depressions indicating where someone had recently been. She observed that the trail ran along the side of the house and without pause to reflect on the wisdom of her decision, stood and followed the tracks.

45

Alpha cursed as he noticed the trail of damp footprints leading from the wardrobe door. 'Bastards must just have been down here.' He looked at Bravo who showed no reaction to his statement. 'No matter. You stand guard up here and I'll fetch the grab bag.'

Bravo nodded and knelt by the open door, facing back towards the main entrance as his father climbed through the wardrobe. Bravo knew Alpha wouldn't be long, the grab bag with the money, passports and other documentation was always ready just to be scooped up in the event of an emergency. *An emergency.* Yeah, with both his brothers dead Bravo was pretty sure that this counted as an emergency alright. He pulled down his hood and tore off the face mask which was proving to be uncomfortably warm now that he was out of the wind. Tossing the white covering to one side, he rubbed his gloved hand through his thick, dark hair and sighed, staring off into the distance.

Alpha saw right away that the police officers must have been looking for medical kit, judging by the mess they had left among the piles of boxes and the items that were missing. *Good.* Might keep them occupied just that little bit longer if one or more of them was seriously wounded. Slinging his weapon around his back and holding the torch in his mouth, he pulled a chair into the centre of the floor and stood on it. Reaching up with both arms, he pushed a polystyrene ceiling tile up then ripped it down, tossing it to one side. His hands entered the dark space above and closed upon an unseen object. He explored the object with his hands for several more moments before finding the handle and dragging the bag from its hiding place. Stepping down onto the floor, he guided the beam of the torch with his mouth and opened the zip of the canvas holdall, examining the contents within. *All there.* He was pretty sure the police would not have found the bag without conducting a thorough search but it paid to make sure. He took the torch from his mouth and headed back towards the stairs.

Tess paused at the gable end of the building studying the disturbed snow at her feet. With her eyes she followed the direction the trail led and realised immediately where it was headed. *Their secret base.* Adams must have something that he needed in there otherwise it made no sense for him to waste any more time than was necessary. Not after killing another police officer and with no real idea how many more were in the area. Her breathing hitched as she remembered Mitch lying dead in the snow not fifty feet from where she was standing. She knelt beside the wall of the building and leant against it as she thought about what to do next. *Kill them. Kill them all.* The coldness of her thoughts settled her breathing and focussed her mind. A small voice inside her urged caution and a retreat to the Police Station but it was overwhelmed by the icy decisiveness of her prevailing mood. Decision made, she stood and advanced across the open ground, carbine in the shoulder ready to be brought up on aim at a moment's notice.

Bravo heard the sound of Alpha coming through the wardrobe and glanced around in time to see his father's leg stretching out of the open door. Alpha pointed towards the large double doors set into the main wall. 'We'll go out that way. I've got the key.'

Bravo nodded and stood, following his father but keeping his attention on the door behind them, well aware that there was another policeman alive out there somewhere. Alpha's decision made sense; the doors opened directly onto the gravel track that led to the jetty and also meant that they weren't exposing themselves to any plod still hanging around by going out the same way that they had come in. He reached Alpha and turned to face the entrance while his father unlocked the large doors. He heard the click of the padlock being opened and the rattle of the lock being removed from the bolt. The harsh crash of the bolt slamming home made him jump but he turned back to his father just as the doors were opened fully. Alpha picked up the bag and strode out of the building, taking a glance behind to confirm that Bravo was following him. Satisfied, he slung the bag over his shoulder and carried the carbine loosely in his right hand as he made his way onto the track. A burst of gunshots split the still night, followed closely by Bravo's yell of surprise. Alpha spun around in a fluid motion, dropping to one knee and bringing the carbine up, the weapon now pointing into the darkness of the building where the shots had originated from.

Tess paused; her night vision completely destroyed by the bright flashes from the muzzle that had seared their image onto her retinas. Her ears rang with the concussion of her shots and she was tempted to wait for a few seconds until they cleared but she remembered her training. *Fire then move; the enemy will return fire at your last known position so don't be there to accept it.* She took two large steps to her right and dropped to one knee, aiming the weapon towards the open stable doors. A burst of flashes from outside the building was accompanied by the thud of bullets slamming into the wall where she had just been and the sound of the returning fire booming off the walls. Almost instantly, she responded, firing a controlled burst of five rounds at the area where she had seen the flash. A moment later she scuttled a further few feet to her left and had only just made it when more fire was returned, the bullets ricocheting and sparking off the floor where she had just been kneeling. She fired back, this time a longer burst with her aim alternating to each side of the flash. She was rewarded with a yell and made out a concerned but unintelligible question from one of the unseen gunmen.

313

Alpha cursed aloud and rolled over several times until he was behind the cover of an old generator. The pain in his side was like fire and he knew he would be bleeding badly. He heard Bravo's worried call but ignored it as he turned on his back and explored the wound with his fingers. The blood was streaming out of the gash just above his waist, hot and viscous. Ignoring the unpleasant sensation, he ran his fingers around his side and back, looking for an exit wound but found none. *Shit*! The bullet was lodged somewhere in his lower abdomen. He knew he had no time to waste so pulled the field dressing from the pocket on his combat jacket and tore the packaging with his teeth. With furious motions he dressed the wound as best he could and screamed with rage against the pain that kicked in as he tightened the bandage around him.

Bravo yelled again in the direction of the scream. 'Alpha, are you alright?'

There was a pause, everything still in the hush of the falling snow then the reply came.

'Bravo, I'm good. Caught a minor in my side but mobile and combat effective, roger so far?'

'Roger Alpha.'

'Okay, break contact here, you get to the boat and prep for exfil and I will follow figures one, over.'

Bravo nodded as he adhered to Alpha's direction. He half stood in a crouch and walked backwards with his weapon pointed back towards the building until he felt confident that no-one inside could engage him. Turning swiftly, he began jogging down the snow-covered path towards the jetty.

Tess cocked her head to one side as she strained to hear what was being said. She believed that she'd hit one of them due to the frantic nature of their conversation and she'd picked out the phrases break contact and boat. *A boat? Is that how they're getting out of here?* It would make sense. With all the roads closed and likely to be that way for at least a day, a boat would be the perfect way to escape. She squinted, trying without success to see through the night and relentless snow outside. *Have they gone?* There was no more movement and there had been no shots for some time. She put herself in their position; one of them was injured, and they had to know that their exfiltration plan was compromised. Tess thought about what she would do in the same situation and didn't think she'd be waiting around. They would know that the police didn't have a vessel with which to follow them and they would want to make the most of their lead in the bad weather before a proper search for them could be implemented. *No, they'll be legging it right now.* She changed the magazine on the weapon for a fresh one, again, reacting to memory born of thousands of training drills a lifetime before. Standing with confidence, she strode towards the door determined to catch her quarry before they made good their escape. Pausing at the door, she leaned her head out slightly, peering into the gloom and listening for any movement. *Nothing.* Satisfied that the coast was clear she stepped out of the building and into the open. The burst of automatic fire shocked her and slammed her against the wall in the same instant, the carbine tumbling from her fingers as she tumbled to the ground, her face retaining a startled expression.

Alpha stood and took a step towards the fallen police officer. The pain in his side was like a red-hot knife skewering his lower abdomen and he screamed and grasped at his stomach. *FUCK!* He tried another step and the agony intensified. Pausing for several moments, he studied the body with feral intensity. When there was no movement, he nodded to himself, having arrived at the decision that the plod was dead. He wanted to check but knew he needed to save his strength for the journey to the boat. It was only a matter of a few hundred metres but with his wound...He turned, took a deep breath and started his awkward shuffle along the jetty track. The pain was instant and took his breath away but he focused his mind and pushed the immediacy of the agony to one side, still hurting, but something he could fight through for the time being.

Tess opened her eyes and felt the snow settle upon her face. Groaning as she pushed herself up to a sitting position, leaning her head back on the wall of the building. She yelped in pain as the back of her head felt like it was on fire. Running a shaky hand over the area, she felt her hair matted in a sticky clump. *Blood.* Confused she tried to remember what happened and a jolt of pain in her chest as she took a breath helped refresh her memory. *Oh shit, I've been shot. I'VE BEEN SHOT!* She became panicky, her breathing ragged as she probed her chest and abdomen for signs of the wounds. Despite her chest feeling painful, she found no blood to indicate where she had taken the hit.

As her panic abated and she could concentrate fully, she put the pieces together. She *had* been shot but the vest had stopped the rounds from penetrating, slamming against the wall and the impact cracking her head. With this knowledge, she examined the wound in the back of her head with a bit more care and was relieved to find that the injury was not deep or wide and the blood was not streaming out, more a slow ooze judging by the feel of her fingers. She reached a shaking hand out to retrieve the rifle and swore as she brought the object up, staring at it as she held it in front of her face. The carbine was broken, the stock shattered and the bolt mechanism in pieces. The weapon must have taken a couple of direct hits from one of Adams' goons, probably saving her life in the process. Problem was, she was now without a weapon as the murderers were making good their escape.

She felt tears of frustration roll down her cheek as she hurled the useless weapon away from her. *So bloody close!* She couldn't believe it: The killers of Mitch, Fletch, Mark and old Liza were about to escape and there was nothing she could do about it. She had no doubt that this escape had been planned and set up well in advance and, to that end, there was probably no chance that Adams and his son

317

would ever be heard from again. They were going to get away with it and all because she couldn't just have waited another couple of minutes and followed their tracks. *FUCK!* Her teeth were gritted in sheer rage as the helplessness of her situation became clear.

With no weapon she had no chance of stopping them. She remembered what she and Mitch had come for originally and decided that her only course of action was to retrieve the medical kit, return to the Sarge and inform him that she'd let the killers escape. Taking it slow, she stood, using the wall behind her as support. She didn't feel any dizziness or nausea, only a tightness in her chest, no doubt the legacy of one of Adams' bullets being stopped by her vest. Giving the useless weapon lying on the snow a glance of contempt, her mind was racing, looking to identify some way she could stop Adams from escaping and causing further harm... Her thoughts ran on as she was prompted to think about how many times the former Special Forces soldier and his team had almost killed her.

Tess remembered that Mitch had a Glock and forced herself away from the wall, moving back towards her colleague's body. Steeling herself for the macabre task ahead, she shut all thoughts from her mind other than the base functions she required to retrieve the gun. On reaching the snow-shrouded body, Tess increased her stride and dropped on one knee without hesitation. She kept her focus small, an intense stare at the uniform around Mitch's hip. She quickly unfastened the holster and pulled the weapon free, ramming it into her coat pocket. She tore open the Velcro securing straps on the side of the holster and removed the spare magazines, putting these into the same pocket as the gun. Standing up, she spun on her heel and strode back towards the building, breathing in short, jerky inhalations. She felt a little better knowing she had a weapon with which to at least consider going after the killers but could see little point in trying to match the firepower of their carbines with the pistol.

A new-found feeling of determination fired her up and she found herself getting angry at her lack of options. Standing on wobbly legs she took a few moments to centralise herself and try to come up with an idea. She looked in the direction that Adams and his accomplice had gone and then turned her attention back to the building. Her eyes widened as she remembered the room with the trip-wire and the possibility that there may still be a rifle that she could use to try and halt the killers. She started walking towards the building when the memory of her last visit to the bottom floor of the building was recalled in full clarity and she stopped dead, eyes widening as the revelation hit her. There *was* a weapon down there. A weapon so perfect for the task at hand that it could have been placed there for this exact situation. Spurned into action, she began running back towards the building, offering up a silent prayer that the item she was depending on was still there.

Tess yelped as she bumped her head hard clambering through the wardrobe and into the dark stairwell beyond. Turning on her torch she descended the staircase as fast as she could, treading a fine line between speed and calamity. Bursting through the first door, she continued her rapid clambering and arrived at the door controlled by the push-button lock. Reaching for it, her brain quickly threw negative scenarios into her mind; the combination had been changed, the door was booby trapped, or, worst of all, they'd taken the weapon with them. Her fingers trembled as she keyed in the lock's default setting as she had done in what seemed like a lifetime before. Clamping the torch under her armpit, with her free hand she twisted the metal door knob and gave an audible sigh of relief when it opened, revealing the dark room inside.

Shining the torch beam into the room she stood still, scrutinising every inch of the area the beam highlighted, hyper-alert to the possibility of more trip-wires. Content that there were none, Tess advanced towards the corner where she had seen the weapon on her last visit and felt her pulse quicken as the torch beam alighted upon the packaging. Working quickly, she unfastened the metal clasps on the crate and hauled the lid open, nodding when she saw the contents inside. She placed the torch on a nearby shelf and positioned it so that the beam fell upon the box and its contents. With two hands she lifted the weapon from its holding cavity and turned it in the glow of the torch light, giving a silent prayer of thanks that it had

320

still been there. Her mouth tightened as a wave of determination engulfed her. She was back in the game. Adams and his boy might be a force to be reckoned with as they were armed and trained, but even they were going to be hard pushed to defend against this weapon. *Yeah, carbines are all well and good gents but let's see how you do against an anti-tank launcher!* Checking to make sure that the instructions remained as she remembered, printed and embossed on the weapon itself, she grabbed the torch and hurried back up the stairs towards the escaping killers.

46

Bravo looked up as his eyes caught the movement where the trees met the jetty. Bringing the carbine up on aim, he sighted on the dark figure emerging from the woods. He let out a small breath he was unaware that he had been holding and lowered the weapon. *Alpha.* As his father's form became clearer, Bravo frowned and moved along the stone jetty towards him.

'I'm good Bravo, I'm good. Fucking plod just winged me. Let's get going, there's no time to waste.'

Bravo stared at his father for a moment before nodding and turning back. He jogged along the jetty, taking care not to slip on the slick cobbles beneath the snow. The boat was secured with lines at the bow and stern and was only slightly lower than the jetty due to the high tide. Bravo slung his carbine across his back and using both hands, climbed down the few rungs of the cold iron ladder until his feet touched the deck of *Minerva.* A thirty five-foot sloop with serious modifications, Alpha had named the boat after the Roman goddess of war and the SAS Regiment's official magazine, *Mars and Minerva.* Bravo opened the hatch that gave access to the quarters below and noted with satisfaction that everything was still in the same position as they had left it during their earlier preparations. *Their.* That word again. The wave of sorrow engulfed him as it hit home once again that he was now alone, his brothers dead. But for Alpha, he would be a single entity, no longer a team. A grunt and a curse caught his attention and he turned to see his father clambering down the ladder with obvious difficulty. As before, his instinct was to assist but he paused and watched as Alpha's dogged determination saw him complete his descent and join him on the deck of the boat.

Alpha grunted against the pain and bent over, his free hand clutching at the area around the wound. He looked up and met Bravo's eyes. 'Help me get below and sort this fucking wound out or I'm going to be more of a hindrance than a help.'

Bravo moved to his father's side and took the carbine from his hand, leaning it against the stern rail. He was shocked to see that, despite the frigid temperature, his father's face was coated in a sheen of sweat. Bravo moved around him and descended the small wooden steps into the cabin below. He waited at the base of the steps for Alpha to begin climbing down and placed his hand into the small of Alpha's back, providing support as his father awkwardly descended. Once he was stood beside him, Bravo guided Alpha to the seating area and lowered him onto the cushions. Content that he was comfortable, he left Alpha sat upright and stretched above him, opening a small, latched cupboard from which he retrieved a medical kit.

Alpha was already removing his webbing vest and jacket in anticipation and Bravo left him to it as he laid out the items he would need on the small table between them. He saw that Alpha was now removing his t-shirt and exposing the bloodied dressing around his lower abdomen. Bravo could see his father's chest heaving as he fought through the agony that he must have been feeling every time he stretched. With the shirt removed Alpha looked at his son.

'You're going to need probe and forceps to get this fucking thing out of me, okay?'

Bravo identified the items among the collection on the table. Reaching back up to the cupboard he pulled out a large bottle of distilled water, well aware that the procedure he was about to attempt would be bloody and require a lot of irrigation to keep the wound visible. He strapped on a head torch and turned it on, nodding with satisfaction at the strong output of light.

Alpha was speaking to him again. 'This is obviously going to be very fucking painful but you know what you're doing, we've trained and practised this hundreds of times. If I pass out, make me comfortable then get us out to the open sea as fast as possible okay?'

Bravo nodded as he pulled on the surgical gloves and selected the scissors from his row of implements. He indicated for Alpha to lay down and waited until his father was prone. Working quickly, he cut the bandage with the scissors and gently pulled away the sopping, blood-heavy dressing. Alpha gave a sharp intake of breath as the wound was exposed once again. Tossing the bloodied dressing to one side, Bravo leaned in and looked at the wound, the seeping blood reflecting the light of the head torch. He could see that it was a steady trickle of blood rather than spurting which would have indicated arterial damage. Grabbing a swab and removing it from its sterile packaging, he opened the water bottle and with a quick glance at his father, poured the liquid on to the wound, immediately following it with a wipe from the swab. Ignoring Alpha's gasp, he examined the wound, stretching the entry hole slightly as he attempted to identify the trajectory of the bullet inside his father's abdomen. He almost grinned with surprise as he saw immediately what he had been looking for; the metal of the bullet reflecting back from within the muscle wall of Alpha's abdomen. Bravo shook his head at his good fortune. The bullet was not very deep at all and would not require the lengthy probing and searching that he had anticipated. He stood up and laid his hand on his father's shoulder.

'You're really lucky Alpha; the round's only in a half inch at most and there doesn't look like there's any other major damage.'

Alpha groaned. 'Well, let's not waste any time congratulating ourselves on how lucky I am, let's just get the fucking thing out and me back on my feet okay?'

Bravo felt a flicker of irritation at his father's remark but it passed in a moment as he concerned himself with the task at hand. He flushed the wound with another squirt from the bottle, his father cursing as a new wave of pain accompanied his son's actions. Crouching down until his face was close to the wound, he swabbed away the mix of blood and water. With a steady hand he pushed the slim forceps into the mouth of the wound and his father stiffened immediately with a roar of agony leaving his lips. Bravo ignored this, knowing that to stop would only prolong the suffering. He felt the tips of the forceps grate against the metal of the bullet head and he drew them back a fraction. Giving his father a quick glance, with a small movement of his fingers, Bravo opened the forceps and pushed them further into the wound. Alpha's scream filled the small cabin and his chest heaved up and down as Bravo continued his attempts to grasp the bullet. It was proving trickier than he had first anticipated, the round lodged tighter against the abdomen wall than he would have thought possible. He had carried out this procedure on pigs, procured by Alpha and used during their medical training lessons, so he was quite familiar with the process. Feeling that he had a good grip of the bullet once again, he clamped down harder on it, determined to make this the last time. *Got it!* He could feel the bullet secure within the tips of the forceps and withdrew the implement slowly, immune now to his father's hoarse cries as he concentrated on removing the foreign object. With the forceps fully removed he brought them up to his eyes and looked at the small metal object clamped in the jaws of the implement. The round had been slightly squashed by whatever it had hit but there was no mistaking the killing end of a 5.56 mm bullet. He placed the forceps on the table and rinsed the wound again with the water. Using the swabs, he cleaned and dried the area as best he could then opened the sutures kit. With a deftness born of practice, he set to work stitching up the open wound. It took him no time at all and he placed a clean dressing over his handiwork and secured it with a bandage around Alpha's abdomen.

Alpha felt the bile rise as the waves of pain rocked him. He was almost about to turn his head to one side and let the vomit come when he realised that Bravo had stopped. Panting from the exertion of enduring the invasive trauma, he raised his sweat-drenched head and looked at his son. 'Good work Bravo, good work. Get us away from here mate, quick as you can.'

47

Alpha heard the engine cough once again and stall. Gritting his teeth in both pain and frustration he called out to Bravo again. 'What the fuck are you doing? I thought you checked this thing?'

Bravo struggled to keep the anger from his voice. 'I did. And it was fine. I don't know what the hell is wrong with it now.'

Alpha pushed himself up into a sitting position and yelled as the pain of his wound sent a river of agony up the side of his body. Panting with exertion, he was just about readying himself for the effort of standing when he heard the engine catch with a deep, throaty cough that smoothed out to an even throb. *Thank fuck for that.* He reached for the bottle of water Bravo had left on the table for him and gulped the entire contents down. His hair and forehead were slick with sweat and his side felt literally like it was on fire. He hoped the antibiotics would do the trick and stave off any infection. Bravo was moving on the deck above him and he heard the thump of the mooring lines as they were cast off. The boat moved a little and he knew Bravo had just pushed off from the wall of the jetty. The footsteps above moved to the wheel and Alpha nodded as he heard the gears engage and the throttle increase as the motion of the boat become more pronounced.

Bravo turned the wheel to set them on a course to get them out of the bay and into the open waters beyond. They hadn't had time to discuss any new plan as their first priority had been to get some distance between themselves and any back up that plod had managed to contact. Their own plan had now gone to shit and, he assumed, would be dropped due to Alpha being combat ineffective. Bravo tried to second guess what they would do now and could only assume that they would bypass the Leuchars leg of the plan and continue with the exfil they'd put together for after the assassination. A frown crept on to his brow as he considered this from Alpha's perspective and the suspicion that his father, against all reason, might still not be willing to let this go. Bravo increased the throttle as they made deeper water, the swell starting to lift the bow as the waves rounded the headland.

Alpha yelled up the small stairwell. 'Stick the autopilot on and come down here.' He heard movement above him and a moment later Bravo descended into the small cabin area and looked him up and down.

'How's the side Alpha?'

'Fucking sore. But that's not what we need to talk about. We need to revisit the plan and come up with an alternative to get this fucker before we disappear.'

329

Despite his previous suspicions, Bravo could still not believe what he was hearing. 'Alpha…you're pretty banged up. There's no way we can still carry this off.' He was about to carry on when he saw the blackness in his father's eyes and the slight cock of the head as Alpha held him in his cold stare.

'There's *always* a fucking way soldier. ALWAYS!' The shout boomed in the small cabin, causing Bravo to flinch. 'We will get this bastard if it's the last thing we do, understand?' When there was no immediate answer he leaned forward. 'I said, understand?'

Bravo shook his head. His despondency was slowly morphing into a cold anger and he met his father's reptilian stare with a glare of his own. 'How? I mean seriously, how the fuck are we meant to do this? You can't do anything. You're combat ineffective Alpha. The operation is over. We have to abort. Come back another day with another plan.'

Alpha could not believe what he was hearing. 'Are you fucking insane? Of course we're going to carry this out; we've worked too long and too hard not to. Yes, Plan A is gone but we'll adapt it and make it work with the assets we have. As we always do. So, get on board with this and start thinking about how we're going to achieve it.'

Bravo remained resolute. 'No. Absolutely no way. This is madness, that's all this is. Think about it; whatever plan you say we're going to come up with will basically involve me doing everything. It's crazy Alpha, you must see that!'

Alpha stood, the rage within him overriding the pain of his wound. 'Don't you fucking dare try to tell me what I must and mustn't see you little shit. Madness? No. We're doing this and we're going to succeed and carry on with our exfil as planned.' He stepped forward and rammed his finger into his son's chest. 'Your brothers didn't die out there just so you could chicken out of the mission when things got a little complicated.'

Bravo's punch was mid-flight before he had even registered his intent. The mention of his brothers had triggered a cold rage and his fist connected with the side of his father's face with a satisfying crunch. Alpha's expression was almost comical as he tumbled to the deck on his wounded side, a bellow of agony and rage emitting from his rictus of a mouth. For a brief moment, Bravo stood rooted to the spot as the consequences of his action sunk in. Torn between respect for his father and fear of the inevitable retribution that would follow, he was unsure what to do. The low, guttural growl from Alpha as he hauled himself up from the deck gave him all the indication he needed to decide on his course of action; *Run*.

48

Tess burst through the trees, heart pounding as she saw the empty jetty before her. She stopped and was overwhelmed with dismay as her first thought was that she had missed them, that the killers had escaped. Then she saw it; around a hundred metres away, a boat heading out to open sea. *Shit!* With no time to lose she sprinted down to the jetty, slipping and almost falling on the slick cobblestones beneath the snow. She could see that the snow was definitely easing and the grey light of a new day was beginning to push in from the horizon.

At the end of the jetty she paused and caught her breath for a moment as she studied the boat. It was still only a hundred metres or so away and she could see it clearly in the muted dawn light. The boat was moving up and down in the swell but not to the point where it would be impossible to hit. *Okay, stop faffing about and get this done.* Dropping to one knee, she laid the tubular device across her thigh and read the yellow instructions stencilled on the olive-green casing. She nodded as the long-ago familiarisation lesson came back to her. The anti-tank weapon wasn't one that she'd ever used or even practiced with again but the operation was designed to be as simple as possible.

She removed the protectors at each end of the device, exposing the hollow tubes. Taking a firm grasp of the fabric loops at each end of the weapon she yanked hard, extending the device to its full length with a reassuring click informing her that she had succeeded. The sight popped up automatically, a small, erect rectangle standing proud of the tube. Ensuring she was keeping her fingers away from the detent trigger mechanism, she raised the device and laid it upon her right shoulder, adjusting its position until she was looking through the sight. She manoeuvred her head around until the reticules in the prism became clear, the lines and numbers now prominent in the display. Turning slowly until she was facing the departing boat, she then lined the sight on to her target. She assessed that the vessel was getting close to two hundred metres away and could actually see two people on the deck near the stern. Her attention was diverted for a moment as she attempted to discern what they were doing but she re-focused her efforts back to the weapon. With the target clear in her sight picture, Tess took a deep breath and gently ran her fingers on to the top of the rubber that covered the trigger mechanism. With a final check through the sight, she lined the boat up with the range line and pressed firmly down on the rubber.

The noise and shock of the projectile shooting out of the end of the tube was instantaneous. She watched as the missile followed a graceful trajectory over the water and towards the vessel and held her breath as the projectile was lost from her sight. She thought for a moment it had dropped into the sea but a brief second later, the flash and the loud bang that carried over the water told her she had struck her target. A plume of smoke obscured the bow of the boat but she could see that the vessel was listing badly already. Releasing her breath, she stared at the sinking boat across from her, the hull now showing its white underside as it toppled into the frigid, grey water. Tess stood and tossed the launcher to one side, its task now complete and safely inert with no projectile inside the weapon. It landed with a soft thud in the snow and she gave it a small smile of thanks for its service. Putting her hand into her pocket, she retrieved the Glock and smoothly removed the magazine from the pistol, checked that it was full, then reloaded. She racked the slide back slightly to confirm there was still a round in the chamber and was gratified to see the brass glint within the dark orifice. With a strange sense of calm, she turned her attention back to the pewter sea in front of her, looking for any sign of survivors.

49

Alpha kicked away from the sinking boat, his breathing loud and rapid as the freezing water assailed his senses. He was confused as to what had happened; one minute he was about to tear Bravo's head off for his insubordinate behaviour, the next he was sliding across the deck and tumbling over the stern rail. He attempted to control his breathing, well aware that he was in danger of drowning if he did not. *What the fuck happened?* He cast his memory back to before he was falling and remembered the bang. *A bang.* He clearly remembered it now but couldn't work out what it had been. The engine was just below where he and Bravo had been stood so it wasn't an explosion down there. And there was nothing he could think of near the bow that could cause such a thing. Swiftly, he put the *what-ifs* out of his mind and concentrated on his immediate survival. By his reckoning he was a few hundred metres from the jetty, wounded and in danger of freezing to death in the frigid water. He groaned as the pain in his side pierced him once again. Every stretch of his arms as he breast-stroked around the sinking boat was a fresh hell. It was only then that the thought of his son hit him. *Where the hell is Bravo?*

Bravo spat and choked on another mouthful of seawater. He continued stroking towards the shore, alternating between a crawl and a breast-stroke. He felt weighted down by his clothing but knew he could make it to shore before it became a serious issue. He had always been a strong swimmer, loved body-surfing the big autumn rollers that broke on the sandbar south of the jetty. It was paying him dividends today. He had picked out the small cairn on the headland as a marker and could see he was getting closer to the shore, grateful that he hadn't been caught in a riptide or outgoing current. A twinge of guilt took him by surprise and he paused again, treaded water and turned, scouring the sea for any sight of his father. The boat was all but gone, the keel upturned and clearly visible just above the swell of the waves. He couldn't really make out much more between the rise and fall of the swell due to his low position and he shook his head.

Shivering hard, he felt his lips tremble and began swimming again, hard and fast to get whatever heat he could back into his limbs. *What the hell had caused the boat to sink?* He remembered simultaneously feeling and hearing a huge explosion before being knocked overboard. He also recalled the crazed expression in Alpha's eyes as he'd cornered him on deck. For a brief moment Bravo had been certain that his father was going to kill him, the cold stare, the lack of any expression whatsoever on his face, despite the agony that his wound must have been causing. Spitting out another mouthful of the freezing sea-water, Bravo reflected that the explosion may just have saved his life.

Tess remained crouched behind the large boulder watching as the figure made its way to the shore. She had initially been surprised to see someone survive but then remembered she had fired the projectile into the bow area and that the men had been at the stern of the boat. The figure was struggling now but she made no effort to move. The last 24 hours had taught her never to underestimate these people, a lesson paid for with the most serious of consequences. It took her a moment to realise that she felt nothing. No regrets for her actions, no jubilation at the success of halting Adams' escape, no joy at the prospect of arresting the lone survivor and taking him into custody. For some unknown reason the thought of her impending arrest report entered her mind and she shook her head at the field day the hand-wringers at HQ would have at the thought of a PC firing an anti-tank weapon at members of the public. She probably would be out of a job after this. Her eyes narrowed at the thought. *No matter.* She didn't give a shit what happened to her just as long as she stopped these bastards once and for all. Snapping back to the present with a jolt, she concentrated her attention on the figure approaching the slick, black rocks on the foreshore.

Alpha could see that he was going to make it. The rocks weren't far now and he still had more than enough strength to cover the distance. While his hands felt numb and his wound still screamed at him, by and large he wasn't in bad shape, all things considered. His mind was already looking ahead to his next move. He needed to get back to base, warm up and get some dry clothes or he would succumb to hypothermia. Glancing around again, he searched for Bravo's face between the peaks and troughs of the waves but there was no sign of his son. He felt conflicting emotions now that they were in a completely different situation. Alpha knew that, back on the boat, he had been close to really hurting Bravo for his insubordination, but now all he really wanted was for his son to have survived.

Bravo hauled himself over the rocks, his numb hands barely registering any sensation. Clambering to his feet he slipped on the slimy seaweed and threw his arms out to balance himself. Taking more care with his footing, he advanced slowly across the slick, round boulders. The wind was cutting through him and his teeth were chattering hard against each other. His instinct was to pick up the pace but he knew he would risk injuring himself. Looking up, he saw that he was now only ten feet or so away from the red earth of the land, a small outcrop of rock and scrubby grass poking out of the blanket of snow. He gave a small grunt of triumph as his hands touched the grass and he pulled himself up the small obstacle until he was standing upright on firm ground. Wasting no time, he started jogging towards the jetty path that would lead him back to the base.

His gait felt awkward and he knew he had to hurry; his legs also numb from the frigid swim. Lurching between the trees, he made his way onto the snow-covered path and was just about to try running faster when the voice stopped him.

'That's far enough you murdering bastard. Don't move another inch.'

50

The gun was steady in her hand as she watched the man turn to face her, hands raised above his head. She saw immediately that he was young, late teens at the most, but any vestiges of sympathy she may once have harboured had dissipated along with the life of her colleague. For a moment she locked eyes with the boy and felt nothing. She could see he was freezing, could hear his teeth knocking against each other and the prominent shivers affecting his body. Again, she was surprised at her utter lack of emotion. 'Get on your knees and keep your hands on your head.'

Bravo looked at the policewoman and saw instantly that she was serious. She showed no indication of any nervousness, her gaze steady and the pistol rock-solid in her grip. He could feel himself starting to fade, the cold now creeping into him with lethal intent. Sighing as he realised he had neither the strength nor inclination to fight anymore, Bravo lowered himself to his knees. He tried to keep his hands on his head but kept losing his balance and had to reach out to stop himself falling over.

The crack of the shot startled Tess even though she had fired it. The puff of snow beside the boy showed her that her aim was true. She wasn't falling for any more of their tricks. 'Keep your hands on your head or I'll put the next one into your stomach.' She watched as the boy eventually made eye contact with her and slowly carried out her directive. Tess moved closer to him, approaching him in an indirect arc until she was behind him and just beyond his reach.

She removed the handcuffs from her webbing vest and was just moving forward when a movement caught her eye. Too late she tried to duck but Adams' punch still caught her on the side of the head. Her vision was suddenly an explosion of stars as she staggered under the impact of the blow. She raised the weapon up as she fell backwards and pulled the trigger, blind to where or what she was aiming at. As her body crashed to the ground her sight returned just in time to see the sole of Adams' boot as it stamped on her face. Tess managed to turn her head slightly but the impact was still horrific and she screamed in agony. She pointed the pistol in Adams' direction and was about to fire when a blow hit her arm and the gun spun out of her grasp and disappeared from view. Her heart was hammering in her chest as her situation became clear: Adams was going to kill her. She rolled over several times to create some space with which to get to her feet, but he was on her, his weight knocking the breath from her.

Alpha straddled the woman, pinning her arms under his legs and driving his fist into her bleeding face. He grinned at the satisfying crunch of shattered cartilage and the yelp

341

from the mashed mouth. He punched the unprotected face just under the eye socket and felt it break, with a scream of agony splitting the air. Placing his hands around the woman's small neck, he applied pressure, digging his thumbs hard into her windpipe. She began choking beneath him and bucking hard, trying to throw him off.

Tess knew she was fighting for her life. She couldn't see and couldn't breathe and she could feel her strength sapping away. Bucking her hips, she tried to twist but there was absolutely no give. She threw her arm out to one side, sweeping the area she could reach, praying her fingers would brush up against the Glock. *Come on, please, PLEASE!* Her sweeping became more manic as she felt herself starting to succumb to the blackness. She had just about given up when the hands removed themselves from her neck and she drew in the most wondrous breath of her life even as her constricted throat choked on the life-saving air.

The gunshot shocked her and she screamed, wondering where she had been hit. When no pain was apparent, she opened her eye and took in the scene in front of her. The boy was stood above her, the Glock hanging loosely by his side. He paid her no attention but was looking off to one side. Tess turned her head slowly, not wanting to give him any reason to shoot again but needing to see what he was staring at. Adams' body lay on its back, arms and legs spread as he stared at the sky. Except she could see that he wasn't staring at the sky. And never would again. The small hole in the centre of his forehead was leaking a steady stream of blood that pooled briefly in the hollow of his eye socket before continuing its meandering path and falling on the pristine snow below.

Bravo felt the tears roll down his face, warm against his frozen skin. He looked at his father, dead by his hand, and was sadder than he remembered ever being in his entire life. It was over. *Everything* was over. He shivered hard again and his head drooped on his chest as the cold and exhaustion finally took a real hold. Turning around, he looked at the policewoman, her face a shattered, blood-covered mess, staring back at him with her one good eye. He wanted to tell her that he couldn't let Alpha kill any more people. Wanted to tell her that he'd had enough. Enough of death, of killing, of loss. But he didn't. As the greyness in his vision expanded, he felt his knees buckle and his body list to one side as he began losing consciousness. His last deliberate act was to use his final reserve of energy to lob the pistol towards the prone policewoman as he collapsed into the snow.

51

The dog bounded back out of the sea; a stick clamped between its jaws as it raced back towards the pair walking along the beach. The man laughed when he saw the animal sprinting towards him, skidding to a halt and dropping the item at his feet. He stooped, picked up the stick and hurled it back into the sea, smiling as he watched the dog chase after it, splashing through the small summer waves. The woman patted his shoulder as she paused to watch the dog's joyous retrieval.

'He'll have you doing that all afternoon if you let him.'

Colin grinned and nodded in agreement. 'I know, I know, but I've always been a bit of soft touch around dogs.'

Tess smiled and turned to continue their walk. Kota bounded past her, the malamute's wolf-grey coat slick and dark with the soaking from the sea. The dog dropped the stick and looked at her, bushy tail wagging furiously. Unable to resist she picked the stick up and threw it for her canine companion, shaking her head as he hurled himself gleefully back into the breakers. Colin walked beside her, quiet and enjoying the peace of being the only people on the beach. Tess loved this place, and the access to such a pristine slice of the coast was just one of the reasons she'd opted to stay after the incident. People had thought her mad when she returned to both active duty and St Cyrus, many of her superiors suggesting she transfer to another area where she wouldn't be reminded on a daily basis of the traumatic events of that winter. But while she was hospitalised, all she could think of was getting back to the village and walking along the beach and the nature reserve.

Colin glanced at her as she strolled beside him. The scars on her face were only noticeable if you really knew where to look for them and he thought, not for the first time, that she'd had one hell of a talented surgeon to piece her back together so well. The thought recalled the memory of her staggering into the station, her distorted, blood-drenched face shocking even him in his semi-conscious state. She'd brought back the intravenous kits and Kenny had rushed to her after the initial shock had worn off but she'd pushed him aside and ordered him to get the lines into Colin, get the life-saving fluids into his veins. Only then had she allowed Kenny to help her, and then he'd seen to the boy she'd brought back in the Rover, who had been closer to death than any of them.

Help hadn't come until later that morning when the coastguard helicopter had reacted to the report of a boat in trouble. Unable to raise any communications with St Cyrus police station, they had flown over the location and saw the signs of violence. Landing in the nearby park they'd made their way to the station on foot and been stunned by the sight that greeted them. Thereafter, Colin's memories seemed to recall a blur of evacuation by helicopter to Aberdeen Royal Infirmary and the relief of knowing that they were going to be okay.

Tess felt Colin's gaze and assumed he was thinking about the tragedy. She didn't blame him; it was never very far from her own mind. But she was never consumed by it, never overwhelmed by the memories. She'd had a tough time during the facial reconstruction surgeries, unconvinced that she wouldn't be left as a grotesque, scar-ridden monster. But as the surgeries progressed, she could see she was going to be okay.

Colin had pulled through, the drips that Tess had brought back that fateful day doing their job. The boy also had survived but only barely, the helicopter getting to ARI just before the severe hypothermia became irreversible. She shook her head as she thought about how those days had shaped and altered the lives of all involved. Adams and two of his sons had been killed, two Firearms' officers and Mitch had been killed and Susan's brother never fully recovered from his internal injuries. The Police funerals had been hard for her. She hadn't known the Firearms' officers very well, but they'd seemed to be really nice guys. *But Mitch.* Mitch had been an annoying git at times but he wasn't a bad bloke and she still felt a real pang of grief at his passing. His girlfriend had taken it really hard and Colin had explained to Tess that she'd broken up with Mitch the same day they'd arrested Adams. All in all, it had been hard on everyone.

The media had a field day with the story and she'd been harangued non-stop for months after the incident. It had been perfect tabloid fodder; crazed, ex-SAS soldier massacres cops and has assassination plot thwarted by hero policewoman. It had been huge news and lasted a long time as more and more was uncovered about Adams and his sons. While she was hospitalised and undergoing surgeries, the investigation into Adams and his activities had uncovered some incredible information. Tess had been stunned to learn that there was no evidence to show that Adams's wife had ever emigrated to New Zealand and no trace of the woman could be found after the divorce. The investigators concluded that Adams had killed her, disposed of her remains and taken the boys. He had then raised his sons as a militia unit, indoctrinating them with his hatred of government and turning them into a tight military unit using his special forces training. The robberies had been going on for at least two years, the use of the younger brothers proving particularly clever when the gang had been conducting their reconnaissance of targets. After all, who would take a second look at a nine or ten-year-old casually riding around the area on his bike?

Whether through an inherited condition or PTSD related, the investigation also concluded that Adams was suffering from an untreated mental illness. His twisted nurturing of his sons showed complete amoral judgement and his capacity for violence and crime underlined this diagnosis. A detective inspector from Serious Crimes had visited her on occasion, both to glean more information on Adams and to bring Tess up to speed with the investigation's developments. He was surprised to find her concerned for the fate of the surviving boy, requesting updates on his situation. She learned that he had been lucky to survive and he owed his life to Tess for hauling him into the Land Rover and getting him back to the station where Kenny had treated him. He was remanded in a secure unit as he had remained completely silent since regaining consciousness. The doctors concluded that it was a psychological issue and were now determining how this would affect his suitability to stand trial for his actions. Tess found herself thinking of the boy, what he had lost and what kind of life awaited him. She wondered what chance he ever had at a normal life, having been indoctrinated and radicalised by his father from such a young age. Not *quite* sympathy for him as she could find no forgiveness in her heart for his role in the killings but perhaps some empathy for the path he'd been forced to walk that had led him there.

The medal had been completely unexpected; the George Cross award coming out of the blue. Her initial fear, based upon her experience of how risk-averse Police Scotland was regarding negative publicity, was that she would be reprimanded for her use of the anti-tank launcher. It had certainly raised eyebrows during her interviews with the investigators and she imagined the sharp intake of breath when the report had reached the Chief Constable's desk. But during her extended convalescence she'd received numerous visits from various officials who had nothing but praise for her efforts that day. And then she had been *invited* to a meeting with the Chief Constable. She'd assumed that this was going to be when the axe fell and she'd be told that her time as a police officer was over. In her best uniform and with a heavy heart, she'd arrived at Headquarters and been escorted to a comfortable seating area outside a suite of offices on the top floor. The division commander arrived just after her and smiled and shook her hand before knocking and entering the office, closing the door behind him. A few minutes later he returned and called her name. He'd indicated that she should follow him into the room and she'd sighed, straightened her uniform and entered. The Chief Constable stood up immediately, a tall, handsome man with an easy smile. He'd moved around the desk until he was in front of her and shook her hand. He took his seat again and nodded at her and then informed her that she was now the official holder of the George Cross, the highest award for bravery for non-military personnel. Tess had been almost too stunned to hear the rest of the Chief Constable's words as he read out the citation which he had forwarded to the awards committee many months before. Essentially it was recognition for her bravery and utter disregard for her own life in the protection of others that was the underpinning justification. He'd gone on to explain about the investiture, when it was, how many guests that she could take and how not just

Police Scotland but the entire Police community were proud of her achievement.

And again, the media frenzy had been incredible. The award had reignited the story and she was front page news on every tabloid and lead item on the news channels. Her parents, under her advice, took advantage of a friend's holiday home in the Dordogne and rode the storm out in relative obscurity, far from the paparazzi circus. Book deals were offered, several of them so lucrative she need never work again and there were moments of very real temptation to pick up the phone and accept. But it had felt wrong. Friends and colleagues had died as had a madman's kids. So, she didn't take the offers. Instead, she got a dog.

She'd found Kota when she was looking at pups online one evening. His litter was coming up to eight weeks old and he and a bitch were the last remaining available pups. She'd been taken immediately by his wolf-like colouring and appearance. And just like that, she'd made her decision, e-mailed the breeders and went to Fort William the next day to pick up her eight-week old Alaskan Malamute. Kota was exactly what she had needed; companionship and something to focus on while she healed and now, she couldn't imagine ever not having him in her life.

The dog loped ahead of them, stopping at interesting patches of washed-up seaweed to sniff and investigate. As she watched she saw him stop and focus his attention toward the sand dunes. She followed the animal's gaze, shielding her eyes from the sun's glare with the flat of her hand. Colin spoke first.

'Someone you know?'

She shook her head. 'Don't think so. You?'

'Nope. Can't say I know him.'

They watched in silence as the man ambled across the sand towards them. Kota wagged his tail and sprinted towards the stranger. Tess almost called to the animal, well aware how intimidating a wolf-like creature in full flow could be but decided to let events take their course. She raised an eyebrow as the man laughed and reached down, roughly rubbing the dog around the neck, to Kota's obvious pleasure. As he got closer Tess realised he looked familiar but couldn't quite place him. He was slightly taller than her with almost Hispanic features, dark stubble and black hair, slightly greying at the temples, stocky and obviously kept himself in shape. Her instincts weren't screaming 'journalist', so she was curious as to who this stranger was as he reached them and smiled at them both, a wide grin with the laughter lines around his eyes prominent in the shadows of the afternoon sun.

'Evening folks. Apologies for the intrusion but needs must and all that.' The man fished through his back pockets as Tess and Colin shared a quick glance. The stranger was English, north-east by the sound of it although not a particularly strong accent. He produced a black leather wallet which he flipped open to display his badge and warrant card.

'I'm DS Cole, formerly of Serious Crimes and I really need a word with Constable Cameron here.'

Tess sighed and shook her head. 'Look DS Cole, I'm pretty sure that I've given your mob everything I remember and even if by some minute chance I forgot something, I don't think tracking me down on my evening walk on the beach is really necessary do you?'

The DS laughed, a deep throaty chuckle. 'Calm your jets Cameron, that is not why I'm here at all. And we've actually met before. I was sitting in the back of several of your interviews you gave to the investigation. Didn't say much at the time but was watching to make sure you were the right person. And that's why I'm here today PC Cameron: I'm here to offer you a job.'

Tess frowned. 'Erm…thanks and all that but in case you hadn't noticed, I actually *have* a job.'

She watched as the detective sergeant regarded her with something akin to amusement. 'No, you don't. You have somewhere to go when you get out of the bed in the morning and occupy yourself for eight hours before coming home, cooking tea, walking the dog, going to bed and then doing the same thing next day and every day after until the weekend. Sound about right?'

She felt her cheeks flush and jabbed her finger in his chest. 'Who the hell do you think you're talking to? You obnoxious bastard! Don't come up here and slag off my job and my way of life just 'cos you think you're some hot-shot from Serious Crimes.'

352

DS Cole threw his hands up in mock surrender, smiling widely again. 'Whoa, whoa. Sorry for the offence, but I'm a straight talker.' He lowered his hands to his sides and became serious. 'Listen; the way you acted throughout the incident is obviously the talk of Police Stations up and down the country. What you did was bloody impressive PC Cameron and beyond the ability of most of the rank and file police men and women up and down the country. And that's where I come in.'

She looked at Colin who shrugged his shoulders, equally as intrigued as she was. She turned back to face the detective. 'I don't understand, what exactly is it you want?'

He nodded in return and met her gaze. 'I run a special Task Force that targets the hardest and nastiest criminals in our little island nation. I answer to a national director and no-one else, I have no budget constraints and I recruit the whole team myself. We're the first of our kind PC Cameron, a unique team doing a unique job that requires unique individuals. And that's why I'm here.' He paused and looked down at Kota, giving the dog a soft caress on the head before continuing. 'While the world and its uncle have been going gaga for the story of Adams and the copper who stopped him, I've been studying it with an altogether different perspective. Actually, to be more accurate, I've been studying *you*. More to the point, what you did and how you reacted in a situation that ninety-nine percent of coppers would have been killed in. You see, you've got exactly the kinds of skills I need for people on my team.'

Colin interrupted by clearing his throat. 'Look guys, why don't I give you some privacy here, let you talk this over.'

Tess was about to answer when DS Cole replied. 'I'd prefer you to stay Colin, if you don't mind me calling you that? And here's the reason; PC Cameron will not belong to a constabulary, will not be paid through the public sector salary process and will never wear a police uniform. In short, she will disappear entirely from any official police records. And I instruct all my team to have one person that they trust implicitly, to know what has happened to them and can help put nosy colleagues and prying friends off the scent when PC Cameron here crosses over.'

Tess laughed. '*Crosses over*? A bit melodramatic isn't it?'

His face grew serious. 'Is it? Think about it: We target all the evildoers that conventional police and national agencies have failed to bring to justice. We also target the corrupt judicial, governmental, political entities and those who regard themselves as untouchable. We leave being a police officer behind us as completely as if it was dead to us. Because it has to be. Our targets have real influence and access and that includes having corrupt cops on their books and the ability to hack our information systems. Believe me PC Cameron, when you join my team, you are definitely crossing over.'

She raised an eyebrow. 'Well, to be fair I haven't said anything about joining your team yet have I?'

He smiled back and knelt beside Kota, taking the dog's head in both hands and roughing up its fur as Kota gave a low growl of contentment. 'No, you haven't *said* as much but we both know you made your decision as soon as I told you what it is we do and why I want you. You *know* this is what you joined the police to do; find the bad guys, get the bad guys and put them away for a very long time. And, no harm to conventional policing, but that's just not happening as well as it should and that's where we come in.'

Tess chewed on her bottom lip as she considered his statement. The thing was, he was absolutely right; she was *very* interested. Living in St Cyrus was wonderful but her duties as a rural police officer were routine and mundane and she had been feeling a void in that area for some time now. 'Okay, let's just say I am interested. What happens next?'

DS Cole stood and wiped his damp hands on his jeans. 'Doesn't work that way PC Cameron. You're in or you're not. You say yes now, you're on the team and I'll tell you where and when we'll meet again. Otherwise I walk away now and you will never see or hear from me or any of my team again.'

She had the urge to laugh at how assertive this guy was. After all, he had approached her, wanted her to join his team but in the same vein sounded like he couldn't give a shit if she said yes or not. He spoke again.

'We're the best the UK has to offer in the taking down of High Value Targets PC Cameron. It's never been done like this before; this isn't just undercover work I'm talking here. We're a completely non-disclosed task force with every asset we want and no jurisdiction or red tape to slow us down. Now, I'm hungry and getting chilly so it's crunch time. In or out?'

Tess looked at Colin but he held his own counsel and just gave her a small shrug of the shoulders. She looked at Kota, tongue lolling from his mouth as he panted, soaking fur dark against his skin. 'Can I bring my dog?'

DS Cole laughed. 'Definitely: That's one of the best-looking mutts I've ever seen.'

Tess took a deep breath to calm the nervous sensation in her stomach and offered out her hand. 'In.'

The detective shook her hand once and met her gaze. 'Welcome PC Cameron, great to have you on board.'

'What happens now?'

DS Cole zipped his jacket up against the stiffening breeze. 'I'll give you a call tomorrow with your joining routine. Some of it may seem a bit bizarre but just go with it; you're about to disappear from the police completely and it takes a lot of strange measures to achieve this but we know what we're doing.' With that he nodded to Colin, turned and began walking away, checking his phone as he went.

Tess raised her eyebrows in surprise. *That's it?* She called out to the departing figure. 'Hey, Cole's not your real name is it?'

She watched as he looked over his shoulder at her with a small smile on his lips. 'It's…*real* enough for my purposes. Just like the badge.' He stopped and put the phone back into his pocket. 'Anything else before I starve to death here?'

'Yes. What are we called? What's our unit name?'

He nodded as though satisfied with the question. '*The Dark*, PC Cameron. We call ourselves *The Dark*.'

She watched in silence as he made his way along the beach and followed the trail through the dunes and eventually out of sight.

THE END

Thank you for reading and I truly hope you enjoyed this book. Please, if you have enjoyed it, take the time to leave a review and let others know how much you liked it.

Thank you once again.

James

www.jamesemack.com

www.facebook.com/authorjamesemack

THE KILLING AGENT

The worst terrorist attacks that the UK has seen. A country in turmoil, a government in disarray. Intelligence agencies with no leads or suspects.

Lovat Reid, a veteran covert operator with the Special Intelligence Group, is tasked to help track down the mastermind behind the attacks. With his partner Nadia, an officer from the Special Reconnaissance Regiment, they soon realise that they are dealing with an individual the likes of which they have not seen before.

When another atrocity is carried out, the entire weight of the Intelligence agencies and Special Forces is thrown behind the effort to find the terrorist responsible. But for Lovat, something isn't quite right. Suspecting a dangerous power-play between the agencies, Lovat digs a little deeper into the background of the terrorist suspect.

And is stunned by what he finds.

With a race against time to halt the next attack, Lovat and Nadia find themselves fighting a war on two fronts as they strive to uncover the depth of deception while hunting the master terrorist.

From the killing fields of Kandahar to the back streets of London, the consequences of a secret assassination program are brutally levelled against an unsuspecting British public.

ONLY THE DEAD

'Only the dead have seen the end of war'

In war-torn Libya, veteran Commando Finn Douglas is forced to commit an appalling act in order to save the lives of his men. Haunted by his actions, he suffers a further blow when he learns that his family has been killed in a terrorist attack in London. Numb with grief and trauma, Finn turns his back on the world of war and killing and flees to an island wilderness to escape his demons.

A team of Military Police are tasked with bringing Finn to justice. But for one of the policemen, the manhunt is a more personal issue; a chance for revenge to right a wrong suffered years before.

When Finn intervenes in a life and death situation, his sanctuary is shattered, and the net tightens. The manhunt becomes a race against time between the forces of law and order and a psychotic mercenary determined to exact his revenge on Finn for thwarting his plans. For Finn, the world of killing and conflict returns with a vengeance on the blizzard-swept mountains of the island.

Only this time there is nowhere left to run.

Only the Dead is a thriller in the tradition of Gerald Seymour and a stand out debut from a new British author.

361

Printed in Great Britain
by Amazon